W9-CTA-709

PRETTY PUNISHMENT

It was bad enough when Meriden goaded Emily into slapping him hard across the face. It was even worse when he threatened to spank her like a child if she did not apologize.

Needless to say, Emily refused to humble herself. Instead she intended to tell him in devastating detail what she thought of him.

But she did not get to utter a single word. For the moment she lifted her chin and opened her mouth, Meriden's right hand moved to cup the back of her head and he bent to stop her lips with his own.

When she stumbled back, striving to regain her composure, he merely grinned at her and asked, "Learned your lesson, or do you want more?"

AMANDA SCOTT, a fourth-generation Californian, was born and raised in Salinas and graduated with a degree in history from Mills College in Oakland. She did graduate work at the University of North Carolina at Chapel Hill, specializing in British history, before obtaining her MA from San Jose State University. She lives with her husband and young son in Sacramento.

SIGNET REGENCY ROMANCE
COMING IN SEPTEMBER 1989

Emma Lange
The Unwavering Miss Winslow

Mary Balogh
Lady with a Black Umbrella

Vanessa Gray
The Lady's Revenge

The Dauntless
Miss Wingrave

by
Amanda Scott

A SIGNET BOOK

NEW AMERICAN LIBRARY

PUBLISHED BY
PENGUIN BOOKS CANADA LIMITED

For Jim
with love from
Mom

Copyright © 1989 by Lynne Scott-Drennan

First Printing, August, 1989

2   3   4   5   6   7   8   9

⊘ SIGNET TRADEMARK REG U.S. PAT OFF AND FOREIGN COUNTRIES
REGISTERED TRADEMARK — MARCA REGISTRADA
HECHO EN WINNIPEG. CANADA

SIGNET, SIGNET CLASSIC, MENTOR, ONYX, PLUME,
MERIDIAN and NAL BOOKS are published in Canada by Penguin
Books Canada Limited, 2801 John Street, Markham, Ontario,
L3R 1B4
PRINTED IN CANADA
COVER PRINTED IN U.S.A.

1

"WE OUGHT SOON TO SEE SOME SIGN OF LIFE, I expect," Miss Wingrave said to her abigail when their post chaise, which had been laboring steadily uphill ever since leaving the cheerful, bustling little town of Thirsk, leveled out and immediately began to move more rapidly on a slight downhill slope. "Sabrina wrote in that very odd letter of hers that Rivindale, which is where the Priory is located, you know, is but eight miles from the crest of this escarpment."

Her plump companion, hands folded serenely in her lap, was looking out her window and only nodded in response. Moments later she said without turning her head, "Startling it is, Miss Emily, the way all them green fields and fertile farms below have given way to this barren land. Naught to see now but bracken, scrub, and dry brown moor grass."

"But look behind us, Martha." Pushing her light mesh traveling veil back in order to suit action to words, Miss Wingrave revealed a charming, pink-cheeked countenance dominated by a pair of expressive light-blue eyes fringed by thick sable lashes. "Why, from here atop these hills, so close do the Pennines appear to be that it looks as though one might reach right across the plain of York to touch them."

"Humph," retorted her companion. " 'Tain't like you to talk so fanciful, Miss Emily. Why, for all them fields below look more like a gentleman's draughts board than a landscape, it must be all of thirty miles to them mountains from here." She sighed. "I don't mind telling you, miss, I will be right glad to have this journey over and done. Two hundred fifty miles in four days is not what I am accustomed to, and that's the nut with no bark on it. Nor do I hold with young ladies staying at common inns with no more than an abigail to bear them company.''

Miss Wingrave lifted her pointed little chin. "Nearly five days it's been, Martha, and the inns we have patronized have been perfectly respectable. Moreover, having attained the age of one-and-twenty, I am quite old enough to look after myself, as even Papa has agreed, and,'' she added as a clincher, "you know perfectly well that we have insufficient time in which to arrange to stay with friends along the way.''

Martha vouchsafed no reply, and a silence fell that lasted until the chaise passed through the little town of Helmsley, beneath the ruins of the ancient castle there. Just beyond the town, they turned northward onto a track, whereupon the abigail expressed her hope that the postboys knew their direction.

"For I don't mind telling you, I'd as lief not be lost on these moors, and that's a fact,'' she said. "Try as I might, I cannot imagine Miss Sabrina living in such a wasteland.''

Miss Wingrave had been experiencing the same difficulty, but a quarter-hour later when the chaise turned onto a neat white-pebbled roadway, then topped a small rise and began to descend into Rivindale, both women gasped in surprise at the lush view spread before them. Where there had been only barren moorland but moments before, there was now dense greenery covering both the eastern and western slopes of the narrow river valley. Cedar, oak, and birch trees abounded, and the pebbled roadway was soon flanked by high, thick green hedges.

Some moments later they passed between tall iron gates set in a gray stone wall and saw before them the large brick manor house of Staithes Priory, surrounded by its lavish and colorful gardens. The pebbled drive swept up to the imposing white-columned front entrance and curved away again downhill, past a verdant, well-scythed lawn, to follow the serpentine shoreline of the deep-blue lake at the bottom of the hill before disappearing into the thick woodland beyond.

When they had drawn to a halt, Miss Wingrave allowed a tall young liveried footman to assist her from the post chaise. Then, her neatly shod feet planted firmly upon the pebbled drive, she shook out the light-gray skirts of her traveling dress, pushed her veil back again, and looked about her with approval. The rose-brick house was clearly not the original structure but an elegant manor house no more than one hundred years of age. Its dimensions were symmetrical, laid out with an attention to detail that pleased Miss Wingrave's passion for orderliness. After the eerie bleakness of the high Yorkshire moor across which she had journeyed, the lush green gardens, well-tended lawns, and the dense, curving woodland framing the picturesque lake below were particularly refreshing sights.

The footman cleared his throat.

"Yes, what is it?" Miss Wingrave inquired, looking up from under the rim of her gray bonnet into his face. She had to look up nearly a foot, for the young man was tall and she was not.

"Tha'll be wantin' to go inside, miss," he said deferentially. "There be a brisk wind off the moors today."

"Thank you," Miss Wingrave said graciously, picking up her train and noting for the first time that a number of other servants had emerged from the house to assist Martha with their baggage. Miss Wingrave looked again at the footman to see that he was regarding her with anxiety. She had seen the expression many times before, generally on masculine faces, faces of men who did not know her well. She smiled. "I am not nearly so fragile as I look, I promise you."

"Indeed, miss, tha' looks as though the smallest breeze would whisk ye right off them little feet."

Miss Wingrave frowned, her light-blue eyes narrowing beneath their heavy lashes. "What is your name?"

"Willum, miss, and sithee, I didna mean to speak familiar, but tha' bein' so small—"

"I think you had better take me inside, William,"
Miss Wingrave said firmly, "before we have a falling-
out. And do not, pray, attempt to fob me off on the
housekeeper or a chambermaid, but take me directly to
her ladyship."

"But her ladyship made sure ye would be wanting to
rest a bit first, miss, and get tha'self settled in like."

"Nonsense. I shall take off my bonnet and spencer,
but then all I shall require is a cup of good hot tea and
some bread and butter. I have taken no refreshment
since breaking my fast this morning. Martha will attend
to all the settling in, I assure you." She did not add her
belief, for it did not suit her notions of propriety to do
so, that her sister, having sent for her, now wished in
her usual fashion to put off, for as long as possible, the
actual moment of confrontation.

William, clearly abashed by her air of calm resolution, bowed and allowed her to precede him up the wide
granite steps and into the stately hall, which was
presided over by an elderly butler, who greeted her
politely and introduced himself as Merritt before
returning his attention to the men who carried her
baggage into the house. While William assisted her in
doffing her bonnet and spencer, she looked about her
curiously.

The hall, the walls of which were hung with a collec-
tion of excellent landscapes, was paneled in golden oak
with a floor composed of alternating blocks of light and
dark oak in a checkerboard pattern. The central, dom-
inant feature was the stairway, which branched at a
wide landing into two wings that swooped upward to an
oak-railed gallery curving around three sides of the two-
story hall. The domed and painted ceiling above was
patterned with carved oak beams which met at the
center like spokes at the hub of a wheel, and from the
point of their joining depended a massive, highly
polished gilt-and-crystal chandelier.

Having satisfied herself that one might command the
elegancies of life even in the wilds of North Yorkshire,

Miss Wingrave glanced at herself in the gilt-framed looking glass mounted over a side table. It was necessary only to tuck one errant wisp of her pale blond hair back into place before she turned back expectantly to the footman.

"This way, miss." Having passed her things to an underling, William now led Miss Wingrave past an open doorway leading into a large, elegant book-lined room that she realized could only be the late Baron Staithes's library, up the right wing of the stairs, then along the railed gallery to a pair of tall white-painted doors. William pushed these open, revealing a spacious, well-appointed drawing room, its walls hung with emerald-and-sea-green-striped silk above white linenfold wainscoting. The furnishings included a set of giltwood chairs and sofas covered with matching needlework that Emily recognized at once as the work of Thomas Chippendale. As they entered the room, the footman announced quietly, "Miss Wingrave, my lady."

"Emily! We did not look to see you before dusk." The plumpest of the three ladies in the room made a movement as though to rise from her sofa, but Miss Wingrave waved her back to her seat as she stepped briskly forward to greet her.

"Do not get up, Sabrina. I declare, you get stouter every year. You would do well to slim yourself a bit, I think. Not that the round look don't become you, for I do not scruple to tell you that it does, particularly whilst you continue to wear your blacks. How do you do, ma'am," she added, turning to the slender gray-haired lady seated erectly upon a giltwood chair near one of the tall, arched, green-draped windows. "I am Emily Wingrave, you know—Sabrina's youngest sister. You must be Miss Lavinia Arncliffe. She has often spoken of you and frequently mentions your name in her letters. And you," she went on, smiling at the youngest of the three ladies, "must be Dolly. Or have you grown so old and grand in your seventeenth year that I must now call you Dorothy? Indeed, you have turned out to be a beauty, as I daresay you know perfectly well. Only wait until London sees you. I promise, you will be a blazing success."

"Oh, pray, Emily, do not mention London," begged the dowager Baroness Staithes as her pretty blond daughter arose and made a wide-eyed curtsy.

No one else had attempted to say a word, and Emily, taking a chair near her sister, turned her attention back to that lady, demanding to know why she should not mention London. "For you must see for yourself that Dolly is a diamond of the first water, Sabrina. Those golden curls, those china-blue eyes, and such long, curling dark lashes. She will have men crawling on their hands and knees in return for the mere favor of her smile."

"Proper place for them," said Miss Lavinia tartly, pushing wire-rimmed spectacles higher on her narrow nose.

Emily looked at her, noting flyaway gray curls beneath her lace-trimmed cap, her neat, prim little figure, and the book lying open on her lap. "On their knees, do you mean, ma'am?"

"Best place for 'em, to my mind. Can't get into mischief that way, at all events. I fancy that if young Oliver had spent more time on his knees, he'd not have got himself into such a fix at Cambridge, and that's a fact. Not that I am at all popish, mind you," she added thoughtfully.

"Then Oliver is the reason for the very affecting letter you sent me," Emily said, looking at her sister. "Really, Sabrina, I cannot think why you will not simply write a proper letter, with proper sentences full of meaningful nouns and verbs. You had the very same governess I had, and considering that Mattie was twenty years younger when she taught you, you ought to have benefited even more from her teaching than I did. Your letter rambled from one emotional outpouring to another, without ever coming to a point. And you crossed your lines like a pinchpenny, though you clearly had someone to frank it for you. I am forced to say 'someone' for the simple reason that the frank was the veriest scrawl. At all events, the tone of your letter was such that I did not know but what your children were dying like flies, all four of them, which is why I made such haste that I still feel as though I were rocking in a chaise. If the problem concerns only Oliver, I should think you would have done better to have asked for Papa's help rather than to have begged me to fly to your side like you did. What has the boy done?''

Lady Staithes, who had winced visibly, first at the mention of her weight and then at the even more tactless mention of the disparity in their ages, now spread her hands and regarded her younger sister beseechingly. "Poor Oliver has been sent down from Cambridge, I fear, but it is not only Oliver, Emily. Everything is at sixes and sevens here, and I don't know what to do. I had hoped that you would help, but if all you will say is that I must starve myself or appeal to Papa, who is never in the least conciliating to me, or write a proper letter or send Dolly to London, which you must know I cannot do until we have observed a full year of mourning for my dearest Laurence . . ." She paused, then added woefully, "Well, if that is your notion of being helpful, I don't think you will be any help to me at all.''

Dolly sniffed and said sullenly, "I hope Aunt Emily will at least persuade you that a year is altogether too long for everyone to be forced to give up all pleasure merely because Papa was so unfortunate as to die.''

"Dorothy Rivington,'' said her mother sharply, "pray remember where you are and who you are, and do not speak in such an unbecoming manner again.''

"I shall not speak at all then,'' said Miss Rivington, getting to her feet and putting her straight little nose in the air. "I can see that you mean to pour all your woes into poor Aunt Emily's ears, and since I have heard them all until I am sick to death of them, I shall leave you to a comfortable coze.'' Whereupon, with a decided flounce of her white muslin skirts, she turned and left the room.

When the door had shut with a snap behind her niece,

Emily raised her slim, arched brows and said quietly, "Do you customarily allow your children to address you so rudely, Sabrina? Really, I—"

"Oh, Emily, please. I cannot bear it if you lecture me," cried Sabrina. She opened her mouth to say something else, but the tall white doors opened again just then to admit the footman and a maid with Emily's refreshment. There were four cups and saucers and a tray of assorted sandwiches, and everything was set out in front of her ladyship. Sabrina had herself well in hand again and poured out without a quiver. But when the servants had gone, she looked directly at Emily. "It is not only Oliver, as you can see. Dolly has been much affected by her papa's death."

"Spoilt her," pronounced Miss Lavinia. "Spoilt Oliver too, come to that. Always giving them things because he couldn't be bothered to give of himself. Just a man like any other, putting his own pleasures ahead of all else."

"I was most sincerely attached to Laurence," Sabrina said stiffly, "and I am certain that he loved all his children."

"But you always left the children here at Staithes," Emily pointed out, piling several sandwiches on a china plate for herself and accepting a cup of tea from her sister. "Though we often saw you and Laurence in town, I haven't ever even met Giles or Melanie, you know, and I am persuaded that Dolly cannot have been above seven the last time you brought her into Wiltshire to visit Papa and Mama. Oliver was at school then, but of course he has stayed with us several times during his school holidays. Giles has never done so."

"Well, I am certain that Laurence and I did nothing that everyone else does not do," Sabrina said defensively. "One doesn't take one's children to London for the Season when one has excellent persons at home with whom to leave them. Only think of the upset entailed by such a move! And one certainly does not take children from one house party to the next during the winter or to Leicestershire for the hunting or to Brighton in the summer. We did take them all to the seashore at Robin Hood's Bay—on the east coast near Scarborough, you know—after Christmas, and only look what came of that! Poor Laurence took a chill and died of it, that's what."

"Good gracious, Sabrina, surely you are not blaming your husband's death on the fact that he finally paid some little heed to his children!"

"No, no, don't be absurd. You have diverted me from what I was telling you. Emily, Giles has written from Eton to say he will not come home for the long vacation because he does not wish to do so, and poor dear Melanie scarcely speaks a word to anyone anymore. I promise you, she was used to be the most delightful, cheerful little girl. She is very like you, you know."

"I pray you will cease to think of me as a child, Sabrina. I promise you that I am as fully grown as I am ever like to be."

"Nonsensical girl." Her sister regarded her fondly. "You know perfectly well that I meant only that the child resembles you. You were just such a fairy creature when you were her age. Her hair is as flaxen as yours and just as straight and fine. Her governess, Miss Brittan, has convinced her to wear it in two plaits, and the look suits her." Sabrina paused, but when no one else said anything, she looked down at her teacup and said hesitantly, "I have not told you the worst of it, Emily. Indeed, I am ashamed to confess that such a dreadful thing has come to pass in my very own house."

"Good gracious, what else can there be? You have cited quite a list of woes to me already."

"But this last thing is really worse than all the rest," Sabrina said, glancing apologetically at Miss Lavinia. "Miss Lavinia's sister, as I believe I have told you before, was Laurence's mother, Letitia Arncliffe. Dolly is named for her. Her full name is Dorothy Le—"

"For goodness' sake, get on with the important part, Sabrina," Emily said impatiently. "The Rivington family tree can be of only the smallest interest to me."

"Very well." Sabrina sighed. "Miss Lavinia inherited some of her mama's jewelry, including a number of excellent pieces—"

"Particularly the rubies," interjected Miss Lavinia reminiscently. "I was always partial to the rubies. Never could wear them, of course. Looked like a mouse with apples tied round its neck, but I liked 'em."

Emily's eyes widened. "You speak in the past tense, ma'am. Can it be that your jewels have gone missing?"

"Stolen," said Sabrina tragically. "Right out of her jewel case in her own bedchamber. And pray do not suggest that one of the servants may have taken them, for if anyone else makes such a suggestion, I am sure they will all leave. Every one! It is quite odious enough that Meriden has called in the Bow Street Runners. Bumptious beasts asking officious questions. Pompous, dreadful, common little men who—"

"Meriden?" Emily ignored the rest, her attention riveting on the name. "The Earl of Meriden, Sabrina? Crazy Jack?"

"Of course, the Earl of Meriden," her sister replied tartly. "Who else should have done such a thing? And I do not think it at all becoming in you to refer to him by that dreadful nickname, though now I come to think of it—"

"But all the bucks in London call him Crazy Jack," Emily said calmly, "and most of the ladies do too, for he is always ripe for mischief. They say he will bet on anything, that he fights duels for the fun of them, and that he is always in the thick of things. I have met him, you know. He is a handsome man, I believe, though I candidly admit that I am partial to men with dark hair and gray eyes. But I liked his quick smile and friendly manner too. Of course," she added, reflecting on certain specific occasions when she would gladly have slapped the earl's flashing grin right off his handsome face, "he can be dictatorial, impertinent, and unbecomingly arrogant at times. However, I do not see what he has to do with you."

"But surely I told you," Sabrina said, staring at her.

"Indeed, Emily, I know that whatever else I may have neglected to write these past months, I did tell you the distressing news about Laurence's will. I simply cannot comprehend any law that permits a man to put his affairs into another man's hands rather than into those of his own dear wife."

Blinking at the thought of her sister attempting to manage anyone's affairs, her own certainly included, Emily said slowly, "You did write about the will and that things were left in a mess. That was months ago, of course, but I remember clearly that you said Laurence had named his cousin John guardian to the children and principal trustee of the estate. I know you wrote 'Cousin John' or 'Cousin Jack'—good God, Sabrina, never tell me . . ."

Sabrina nodded. "John Rivington is the seventh Earl of Meriden. Indeed, it was he who franked my letter to you. Cousin Jack and Crazy Jack are one and the same."

Emily took another sandwich, chewing thoughtfully. "So Meriden calls the tune here," she said at last. "I cannot imagine such a thing. Is he a strict guardian, Sabrina? I'd not have thought it."

"You wouldn't know him now," said Sabrina, "for he's changed beyond recognition, although I, too, have a memory, my dear, and I distinctly recall one or two *on-dits* after Christmas, linking your name with his. Indeed, I am surprised to learn that you knew nothing of our connection with him. But truly, Emily, he is the cause of all our troubles. He has expressed himself most unfeelingly over poor Oliver's troubles, considering that he is as much to blame for them as the boy is. He expects Oliver to get on at Cambridge on the merest pittance. Laurence was always generous, so it is no wonder that the poor boy went to the money lenders when he ran short. And with his expectations, it is even less wonderful that they broke the law just a trifle and lent him the money he required. But the authorities at Cambridge found out and ordered Oliver home till Michaelmas term."

"What expectations?" Emily demanded. "Unless I'm out in my reckoning, Sabrina, Oliver is barely turned eighteen. Surely everything is in trust until he is twenty-one or older. That is the usual method with such estates as Staithes, I believe."

"Twenty-five," said Sabrina.

"Then—"

"He is Meriden's heir as well," Sabrina explained, "just as poor Laurence was before him, although Laurence, bless him, rarely mentioned the fact to anyone."

"But how can that be? Oliver is Baron Staithes. Surely that is not a mere styling, not one of Meriden's lesser titles."

"No, no, the barony derives from Laurence's grandmother, who was a baroness in her own right. Laurence's great-grandfather was the fourth Earl of Meriden. His elder son was Meriden's grandfather, and his younger son married Baroness Staithes. The properties march together, you see, so it was an excellent match, but although both sides produced large families, very few of the males survived. Laurence and Jack were second cousins, the only ones left, so Laurence, although he was the elder by nearly twenty years, was Jack's heir. Now Oliver holds that position."

"But expectations, Sabrina?" Emily stared. "Meriden is not yet thirty, I believe."

"But the earls of Meriden have all married young, and he shows no inclination to marry at all. Moreover, I am sure men have died younger than thirty before now," Sabrina said.

Emily took her temper firmly in hand and changed the course of the conversation abruptly by asking, "Is Meriden also responsible for Giles's refusing to come home and for the drastic change you describe in little Melanie?"

"As to Melanie, I cannot say. I daresay Jack has always been kind to her in his own careless fashion, but yes, he is certainly responsible for the very unhappy letter I received from dearest Giles."

"Boy wants smacking," said Miss Lavinia, speaking up in what Emily was coming to recognize as a characteristically elliptical fashion. "Don't do to coddle boys, Sabrina. They grow up to be men no matter what you do."

"I don't coddle Giles, Miss Lavinia," said Sabrina, straightening indignantly in her chair. "Really, I do not know how you can say such a thing of me. I am certain Laurence's school reports can never have been anything special, because he was used to laugh at the cutting things the masters wrote about Oliver. And all they have said about Giles is that he lacks application, whatever that means. Surely there was no reason for Jack to write him a severe scold, as he must have done, for Giles wrote to me that he read only bits of the letter because he didn't like the tone of it, and I am certain that can be nothing to wonder at. No one would have liked to receive such a letter."

"But why is Giles not coming home?" Emily asked.

"Because," Sabrina said, "if he does, Jack has said he must have a tutor for the whole of his long vacation. Can you credit it? Keeping poor Oliver short of money and then expending heaven knows how much on a tutor for Giles—"

"A very strict tutor," added Miss Lavinia on a note of satisfaction.

"I see." Emily applied her attention to her tea for some moments while she turned the matters thus described to her over in her mind. Despite the difference in their ages, she felt that she knew Sabrina well, for they saw each other frequently during the year in London and at other people's homes, and they were avid correspondents. This last fact was true of the entire Wingrave family, of which Emily was the youngest member. But Sabrina was no doting mother, and until the last few months—until the death of Baron Staithes, in fact—she had rarely written about her children.

Emily had dutifully sent each one a small gift on the anniversary of his or her birth and at Christmas, and had received formal notes of gratitude in return. She occasionally received stiff, dutiful missives from one or another, including one letter written in Latin by young Giles from Eton that she had submitted to her brother Ned for translation. When the letter had proved to be no more than a copy of one of Caesar's letters from a Latin textbook, Ned and Emily had composed a satiric reply and sent it off to the boy, hoping to hear from him again, but there had been no response. Thinking about this episode now, she realized she knew very little about her sister's children. Even Oliver, whom she had seen most often and who was, after all, no more than a few years younger than she, was nearly a stranger. She remembered a boy with eyes like her own, light blue with dark rims around the irises, and with light-brown hair, who had visited Wingrave Hall briefly at infrequent intervals. All she really remembered about him was a mischievous laugh and an avid interest in hunting and shooting.

"Is Oliver at home now, Sabrina?" she inquired.

"Yes, of course. Haven't I just been telling you?"

"Well, he might have been rusticated and gone to London or even gone sailing in the North Sea like our John did that time he was sent down from Oxford for playing off one of his pranks and Papa was so out-of-reason cross with him," Emily pointed out.

"Good gracious, Emily, never put such a notion as that into Oliver's head," begged Sabrina. "I don't know what he will do, though he says he desires to cut some sort of dash and then go into Leicestershire when the hunting begins. Meriden will not hear of it, of course, so it will all be dreadful for me, just as it was when he would not let Dolly go to London in June."

"But surely you would not have permitted her to do such a thing either," Emily said.

"No, of course not," Sabrina replied, eyeing her doubtfully, "though I am persuaded that after six months of deep mourning, no one would have been dreadfully shocked if she had gone with me or with her friend Lettie Bennett from Helmsley to a concert or to a play—not to a comedy, of—"

"Sabrina, what are you saying? Surely you would not have taken Dolly to London at the height of the Season and then expected her to sit quietly at a concert or two. What do you suppose Mama or Papa would have had to say to that? Why, I was in black gloves myself till the end of June."

"Oh, I know," said Sabrina with a sigh, "but you do not know what Dolly can be like, and I promise you I feel for her because her best friend made her bow this Season and Dolly truly does not understand why her own pleasures must be curtailed. It does seem such a pity when she so seldom even saw Laurence."

"That does not signify one whit," Emily said severely. "Laurence was her father."

"Yes, and so Jack said to her. What a dust-up we had, to be sure. But Jack's will prevailed, as it always does. And, Emily, he is *not* always right. I am certain he is not."

"Of course he is not. Very few persons are always right," Miss Wingrave said fairly. "But when you know he is wrong, Sabrina, surely you have only to point out his error to him."

Sabrina stared at her.

2

AFTER A MOMENTARY SILENCE MISS LAVINIA SAID TO Emily, "Must see she can't do such a thing as that. Can't say boo to a goose. You must know that if anyone does."

Emily nodded. "How right you are to remind me of that fact, ma'am." She leaned forward to pat Sabrina's knee. "That is the reason you sent for me, after all, is it not? I will soon see just what is to be done, and then you need trouble your head no more, for once I see my way, I shall simply point out the error of his methods—tactfully, of course—to Meriden." Drawing an invigorating breath, she reached for another sandwich.

Lady Staithes stared at her in awe, much as though she feared she had conjured up a genie out of a bottle and didn't know if she would be able to get it back inside again.

Miss Lavinia, looking from one sister to the other, suddenly chuckled and picked up her book.

Emily smiled at her. "What is that you are reading, ma'am, if I may ask?"

"Oh, some bit of nonsense Dolly lent me," Miss Lavinia replied. "The heroine is presently living in a castle in Italy, a place that appears to be infested with mysterious dukes and ferocious bandits. I am attempting to ascertain which category best suits the hero. At the moment he appears to be a bandit, but I suspect he will turn out to be the real duke in the end."

"Miss Lavinia," said Sabrina fondly, "dotes on those foolish novels quite as much as Dolly does, and neither Oliver nor Harry Enderby dares to tell *her* that she is stuffing her brain with rubbishing nonsense."

"Harry Enderby?"

"Oh, he is a friend of Oliver's. Enderby Hall lies further up the dale, north of Meriden Park. Very respectable antecedents, Mr. Enderby has, but he and Dolly no sooner lay eyes upon each other than they come to cuffs. He is up at Oxford just now, but he will be home in a week. He told her the last time he was here that she was nothing but a selfish ninnyhammer. Can you credit such a thing?"

"Perfectly right, too," said Miss Lavinia, glancing up from her book. "Never looked for such good sense from that young man. Dolly won't have him, though. She prefers the worst of the lot to the best. You'll have her running off with some fortune hunter if you don't keep her tied by the heels, Sabrina. Like so many young girls today, she thinks this nonsense"—she hefted her book—"is real. And say what you like about me, I have read a deal more and seen a deal more than what is written here. My head ain't like to be turned by mysterious dukes."

The doors opened before Sabrina could respond to this candid speech, and a handsome young man in a bottle-green coat, buff pantaloons, and gold-tasseled Hessians entered the room. His stiff shirt points, intricately tied neckcloth, and gaily embroidered waistcoat identified him to the experienced Miss Wingrave as a would-be member of the dandy set. Lifting his quizzing glass to his eye, he peered at her and drawled lazily, "Dolly said you had arrived, ma'am, but surely you cannot be my Aunt Emily. You are far too young and pretty."

"Oliver," begged his mama, "pray do not be absurd. Of course she is your aunt."

Emily regarded him critically, saying calmly, "You have not got the precise knack of it, you know. Your quizzing glass ought properly to be used to depress pretension, not to underscore your own lack of civil manners."

Oliver flushed, letting the glass fall so that it swung inelegantly from its black silk cord to bump against his well-muscled thigh. "I beg your pardon. I didn't mean to be rude."

"I am aware of that," said Emily. "That is why I ventured to give you a hint of your error. One should be rude only when one intends to be rude. When you peer at someone through your glass like that, you are either doing so to criticize him or to praise him. For example, you might examine the elegance with which a bow is tied or the preposterous pattern of a gentleman's waistcoat. Indeed, if you wish to do the thing properly, you could do no better than to observe how Meriden does the trick. He is nearly as skilled with a quizzing glass as he is with a sword or a pistol."

Oliver stiffened. "I do not choose to take my tone from Meriden, ma'am."

"No, of course not," said Emily apologetically. "To

have suggested such a thing was a thoughtless error on my part. I know that you are out of charity with him at present, for your mama told me so, but I was thinking only of the quizzing glass, you see, and spoke without thinking. It is a fault of mine, I fear, that I often focus my attention on one small point and forget the larger issue." She smiled. "I trust you will contrive to forgive me."

Oliver blinked at her, clearly unaccustomed to such apologies from the adults in his life. But then he smiled, looking singularly boyish despite his fashionable attire, and said as he drew up a giltwood chair and sat down beside her, "My pleasure, ma'am. No offense taken."

"I declare," Emily said then, turning back to Sabrina, "I am anxious to meet Meriden again. He must have changed a great deal indeed since last I saw him, though I have not done so, to be sure, since Christmas. My own activities this Season have, like your own, been sadly curtailed."

"Meriden hasn't gone out of Yorkshire since February," Sabrina said. "He went down to London for the opening of Parliament and stayed through the first sessions because of some trifling matters of probate that he said would be more easily attended to there than in York, but otherwise he has been here."

"He practically lives here," said Oliver acidly.

"You exaggerate," his mother told him.

"No, he don't," said Miss Lavinia. "Dines here, often as not. Can't be wondered at. Must prefer company to dining in solitary splendor at Meriden Park. Ain't here today, though."

"No, thank God," said Oliver. "We are spared his carping for one night at least. He rode into York this morning and won't return to Staithes until tomorrow. You will have to postpone your reacquaintance with him till then, Aunt Emily."

"Then I trust," said Emily to Sabrina, "that you will allow Melanie to join us for dinner this evening. I should like to meet her at long last."

"To be sure, my dear. She and Miss Brittan often

dine with us when we are *en famille*. I believe it is good for children to grow accustomed to dining in company, do not you? I recall that we Wingraves were used to do so often.''

Emily was as certain as she could be that the forthcoming evening meal would bear little if any resemblance to the merry family dinners at Wingrave Hall, and it proved to be much as she had anticipated. Oliver and Dolly expressed, rather too often for her taste, their delight in the "peaceful" tenor of the gathering, while Melanie sat silent as a wraith.

At nine years of age, with her silky blond hair tied back with a blue ribbon to hang in waves down her back, the slender child did indeed have a fairylike appearance. Prodded by her mama and the prim, dark-haired Miss Brittan, she murmured a polite greeting, but with that small exception, she sat silently, pushing her food about on her plate, looking at no one.

Since Emily was not sitting next to the child, she made no attempt to draw her out, believing it would be better done at a more propitious time and place.

The governess appeared to keep a watchful eye upon Melanie without losing track of the conversation, and when Dolly expressed herself rather too impetuously at one point, Miss Brittan assayed a mild reproof. Dolly's eyes flashed defiantly before she looked away from the woman and went on with her conversation as though there had been no interruption. Encountering Miss Wingrave's frown, Miss Brittan flushed and returned her attention to her plate.

The response did not please Emily any more than her niece's impertinence had pleased her, but she resolutely held her tongue and did not dwell on the incident, knowing that to do so at that moment would serve no good purpose. Instead she found herself wondering if Miss Brittan would not be prettier and younger-looking if she were not forced to wear spectacles or if she were to arrange her tightly coiffed hair in a softer, more becoming style. Perhaps, Emily mused, she ought out of kindness to suggest the latter course to the woman.

When Miss Lavinia addressed a comment to her some moments later, Emily turned her attention without regret to that lady, and the rest of the evening passed amiably, although Oliver took himself off on some errand of his own, declining to respond to his mama's feeble attempt to discover whither he was bound. Neither did he deign to reply to her suggestion that he would do better to remain at home and help to entertain his aunt on her first evening at Staithes.

When Emily retired to her bed in the spacious blue-and-white bedchamber allotted to her use, she had much food for thought. Her sister's household was, without question, at sixes and sevens. A good deal of the blame, she was certain, could be laid at the door of Sabrina herself and at that of her late husband. Neither seemed to have attended very skillfully to parental duties. But that could not be helped now. Once she had ascertained how much blame might be fairly allotted to Meriden, she would know what to do to sort matters out. She had no doubt that before she returned to Wiltshire the household at Staithes would be running smoothly.

Emily did not see the Earl of Meriden until the following afternoon. She knew, for William had told her when she asked him, that Meriden had arrived at Staithes before ten o'clock. But when the young foot-man also told her, most earnestly, that his lordship would be like a lion with a thorn in its paw if she interrupted his business with Staithes's bailiff before he had finished, she remembered her own papa's testiness on like occasions and bided her time.

Donning a Wedgewood-blue walking dress, she decided to take a turn about the splendid gardens to pass the time. She had learned the previous evening that the gardens at Staithes were Miss Lavinia's pride and joy, that she bullied the gardeners over each delicate detail, even supervising the annual coppicing of a portion of the home wood. Emily was particularly fascinated by the large square knot garden she discovered near the southern end of the lake. As she bent to examine an intricate thread of red geraniums woven through the twisting border of dwarf yews, she noticed her elder niece sitting alone on the steps of a small marble temple overlooking the lake just beyond a rustic wooden footbridge, beneath which the lake spilled into the brook that raced from north to south at the bottom of the dale.

"Good morning," she called.

Dolly looked up, hesitated for a moment, then got politely to her feet. She wore a dark blue cloak over her white muslin dress, and she clutched it tighter when the breeze dancing down off the moor caught at its folds. "Good morning, Aunt Emily."

"Is this your private place?" Emily inquired, drawing nearer along the white-pebbled pathway and adding in a more gentle tone when she stood beside Dolly and chanced to note the girl's reddened eyes, "I have my own place at Wingrave, you know—a delicious hollow near the river Avon. It is nestled amongst the rocks, one of which is large enough to form a natural armchair even now that I am grown. The river creatures swim in to talk to me when I sit there—dabchicks and swans and . . . oh, all manner of things. I found the place when I was very small, and at first my father punished me whenever he discovered I had been there, for he was afraid that I would fall into the river, you know. But I liked my private hollow, and it drew me despite Papa's profoundest displeasure, so he gave in at last and made my brothers teach me to swim instead."

She had been talking to give Dolly time to compose herself, for it had become immediately apparent to her that the girl had been weeping. Now Dolly looked at her with some interest, even amusement in her damp china-blue eyes. "Did you really defy your papa until he let you have your way, Aunt Emily? Mama has always said Grandpapa frightened her witless whenever he was angry."

Emily sat down on the top step of the little temple, patting the place beside her. "What a splendid view of the house and the lake you have from here." She looked at Dolly and smiled as the girl sat down beside her. "I daresay it was different for your mama than for me, you know, for she was the eldest and thus particularly precious to them, so they were no doubt stricter with her. She was two years old before Thomas was born. But before I came along, there were Eliza, John, Bella, Ned, and Nellie. With so many others to look after me, and our dear Mattie as well—I know your mama must have told you of our governess, Miss Matthews—well, no one paid me much heed, you see, everyone always thinking someone else must be watching me."

"But how lonely you must have been!" Dolly exclaimed.

Revising her first impression of her beautiful niece, Emily said gently, "But I wasn't lonely at all. There was always someone if I wanted someone. In that houseful of people, the hard thing to find was solitude, and I am strangely addicted to occasional periods of quiet."

"I see," Dolly said, withdrawing a little. "Like Melanie. She avoids everyone of late."

"And like you, I daresay," Emily said with a chuckle. "Since you are too kind to tell me to my face that I am intruding, I will take tactful leave of you now and let you enjoy yours." She moved to stand up.

"Oh, no," Dolly said quickly. "This place has no special meaning to me. Indeed, I was sitting here thinking how very lonely it is here at Staithes."

"But surely with your mama and Miss Lavinia, and now Oliver at home, not to mention Miss Brittan—"

"Oh, I do not count Miss Brittan. She has never been my governess, only Melanie's, for she came to us out of Kent after Miss Jennings left in November, just as I was about to emerge from the schoolroom. Papa had even agreed to permit me to go to Woburn for Christmas, though Mama had said it would not be quite the thing since I had not been presented. But then I came down with a putrid sore throat, so those plans all came to naught, and Mama and Papa went to Broadlands instead. But then, to make it up, Papa took us to Robin

Hood's Bay, and then—'' Dolly broke off and stared grimly at the lake.

"I'm sorry," Emily said quietly, "but you must not dwell upon your sorrow, my dear. You ought instead to look about you for other things to occupy your thoughts."

Dolly turned toward her then, her eyes perfectly dry and calm. "But do you not think it was all very unfair, Aunt Emily?"

"We must all feel that, my dear. Your father was very young to die."

"I don't mean unfair for Papa!" Dolly exclaimed. "I mean for me! Why cannot anyone else see how dreadful it is for me?"

She jumped to her feet and ran toward the house without a backward look, her dark-blue cloak billowing behind her, and Emily watched her go, making no attempt to call her back. A few moments later she got up and walked to the shore of the lake, where she sat upon her heels and drew off a glove in order to test the temperature of the water with her fingertips.

The lake was icy cold, and when she reached the northern end, she discovered why. It had been created by damming up the tumbling little brook, and the water in the brook was extremely chilly. A triple-arched stone bridge, much more elaborate than the wooden one she had crossed earlier, spanned the brook where it fed into the lake, making it possible to cross back to the western side and the white-pebbled road. On the east side, several paths led invitingly into the home wood, including one which seemed to follow the course of the brook, but Emily, deciding to postpone her exploration of the woods and the moors beyond them until another day, crossed the bridge, completed her round of the gardens, and returned to the house.

When she discovered that Meriden did not take a nuncheon with the family, she decided that nothing would be gained by putting off their meeting any longer. Directed by William, she approached the estate office, located at the rear of the house in a separate building near the stables, then hesitated when she saw Oliver rush precipitately out the very door through which she intended to pass.

The young man's face was flushed bright red, and he looked to be both angry and on the verge of tears. When he saw her, he changed course abruptly and hurried away.

Drawing a deep breath, Emily squared her shoulders and went up the stone steps to the door. Finding it ajar, she pushed it open before she could change her mind, and stepped inside.

The office was warm and arranged in a utilitarian fashion with papers and books stacked neatly on the shelves that lined three walls. There were two desks in the room, one against the window wall that was piled high with ledger books, an example of which lay open with a quill thrown down across its pages. The other desk was larger and occupied space in the center of the room. Propped atop the welter of papers spread across it was a pair of large booted feet, crossed at the ankles. Although the door squeaked loudly at her entrance, the feet stayed where they were, and from behind the tall ledger propped open and upright on the knees beyond them came a deep, stern voice.

"I have said all I intend to say on the subject, Oliver, so I will be grateful if you will take yourself off again without subjecting me to more of your infantile whining."

Emily said crisply, "I do not whine, Meriden, nor am I accustomed to being addressed by men from behind open books or with their feet rudely propped upon a desk. You will oblige me, sir, by attempting to behave in a more civil manner."

The ledger fell as the chair's front legs and the booted feet crashed to the floor, and Meriden leapt hastily to his feet, his hands scrabbling to adjust his coat and neckcloth. He was two inches over six feet in height, and he was dressed in a dark-brown coat, white shirt and neckcloth, buckskin breeches, and topboots. His dark-brown hair was tousled, not as though he had spent hours creating the fashionable look, but as though he had recently shoved a hand through the thick locks in frustration.

Although Miss Wingrave had previously expressed her approval of his looks, she knew that his was not the sort of countenance generally described as handsome, for his gray eyes were set too deeply beneath his thick dark brows. His nose, though straight, was overlarge for beauty, and his chin was far too prominent and firm for his expression easily to appear conciliating. His breadth of shoulder, however, was unexceptionable, and his figure, though large, was trim and pleasing to the eye.

His lips were pressed together in a rueful grimace, but he recovered himself quickly and grinned at Emily, his teeth flashing white and even, his face changing dramatically. Indeed, she thought, he looked for a moment much like her brother Ned had looked when he had, as a boy, got into one of his frequent scrapes and hoped she would help him explain it all to Papa.

"Forgive my bad manners, Miss Wingrave," he said, clearly assuming that there would be no difficulty about that. "I was out of sorts and, in fact, had no anticipation of receiving a visit from a member of the fair sex. This chamber rarely enjoys the privilege of serving as—"

"I saw Oliver," Miss Wingrave said, seeing no good purpose to be served by submitting herself to long, windy, albeit polite periods and every reason for getting directly to the point. "I realize that the moment is not a propitious one"—she glanced around, noted a straight chair near one wall, and pulled it forward, dusting it with her lace handkerchief and sitting down, talking all the while—"but I have heard so much, you see, and since Sabrina wrote to request my assistance, which is why I am here, after all, I can see no advantage to be gained through procrastination. In effect, my lord, I have determined that the quicker we put our heads together, the quicker matters will be suitably resolved."

Noting that he still stood and that he no longer looked either apologetic or amused, she added graciously, "Won't you sit down, sir? Perhaps you might begin by telling me what subject it was you raised with Oliver just now that put you both so much out of temper. If we discuss the matter thoroughly, no doubt we will soon discover where you went awry." Folding her hands primly in her lap, she regarded him expectantly.

Meriden opened his mouth and shut it again. His brows snapped together and his eyes narrowed dangerously as he returned Miss Wingrave's look with an ominous one of his own. For a long moment, silence reigned in the little office. Finally, in a commendably even tone, the earl said, "Would you mind explaining to me just what business this is of yours, Miss Wingrave? I seem to have missed a step somewhere."

"Do sit down, Lord Meriden," she repeated. "You are entirely too large to pace in an area so crowded as this is, and I shall not be the least bit intimidated by your looming over me like some predatory creature, I promise you."

With no indication that he did so to oblige her, Meriden perched on the front corner of his desk, rather closer to Emily than—for all she had said to the contrary—was commensurate with her comfort. Firmly suppressing a desire to move her chair back a foot, she forced herself to wait for him to speak.

"You have not answered my question," he said calmly.

"Nor you mine, sir," she pointed out. "And I asked my question first."

"Now, look here, my lass—"

"I am not your lass, sir, despite your obnoxious behavior at Woburn Abbey last Christmas, and I take leave—"

"So that still rankles, does it?" He grinned again. "I wondered. 'Twas only a wager, Emmy love, nothing more. You behaved as though you'd been stung, not merely kissed."

Repressing an errant thought that the kiss had been

anything but mere, Emily lifted her chin and said scathingly, "To sweep a lady off her feet and carry her under the mistletoe to steal a kiss before a roomful of jeering people, and all for the sake of a stupid wager, is not the behavior of a gentleman."

"You had been behaving as though the rest of us had some dread disease—those of us who had the misfortune to be men, if not gentlemen. The temptation, Emmy love, was irresistible."

"You were sadly foxed, Meriden, and so you would own if you had the least grain of truth in you."

"Aye, so I was. I own it freely. Needed all the courage the lads could pour into me—"

"You did not. You'd have taken the bet stone sober."

He chuckled. "Right you are, Emmy love."

"Don't call me by that detestable name!" She was remembering all too clearly how tempted she had been to slap him at Woburn, how pleased she had been with her self-control when she had not done so, and how much she had regretted the lost opportunity later.

"Right." He frowned at her. "Suppose we get back to the subject at hand. Just what makes you think for a moment that I will permit you to interfere with my affairs here?"

"They are not entirely your affairs," she said, wishing he would sit properly or at least move a little so that she might stand up and put some distance between them. "My sister has every right to confide in me and every right to request my help with the bumblebroth you have created here."

She suddenly got her wish, for Meriden stood abruptly and walked away toward the shelf-lined wall behind his desk. "You may well call it a bumblebroth," he muttered.

"Just so," she agreed, getting to her feet and moving to stand behind her chair, placing her hands upon the chair back as she added, "You have turned everything upside down, sir, but I believe it has not been from lack of good intent. I daresay you never have had such responsibility thrust upon you before, which is why you have set up Oliver and Dolly's backs and frightened poor Giles and Melanie out of their senses. As for dear Sabrina, you simply must realize—''

"Enough!" He turned to face her again, his hands on his hips, his gray eyes flashing fire from their depths. "Not another word," he bellowed when she opened her mouth to protest. "I realize all I need to realize, Miss Wingrave, and despite any opinion you may have formed to the contrary, I know precisely what I am doing. Responsibility is no stranger to me, though I'll confess that when my father passed to his reward, he did not leave me with such an unholy mess as that which my idiotic cousin left me to sort out.''

"Laurence was not an idiot," Emily said sharply, "and it does not become you to speak ill of the dead."

"Oh, forgive me, ma'am, for trampling on that precious convention, but if anyone has the right to speak ill of Laurence Rivington, it is I, who have inherited those responsibilities he never chose to shoulder. And under that heading, I must respectfully include his wife and his offspring."

"You are insulting, sir."

"I am truthful." He glared at her. "Look here, why don't you just pick up your skirts and get back to your sister's drawing room. I don't mind if she pours her megrims into your ears rather than to mine. In that respect, you *can* be useful.''

"Sabrina asked for my help," Emily said angrily, "and I intend to look after her interests. She believes she ought to have been named guardian to her own children, and I—''

"And you, Emmy love?" His expression changed again. "You will have altered a good deal if you can look me in the eye and tell me in all candor that my cousin would have done better to have named Sabrina to act instead of me.''

She grimaced but remained firm. "He certainly ought to have named her co-guardian, at least, to her own children.''

"Nonsense, he'd have done us both a great disservice thereby. Your sister is incapable of making a decision. She thinks mostly of herself and is accustomed to depending upon others to look after her. She cannot even decide what gown to wear without discussing the point at length with anyone who will listen and advise her."

"Perhaps there is some truth in what you say," said Miss Wingrave, nettled but fair, "but you have treated Oliver—"

"Oliver is as self-centered as his mother without possessing an ounce of her charm," said Meriden grimly, "and he's a foppish wastrel besides. I'll have you know that, not content with being sent down for his debts, he stopped in Cambridge long enough to run up a staggering account with his tailor, which he has just been informing me was necessary because he wishes first to cut a dash in Brighton before moving on to hire a neat little hunting box in Rutlandshire for the entire winter."

"But surely that is what Laurence would have done himself and what he would expect his son to do," said Emily, adding conscientiously, "Not that he would have expected Oliver to be sent down from school."

"Now, there you're out," Meriden said sardonically. "It is precisely what he would have expected, though he would no doubt have insisted that Oliver return to Cambridge rather than chance having to look after the lad himself. Nonetheless, the estate will not tolerate such heavy claims upon its resources. 'Tis bad enough that Sabrina declares she cannot stand the odor of burning tallow and insists upon burning wax candles in every room of the house. There is little I can do about that, but I will not frank Oliver's excesses. He will remain here until Michaelmas term, when he will return to Cambridge."

"But Staithes has always—"

"The income has declined steadily over the past years," he interrupted sharply. "Laurence cared only for his pleasures, nothing for his land, and one cannot consistently take from the land, Miss Wingrave, without giving something back. Certainly not when there is a war on. There have been tremendous demands made upon the estate, and it will take a great deal of effort if it is ever to be restored to its former level of productivity, and so I have told Oliver. I might add that he took the news as a personal affront."

"I daresay you were not tactful," Emily said vaguely, her mind rapidly processing this new information. She was well aware that Meriden would not have told her so much if she had not caused him to lose his temper. When she looked at him to discover that he was glaring at her again, her own last words echoed through her mind. She said firmly, "You are never tactful, so do not look at me as though I have insulted you. You may have some excuse for your handling of Oliver if he has behaved as you say he has, but there can be no excuse for bullying Dolly or for frightening Giles and poor little Melanie."

Meriden snorted. "Your niece Dolly is a pretty pea-goose with a head full of romantic nonsense and an amazing lack of consideration for anyone but herself. Young Giles is a scamp whose school reports teem with such phrases as 'lacks application,' 'will not try,' 'inattentive to studies,' and 'insolent to his masters.' Need I continue?"

"No, but I am certain he is not the first child in his family to receive such reports. Indeed, I daresay you received your share of them if the truth were known."

"I did, and Giles ought to be grateful that my fore-bearance is greater than my noble sire's was. Since my father didn't see humor in misbehavior at school, I quickly came to see the error of my ways. Giles will do likewise."

"Not if he goes to Somerset, he won't," Emily said, "or did you not know that he intends to spend his long vacation there?"

"I knew. He extended his insolence to the point of addressing a letter to me, informing me of that fact. I have already dispatched a carriage and a good stout servant of mine to collect him. I also took the precaution of writing to his headmaster and to the father of the boy he meant to visit. Master Giles will come home, and when he does, he will be placed, as promised, in the hands of a good strict tutor, hopefully one who will make him smart. I have already set inquiries in train to find just such a suitable young man."

"You might at least have asked Sabrina for her opinion of that course of action," Emily said tartly.

"Why should I?" he demanded. "The children and the estate are my responsibilities, and I will manage them perfectly well without Lady Staithes's interference or yours. And before you fling young Melanie's odd behavior in my teeth, let me assure you that whatever your sister may have told you, there is no immediate cause for concern. Melanie is merely suffering from an overreaction to her father's death. Time will heal her wounds much more effectively than well-meaning interference will. So if that is all, Miss Wingrave—"

"Well, it isn't," retorted Emily. "You will not tell me, I hope, that there is no cause for concern about Miss Lavinia's missing jewelry, and certainly you must own that you ought to have asked Sabrina's permission before calling in the Bow Street Runners, as you did. She is distraught."

"And would she have been less distraught to see her servants leaving *en masse*? That is precisely what would have happened had I not called a halt to her foolish whining and complaining and suggesting to one servant that another might be the guilty party. Bringing in professional help was the only course that made sense. And now, Miss Wingrave, since you have discovered all there is to discover, I must ask you once again to refrain from interference. I will manage everything perfectly well on my own, so if you will excuse me now so that I may return to the work you interrupted, I will be grateful."

Once again she was conscious of a strong desire to box his ears, and her knuckles whitened with the increasing tension of her grip on the chair back. But he still stood across the room, his arms folded now across his broad chest, his expression utterly implacable. Since she could hardly fling the chair at him, she smiled instead and said, "I do hope you will find it possible to forgive my intrusion, sir. Had I known you were feeling bilious this afternoon, I would have been glad to postpone my visit to a more propitious occasion. We will discuss this matter more thoroughly, no doubt, when you have recovered your equanimity." And with that Parthian shot she took dignified leave of him, carefully ignoring the leaping flames of wrath in his eyes and the two purposeful steps he took in her direction before the bulk of his desk impeded his progress.

3

EMILY FOUND HER SISTER AND MISS LAVINIA IN THE drawing room, occupied with their needlework, and passed the rest of the afternoon comfortably in their company. When they retired to change their clothes for the evening meal, she found her tirewoman awaiting her in her bedchamber.

"I shall wear the gray silk, Martha," she said. "Since Sabrina still wears her blacks as often as not, I must take care not to offend her by wearing brighter colors just at first. I'll wear my gold bracelet, however, and carry my pink cashmere shawl. The dining room was chilly last evening."

"Pure affectation, if you ask me," said Martha with a sniff.

"What, Sabrina's mourning? Nonsense. I am persuaded that she was much attached to Baron Staithes, just as she says."

"Miss Sabrina," said the henchwoman who had

known both of them from the cradle, "only knows that black becomes her better than mauve or gray would do. You ought to dress as you please, Miss Emily. Not that that gray silk don't become you a treat, for it does. Things be in a shocking way here at Staithes, I'm thinkin'," she added abruptly.

"Well, you needn't think I mean to sit gossiping with you, for I don't," Emily said. "I daresay you have learned no more since our arrival than I have, unless"—she glanced sharply at the woman—"unless you have learned something to the purpose regarding Miss Melanie. Have you, Martha?"

The tirewoman shook her head, frowning. "That I haven't, miss, for no one don't know nothing about it. They say Miss Melanie just went quiet all of a sudden and that she don't talk 'less someone speaks to her direct. Mrs. Crake—she's the housekeeper—she thinks Miss Melanie be frightened of something."

Emily looked at Martha, frowning. "Frightened? What sort of woman is Mrs. Crake, Martha? Do you believe her?"

Martha shrugged. "Could be she's puttin' on airs to be interesting, Miss Emily. For certain sure, she's in a dither over this business of Miss Lavina's jewels as has gone missin', and having Bow Street Runners in the house. But that sort of thing would put most any respectable woman in a fret. Not but what," she added militantly, "I'd like to see that Mr. Tickhill nor yet his fat assistant, Mr. Earswick, try to get round me with their impertinent questions."

"Well, they won't bother you because you weren't even here when the thefts took place," Emily said, hiding a smile at her tirewoman's look of disappointment at being denied the treat of giving not one but two Bow Street Runners a sharp set-down.

Downstairs, Emily met Oliver at the entrance to the drawing room, and it quickly became apparent that the other members of the family had only been waiting for the two of them to arrive. They went directly across the gallery to the dining room. Neither Melanie nor Miss

Brittan was present, but Meriden was there, wearing the same clothing he had worn earlier, although his hair was brushed and he looked a good deal tidier.

Emily nodded graciously at the earl, and he returned the nod with punctilio. Since the meal was being served well before six o'clock, she decided she could not really cavil at Meriden's lack of proper evening attire. Nor would she have done so aloud in any case, for it was certainly not any part of her duty to tell him what he should wear to dine with four ladies and another gentleman. Oliver, she was pleased to note, was dressed with care albeit with an eye for bright colors.

"What the devil is that thing you are wearing?" Meriden demanded as the younger man moved past him to take his seat at the head of the table.

It occurred to Emily to hope that Oliver was paying particular heed just then to Meriden's masterful use of his quizzing glass. There could not be the slightest doubt in anyone's mind as to his opinion of Oliver's choice of attire.

The lad bore up staunchly. "Since you refused to countenance my driving down to Brighton with my friends, sir, I made sure you would not object if I wore my new clothes here at Staithes." He looked down at his pale-pink pantaloons and shiny red-tasseled Hessians, smoothing the gaily embroidered red silk waistcoat and tugging gently at the rolled lapels of his tightly fitting dark-purple coat. When he looked up just as Meriden's eyebrows snapped together, Oliver's right hand groped for his high, heavily starched neckcloth, and the tugging fingers became less gentle. Indeed, his neckcloth appeared suddenly to be too tight for comfort.

"You thought wrong," Meriden said grimly, taking his own seat opposite Emily. "Those colors are an affront to your father's memory. Indeed they are offensive to anyone with an ounce of sartorial taste. When next you present yourself at your mother's dining table, I trust you will dress as a proper gentleman dresses."

"Like yourself, perhaps?" Emily suggested, her eyebrows arching slightly as she looked him over with an air of gentle reproof.

Meriden returned her look. "Yes, if he chooses. But something tells me, Miss Wingrave, that I am meant to infer from your tone that you do not approve of my choice of attire."

"Buckskins are scarcely what a gentleman wears to dine with ladies, sir," she said, "though I had certainly not intended to comment upon the fact."

"Somehow, I doubt that." His mouth turned down at the corners. "Are you honestly going to try to make me believe that your father and brothers don full evening rig every day to dine at Wingrave Hall?"

"Not likely," observed Miss Lavinia.

Sabrina cut in swiftly, placatingly, "They don't, you know, Emily. Why, it was used to be all anyone could do to get John or Ned to wear evening dress at all, though Thomas revels in it. They all wore riding clothes at home, however, unless we dined in company, and well you know it."

The earl had not taken his eyes from Emily, and she saw their twinkle even before he spoke. "Trying to give me a set-down, Em—Miss Wingrave—or merely taking up the cudgels on Oliver's behalf?"

Emily caught Dolly's eyes upon her just then and felt warmth creeping into her cheeks. She wished, not for the first time, that she did not change color so easily, but her voice remained admirably calm when she replied, "I had no right to take you to task for such a thing, sir. You may certainly wear what you choose upon this or any other occasion."

"Very prettily said," Meriden told her approvingly.

"In my opinion, Aunt Emily," Oliver said, signaling for wine, "it was not at all necessary to apologize to him." He looked at Meriden. "Pretty cool to take me up over my attire when I daresay you scarcely ever care a pin for your own. No one has ever called you Beau Meriden, and that's a fact. And what's more," he added, clearly taking courage from his position at the head of the table, from Emily's support, or from both,

"I supose a man can wear what he likes at his own table, and you certainly cannot pretend to be up on what's all the crack when you've scarcely set foot out of Yorkshire these past six months or more. I assure you, sir, everything I've got on is just the style at Cambridge now, and I ain't even one of the out-and-outers. Only wait until you meet my friend Saint Just. I hope you'll have better sense than to take him up on what he wears."

"You are impertinent, Oliver," the earl said with a look that made the young man flush deeply and fall silent.

"Is Mr. Saint Just coming to visit us soon, Oliver?" Dolly asked lightly.

Her brother turned to her gratefully, his enthusiasm returning in full measure. "He will arrive within a sennight, as soon as the long vacation begins. He is meeting Harry Enderby and Ted Bennett at Leeds and traveling the rest of the way with them. You will like him, Doll. He's a great gun, up to every rig and row."

Sabrina said blankly, "You have invited a friend to stay here, Oliver? Now?"

"Well, and why should I not?" Oliver demanded. "I am certain I have every right to do as I please in my own home."

"Men," observed Miss Lavinia, nodding to the footman to serve her some spinach soufflé, "generally do do as they please, in their own homes or elsewhere."

Meriden paid her no heed, turning a stern eye upon Oliver instead. "Regardless of what you seem to think, lad," he said, "you are not the master of Staithes just yet, a fact it would behoove you to remember. Until that day comes, you will oblige me by asking your mother's permission, and mine, before you extend invitations to persons unknown to us, or in fact before you do anything else that affects this household."

"Well, really, Meriden," protested Emily, more hotly than she had intended, "you do take a great deal upon yourself, indeed you do."

The earl turned to face her, his look still hard but his

words carefully mild. "Keep your oar out of my waters, Emmy love."

"Don't call me that," she said fiercely, glancing at Sabrina and then at Miss Lavinia, both of whom were clearly intrigued by the sudden endearment.

Wide-eyed, Sabrina said, "I am certain that no one ever called her Emmy at home. Did they, my dear?"

"Never mind about that, Sabrina." Emily rounded swiftly on the earl. "You are behaving abominably, sir, and I do not scruple to tell you so to your head. I daresay that if poor Dolly should have been so misguided as to express more interest than she has already expressed with regard to this visitor, you would have taken her to task just as you have Oliver."

"Very likely," agreed the earl, his tone grim and the look in his eyes a clear warning.

Emily ignored both. "You take too much upon yourself, Meriden," she said. "You dare to criticize Oliver for bringing a friend home from school, a young man, I daresay, with a perfectly respectable background, and you say it is because Oliver has done so without first begging his mama's permission. That, may I tell you, would come better from one who had not already introduced a pair of low, bumptious Bow Street Runners into this house without extending to Sabrina that same courtesy."

"I wish you will be silent," muttered the earl, glancing pointedly at the hovering servants.

"I daresay you do wish it," Emily replied, awarding those same servants a look of studied indifference, "but I should think myself very poor-spirited to fall silent merely to indulge a whim of yours, my lord, when the need for a little plain speaking is so clearly indicated." She paused long enough to allow William to fill her wineglass; then, Meriden having clamped his lips tightly shut, she continued with airy calm, "I daresay that because no one here ever dares to go counter to your wishes, sir, you have become entirely too confident of the rightness of your every action. I daresay also—"

"If you dare say one more word, Miss Wingrave, I shall probably throttle you," snapped the earl.

"Oh, please, Emily," Sabrina begged, "please say no more. The dining table is not the place for such an uncomfortable discussion as this. Indeed, it is not."

"Don't see why it ain't," Miss Lavinia said fairly. "Most likely place for members of a family to fly out at one another, in my experience."

Emily said stiffly, "I am not, I thank Providence, a member of Meriden's family, Miss Lavinia." Keeping her temper with difficulty, she added, "Sabrina is right insofar as to say that Meriden has no business to be criticizing Oliver at her dinner table. It is the outside of enough for him to disdain Oliver's clothing at any time, but to be picking at him in front of all of us over so trivial a matter as his having invited—"

"Be silent!" Meriden roared, bringing his fist down upon the table with enough force to make the plates and cutlery jump.

"I will not be silent," Emily retorted, her tone rising, if not to meet his, at least enough to make herself heard. "You have behaved like Henry the Eighth, threatening—"

"If you dare to imply," bellowed Meriden, "that I have suggested beheading anyone, my lass, I shall have you bodily removed from this dining room."

"Oh, no!" cried Sabrina.

"You cannot," Oliver declared bravely.

"No, of course he cannot," Emily said tartly. "Really, Meriden, you are too absurd."

"I told you to be silent," snapped the earl, "but since you seem to heed no one's wishes save your own, Miss Wingrave, I take leave to tell you that these last months have improved you not one whit. You are still the same arrogant, sharp-tongued, cold-blooded little witch I kissed last Christmas, and the best thing for all of us would be if you were—"

He had no chance to finish, for Emily rose from her chair in a blind fury and dashed the entire contents of her wineglass across the table, into his face.

Turning on her heel, she snapped over her shoulder, "When you are quite ready to apologize for those insufferable remarks, Meriden, I trust that I shall receive your apologies with grace. At the moment, however, I have nothing more to say to you, nor can I tolerate more of your company today."

As she neared the door, she heard a growl of rage and the crash of a chair behind her, sounds which made her quicken her pace, but she got no further than the gallery before he caught her. Even hearing Sabrina's horrified shriek did not prepare her, however, to find herself lifted bodily off her feet and flung over Meriden's shoulder. The position was both humiliating and uncomfortable. Emily protested vehemently.

Meriden said not one word even when she began pummeling his broad back with her fists and shrilly shouting at him to put her down. He carried her down the stairs to the hall, where there seemed from her unusual vantage point to be a great many more servants than usual. Yelling louder, she tried to kick him but succeeded only in scraping her hipbone painfully against his shoulder. There would be a bruise there, she was sure.

"Put me down!" she cried, flailing at him with her fists again, this time getting in a good, solid hit on his spine that rattled her knuckles. His response was a hard smack of his free hand to that portion of her anatomy that was uppermost. "You villain," she yelped, "put me down this instant! Oh, what are you about?"

He had carried her outside and down the broad front steps. She saw the pebbled drive beneath her, then the smooth green lawn. They were headed downhill. She caught a quick glimpse of Miss Lavinia's knot garden and the little marble temple beyond the footbridge before she felt his muscles tense and experienced a sudden, clear knowledge of what he intended to do. He lifted her from his shoulder, and as she sailed through the air, she let out a scream of rage, only to find her open mouth filled with icy water when she splashed into the lake and sank forthwith.

She came up sputtering and spitting, gasping with the cold, her hair wrapping itself in wet ropes across her face, her silk skirts billowing around her legs one minute, then clinging heavily to them the next. Behind Meriden, hurrying down the lawn, she could see her sister and several others.

"That ought to cool you off!" the earl shouted. "Don't you ever do such a thing to me again, my lass, or it will be much the worse for you."

Emily opened her mouth to shout a reply in kind, but her gyrations had stirred the water and she only swallowed more of it. Her skirts were interfering with the movements of her legs now, so she ducked underwater to do what she could do to make it easier to swim, realizing as she did so that the lake was deeper than she had expected it to be, and colder. And the earl, in his fury, had hurled her a good many feet from shore.

Coming up for air, she saw that he was frowning. Indeed, he looked worried, she thought, almost as if he might think she . . .

She screamed, flailing her arms, letting herself sink again, then kicked wildly, surging upward, shouting as soon as she was clear of the water, "Jack, help me! I can't touch bottom. Oh, help me! Help me!"

She let the last words end in a watery gurgle, but she needn't have worried. Meriden didn't so much as pause to take his boots off before plunging into the icy water after her. She soon felt his strong grip on her upper arm, and then she was raised up out of the water in much less time than she had thought it would take him. With no real effort at all, Meriden swam with her to the shore and hauled her out.

"My God, Emmy," he said remorsefully, "I never thought." Turning his head, he shouted, "Here, someone, run get a blanket!" and then turned back to her. "How could I have done such a thing? You act as if you can do anything at all. I never thought for a moment that you couldn't swim."

"But she can swim," said Dolly clearly above her mother's agitated reproaches. Sabrina was demanding

to know at one and the same time what had possessed
Jack and why Emily had dared to do such an uncivil
thing as to throw her wine at him. No one heeded her,
however, for Dolly, who was standing behind Jack,
gazing down at Emily, went right on in that same
ingenuous tone, "Don't you remember, Aunt Emily?
You told me your brothers had taught you to swim
when you were a child."

Emily had turned her face into the earl's shoulder in
order to keep from betraying her rising mirth, but any
inclination she felt to laugh dissipated abruptly when
she felt Meriden go still upon hearing Dolly's innocent
words. She didn't move either. Indeed, she tried very
hard not even to breathe.

"Look at me," Meriden commanded in a tone that
told her she had better obey him, and at once. When she
had done so, he asked, "Is that true?"

Swallowing carefully, Emily realized she was more
aware of his size at that moment than she had ever been
before. Nodding slowly, she said with as much dignity
as she could muster, "It is true that I can swim, sir,
but—"

She got no further before Meriden threw her back in.

The only difference this time was that the water felt a
degree warmer and she thought he had flung her a few
yards farther. When she surfaced, sputtering, the earl
was already striding up the lawn, his buckskins clinging
damply to his heavily muscled thighs. He had taken off
his coat, which hung limply over his arm. By the time
she had swum to shore, he had altered his course,
heading not for the house but for the stables, anger
showing in every line of his body. Shivering in the chilly
air, Emily thought of the ride he had ahead of him.

"I hope he catches the ague," she muttered wrathfully.

"Oh, he won't," Dolly said, offering Emily the pink
shawl she had left behind. "Cousin Jack is never ill. He
said he got sick once at school but didn't care for all the
fuss, so he never did so again."

"Well, he's likely to take a chill at least if he rides any

distance in those clothes," Emily said, not without a certain amount of grim satisfaction.

Oliver said, "He won't ride home in them. He will get dry clothes from one of the men in the stables if he can find one whose rags he can squeeze himself into. Oh, indeed," he added, laughing at Emily's astonished expression, "I tell you the man never cares a whit for what he looks like. None of the lads is nearly as big as he is. No one hereabouts is. Here, that shawl is useless, ma'am. Take my coat before you freeze."

Sabrina said, "You are wrong, Oliver. You forget Mr. Scopwick." She looked at Emily, her blue eyes dancing. "He is a cousin of Miss Lavinia's and our local vicar, a most formidable man. I promise you, my dear, he would be better named Goliath than Scopwick, for his clothes would hang even on Jack. But come now, you must hurry inside and change into dry clothes yourself. I fear your lovely dress is ruined, but no doubt Meriden will buy you a new one when he regains control of his temper."

"Sabrina, don't talk nonsense," Emily said, gratefully wrapping Oliver's heavy purple coat around her shoulders and gathering up enough wet skirt to enable her to walk up the grassy hill. After some moments of squishing discomfort, she bent down and removed her sandals, which, tied as they were around her ankles, had neither impeded her swimming nor come loose in the water. Carrying them by their strings, she followed the others across the lawn, only to wish she had not removed them at all when she reached the pebbled drive.

"Emily," Sabrina said, watching her pick her way carefully over the stones, "I do wish you had not come to cuffs with Jack like that. It makes matters very awkward."

Oliver said grimly, "I, for one, think she did exactly the right thing, calling him to account as she did. I only wish I might have stopped him from throwing her in the lake."

"You didn't even try," Emily pointed out caustically as she reached the steps at last. "Not either time."

"But what could I have done?" Oliver asked. "Cousin Jack spars with Gentleman Jackson in London, and the only one around here who can give him a match is Harry Enderby, so you cannot have expected me to knock him down. I've no pistol or sword by me at the moment, and I am not such a gudgeon as to challenge him with either one, so what ought I to have done, if you please?"

"Nothing at all," Emily admitted, smiling ruefully at him. "I ought not to have teased you, Oliver. The fight was my own, and so, rightly, were the consequences. When I lost my temper, however, I never expected such a violent reaction."

"Dear Emily," said Sabrina, following her into the hall, "pray tell me you will apologize to him tomorrow. I cannot bear it if the pair of you remain at outs with each other."

"No, Mama, that is too bad of you." Oliver was clearly aroused. "Aunt Emily is the injured party. You cannot say that a glass of wine is worse than a lakeful of water."

"But then she said she couldn't swim," Dolly pointed out, "and he jumped in and got all wet. I do not think he was pleased to discover that she could swim after all, do you?"

"No, I don't," retorted her brother, "and I cannot think how you could have been such a blockhead as to spoil a splendid joke by telling him."

"But I didn't think about that," Dolly protested, her eyes welling with tears. "I just heard him say he was surprised to learn she couldn't swim and I remembered that she can. The words came out just as I thought them. You aren't angry with me, Aunt Emily, are you?"

"No, Dolly," Emily replied quietly. "Indeed, if I had chanced to recall telling you, I would never have tried to trick your cousin, for if you had kept silent and he had later learned of your knowledge, he would have been angry with you too. I do try very hard never to involve others in my bumblebroths. Now, if you will all excuse

me, I do need to take off these wet clothes. Sabrina,
don't trouble your head over any of this. At the
moment, the last thing I wish to do is to apologize to
that odious wretch, but I daresay that by tomorrow I
shall feel differently. I cannot and will not allow him to
replace my dress, however. It would be most improper.
Hello, Miss Lavinia," she added, encountering that
lady at the top of the stairs. "I am sorry to have spoilt
your dinner."

"Didn't spoil it," declared Miss Lavinia, looking her
over from top to toe. "Stayed and ate my meal like a
Christian. Food's cold now, though. Did you enjoy
your swim?"

"Not in the least," said Emily wryly, "but the honors
did not all go to the opposition, ma'am."

"Glad to hear it. Best you get dry, my dear."

"I'll go along and help," Dolly said, paying no heed
to her mama's suggestion that she ought to finish her
dinner, but any gratitude Emily might have felt for her
niece's concern vanished when she realized that Dolly
wanted only to enlist her help in convincing the earl that
his attitude with regard to her own wishes was gothic.
Since Emily was wholly in accord with Meriden's
opinions regarding the proper activities for young ladies
in mourning, she was unable to acquit herself well in the
conversation that followed. Indeed, she rather feared,
once Dolly had gone, that she had let her niece see that
she found her complaints tedious.

While Martha helped her finish changing, Emily considered the events of the evening. That Meriden had
been entirely accurate in his assessment of both Oliver
and Dolly she could no longer doubt. The evidence of
her own eyes and ears were plain. Still, the realization,
though it gave her pause, did not change her opinion of
his methods of dealing with the two young people.
Meriden, she decided, needed to learn to be more
patient with both of them, more tolerant of their faults.
Emily herself had learned a great deal already. She had
certainly learned that she would gain little in head-on
conflict with the earl. Meriden was clearly more

assertive than she, more bellicose, and even less afraid to behave outrageously.

The last thought brought a flush to her cheeks, for she remembered having once thrown a book at her brother Ned after just such extreme provocation as that offered by Meriden tonight. That time, however, though Ned might have been tempted to retaliate, her father had sent them both to their respective bed-chambers with orders to contemplate their lack of conduct. Certainly no one had tossed her into the river for the mere venting of a little temper. And although there had been yet another lecture from Papa the following morning, ending with the oft-repeated suggestion that she learn to control her explosive rages, Emily had known his heart wasn't in it. No one knew better than her family how hard she tried to behave in a civil manner, and no one knew better than they that the harder she struggled to contain her temper, the greater the explosion when she lost it.

Emily sighed. The rules of proper conduct were so clear, so carefully laid out. Presumably all one had to do was to memorize them and act accordingly. The only thing not taken into consideration was the power of one's own emotions. One thing was certain, however. Those rules of proper conduct nowhere allowed for the flinging of wine across a dinner table, no matter how great the provocation, no matter how deserving the victim. Such behavior was unacceptable.

Allowing Martha only enough time to soak up the worst of the water from her hair with a rough towel and to braid it into two plaits fastened in loops at the nape of her neck, Emily smoothed the skirt of the simple blue round gown she had donned and went downstairs in search of her sister.

4

THE ONLY MEMBER OF THE FAMILY PRESENT WHEN EMILY entered the drawing room was Oliver. The young man had drawn an armchair up before the cheerful fire and was slumped in it, his long legs stretched out before him, his right elbow resting on the arm of the chair, his chin propped up in his hand. He did not notice her until she spoke his name, but then he turned sharply, getting quickly to his feet and feeling to be sure that his neckcloth was in place.

"Aunt Emily, how are you? I trust you took no hurt."

"No, Oliver, I am perfectly stout, thank you, barring damp hair. I was looking for your mother."

"She is in her sitting room." He grinned. "She is studying the lesson for the service tomorrow, for she says old Scopwick bellows so that she cannot attend to what he is saying. He frightens her witless, if you want my opinion."

"If that is your opinion," Emily said sternly, "I do not wish to hear it." Privately she knew Oliver was probably right. Everything frightened Sabrina witless. But Emily would certainly never encourage a young man to speak so rudely about his mother. She was pleased to note that he looked chastened. But still, what was it that he had said? "Services, Oliver? Goodness, I've lost count of the days. Tomorrow is indeed Sunday, is it not?"

"Oh, yes," said Oliver, "but it needn't be, you know, for Vicar Scopwick holds an evening service every day. I suppose you know that country families were used to have their own prayer service before retiring each night. Many still do, of course, but one of Scopwick's pet causes is the lack of religious education for those servants and families in households where the custom no longer prevails."

"But surely people do not simply give all their servants leave to attend daily services," Emily protested. "How would one run one's household properly?"

"Just don't ask Scopwick that question unless you want your ears to ring for hours afterward with his reply," recommended Oliver. "Our servants could go, I'm sure, simply because Mama is terrified of having him descend upon her in righteous wrath. I know for a fact that she has made generous donations to several of his private causes, for I once heard Cousin Jack taking her to task over the amounts. Scopwick has a clothing fund for poor children, another for the French prisoners of war at the detention camp at Stilington, one to provide postal costs for those prisoners who wish to send letters home to their families, and yet another to provide medical care for anyone who needs a doctor and cannot afford to pay one. I daresay Mama has contributed to all of them. Scopwick probably even pays the smugglers who carry the prisoners' letters into France," he added, chuckling. "I doubt that the post still crosses the Channel on English packets."

"I believe neutral ships carry such letters," said Emily repressively. "Does Sabrina go to these services every evening? She did not go last night."

"Oh, no, only on Wednesday evenings. Many of the local gentry attend then, so she is sure of learning all the gossip as well as receiving her religious teaching."

"Does Miss Lavinia go?"

"Occasionally, I believe, though she would scorn to make a practice of it. Says she reads her Bible every night before she puts out her candle, and that that plus Sunday ought to satisfy anyone." He paused, regarding her searchingly. Then, his voice lacking its normal confident tone, he said, "I say, Aunt Emily, I do hope you ain't still vexed with me about what I said earlier. Cousin Jack fair makes my blood boil, but I know I'm no match for him, and I could see nothing to be gained by putting my oar into the business and making him all the angrier."

"Do not let such reflections prey upon your mind," Emily advised. "When I told you earlier that I did not blame you in the least, I meant it." Deciding not to seek out Sabrina for the moment, she pulled another chair close to his. "Sit down, Oliver. I wish to speak with you."

He obeyed, watching her warily, and not looking the least bit reassured when she frowned, collecting her thoughts. When she looked directly at him and smiled, however, she had the satisfaction of seeing him relax. "I shan't eat you, you know. I daresay your position is a most difficult one at present."

"Ain't it just!" He leaned toward her eagerly. "You cannot imagine what a fix Papa's death put me in. For a time, I had my first quarter's allowance, of course, but when that was gone and I applied to Cousin Jack for more, instead of sending me a draft like Papa always did, he wrote telling me I must learn to practice economy. I'd certainly never taken him for such a sobersides, I can tell you that. I was dished. Went to the money lenders, of course, so by second quarter my allowance was already spoken for, which meant I just got in deeper, which anyone ought to have known would be the case. Same thing happened when I received my third quarter's allowance, which is when the proctor discovered the whole. I must say he put the wind up the Shylocks, for he's a great gun when all's told, but he made me write a full account of my debts to Cousin Jack and he wrote to him also, and then I was sent down. There was the most awful row when I got home," Oliver added, shuddering at the memory. "Cousin Jack don't seem to understand how it is, but Lord, I've never heard anyone accuse him of being stiff-rumped or tight with a shilling."

"No, I don't think he is either of those things," Emily said. "Has he ever discussed the way matters were left here at Staithes when your father died, Oliver?"

"Lord, no. He don't want me plaguing him to death with impertinent questions, either."

"Have you tried asking pertinent questions?"

Oliver shook his head. "Wouldn't want to vex him. He don't heed what I say, and he don't care about my pleasures, so here I sit, kicking my heels. I'll be glad when Saint Just and the others arrive. Ted Bennett's a quiet sort, and Harry's always got his eye on the proprieties, but Saint Just's always ripe for fun and gig."

"Oliver, you are Baron Staithes now. I think you ought at least to express an interest in your estate."

"And do you think for one moment that Cousin Jack won't snap my nose off and send me to the roundabout?"

"Pray do not take that sarcastic tone with me," she said sternly. "Meriden can scarcely refuse to explain to you how matters stand with your own property, and I think he will be pleased if you show an interest."

"Well, I do not have any interest, since I have no power to change anything, so I cannot think for a moment why I should make an ass of myself."

"You are a very intelligent young man," Emily said casually. "I saw that right off, of course, so I am persuaded that you will know the exact course to follow. And I suspect that you can see for yourself that if you were to pretend an interest, even if you do not truly have one, and were to continue to ask about things even if your cousin puts you off at first, that eventually you will learn a great deal. But perhaps what you really mean to say is that you do not want the responsibility of running this great estate, not now or ever."

"Well, of course I want it. It is my privilege, after all. It just seems pointless . . ." He paused thoughtfully, then said, "Do you really think he would tell me such things?"

"I do not know," replied Miss Wingrave, ever truthful. "I should think he would. And I will tell you something else, Oliver. You are neglecting your duty toward Dolly, and that is something Meriden would never encourage you to do.''

"Dolly? Good Lord, ma'am, what have I to do with Dolly?''

"She is your sister. At present she is lonely and feeling greatly put upon. She does not understand all that has happened, and she may do something foolish out of her frustration. You, being close to her in age, are more likely than anyone else to comprehend her feelings and to guide her.''

"Much she would listen to me,'' snorted Oliver. "Why, Harry Enderby—he's my best friend and he don't have a sister of his own like Ted Bennett does—he always notices what Dolly's doing, and though he don't approve of her above half, she pays no heed to him or to me either when we criticize her behavior.''

"Then you must exert yourself to win her trust. Truly, Oliver,'' Emily went on earnestly, "you can do it, and it will keep you from being bored. I believe Dolly is starving for attention, and you certainly seem to me to be clever enough to bring her round your thumb in a trice if you wish to do so.''

She knew immediately that she had been right to appeal to his vanity, for he stirred and straightened in his chair. He did not agree with her in so many words, nor did he say he would attempt to do as she asked, but when she left him, still staring into the fire, Emily felt as though she had accomplished a good deal. Really, she told herself as she went back up the stairs, Oliver was no more difficult to manage than Ned or John, not nearly so difficult as Papa.

She found Sabrina preparing for bed in her dressing room and stayed only long enough to apologize for causing her distress and to promise faithfully to make amends to Meriden on the following day. Then, her conscience clear, she took herself off to her own bedchamber to read two chapters of a book borrowed from Miss Lavinia before retiring to her bed to sleep peacefully through the night.

The following morning, Emily arose early and decided to enjoy a brisk walk in the gardens before breakfast. She followed the drive around the dew-dampened lawn to the lakeshore path, past the knot garden, across the wooden footbridge and past the temple, around the far side of the lake to the triple-arched stone bridge. From the center of the bridge, looking back, the little temple resembled a miniature Pantheon, while the house on the hill to her right looked like a child's large dollhouse. The prospect was a pleasing one.

On the other side of the bridge, the lakeside path joined the pebbled drive. One could continue around the lake, back to the house, or one could enter the home wood, where the drive became a roadway leading farther up the dale. Sunlight danced in golden, dust-laden beams among the leaves and shrubbery of the lush woodland, beckoning Emily to explore.

She had walked for only a few minutes along the narrow road before her sharp ears noted the sound of approaching hoofbeats. The voices of the woods continued undiminished, however, which told her that the approaching rider was no stranger to the denizens of the place. The rhythm of the hoofbeats was steady, but her heartbeat was not, for her pulse quickened erratically. A firm believer in doing what had to be done as quickly as possible, she stood her ground, peering ahead through the overhanging tree branches and encroaching shrubbery, as certain as she could be of the oncoming rider's identity.

Nor was she mistaken. Looking powerful and dominating astride a large chestnut gelding, Meriden hove into sight out of the shady gloom into a patch of sunlight. As soon as he saw her, he reined in and dismounted, his quick smile flashing welcome as he said, speaking more rapidly than usual, "I am very glad to encounter you, Miss Wingrave."

"I, too," she replied, returning his smile. "I meant to look for you directly after breakfast. I have something of a decidedly important nature to say to you, sir, though I must confess it goes sorely against the grain with me."

"Please, for once you must let me speak first," he said. "I am a poor hand at apologies and if you interrupt me, I shall be sure to lose my thread."

"But 'tis I who must apologize to you!"

"What? Have you been ordered to do so, Emmy love?" He grinned at her. "Who would dare to command you, I wonder?"

She stamped her foot. "Do not call me by that odious name, sir, or by heaven I shall—"

"I am sorry, Miss Wingrave," he said contritely, taking a step toward her, his hand held out. "I ought not to have offered provocation now or last night. It was very ill done of me. Will you forgive me?"

"Goodness," she said, hardly noticing when he took her hand in his. "For someone out of practice, you do the thing prettily, Meriden, though I perceive that you have apologized only for provoking me, not for throwing me in the lake and ruining a practically new gown."

"Well, you see," he said gently, looking down into her eyes with an impish smile tugging at his lips, "it is first your turn to apologize for the wine. By my reckoning, we can exchange apologies with each other for quite some time before we run short of subject matter. At least I did not tell lies to you."

"Nor I to you," she retorted. "I never tell lies."

"You said you couldn't swim."

"No, sir, only that I couldn't touch bottom. I couldn't. Not without going underwater, at all events," she added conscientiously.

He laughed. "I beg your pardon." When she tried to withdraw her hand, his tightened. "Friends, Miss . . . Look here, I won't go on being so dashed formal all the time. If I agree to try very hard to remember not to call you 'Emmy love,' which I freely admit I do only to get a rise out of you, and if I add to my other apologies one for behaving like a schoolboy at Woburn last

Christmas, will you allow me to call you Emily?"

"I will, my lord. It does seem foolish to remain so punctilious with each other when you are practically a member of the family."

"I *am* a member of the family, and both the family and my friends call me Jack, Emily."

"Well, but I cannot call you Cousin Jack, and—"

"You are quibbling. I distinctly heard you cry out my name last night. If you can do so to make me look foolish, surely you can do so when I particularly request it."

She blushed, for until he reminded her, she had not remembered calling him by name. Indeed, she had not thought at all about what she had shouted, not at the time, nor afterward. She did not doubt his word, however, and there being nothing she could say in her own defense, she yielded gracefully. "Very well, sir, if you wish it." She tugged at her hand again, and this time he released it.

"So now we are friends," he said, "and you will allow me to attend to my business here at Staithes without interference."

She stiffened. "If we are friends, sir, you ought to be willing to hear my opinions."

He frowned, but he did not answer her immediately. Instead he stood looking down at her with a probing expression in his eyes that made her wonder at first if she had smut on her chin or a button undone. It was all she could do to keep her hands at her sides and her tongue behind her teeth. Finally he said, "From what I have learned about you, I doubt that I can force you to keep your opinions to yourself, but I believe I must warn you to have a care for the manner in which you express them. You see," he added, smiling in a way that sent tremors rippling through her body in a most unfamiliar manner, "I know myself, and I know for a fact that I don't respond well to criticism or to uninformed interference in my affairs."

"Then you must exert yourself a trifle to be more receptive, must you not?" Emily said, giving herself a shake, as though by doing so she could rid her body of the disturbing sensations. "Tell me something," she added sweetly. "Do you recognize arrogance when you encounter it in others, sir?"

He chuckled. "That shaft flies wide, Emmy . . . ah, Emily. You must take care never to ask questions that may then be asked of you in return. 'Tis the mark of an amateur squabbler to give one's opponent use of one's own best ammunition." When she flushed, he chuckled again. " 'Twould be best an I see you safe back to the house now, I think, as I have pledged to escort you all to Scopwick's chapel after you have broken your fast. Do we cry truce?"

She smiled up at him. "I believe we must, sir, for the present at least."

The rest of the day passed without incident if one discounted Emily's astonishment at Vicar Scopwick's prodigious size and energetically bellowed sermon; and, surprisingly, her truce with Meriden lasted for a little more than a week. During that time, she exerted herself to make friends with her sister's children and learned that the earl was capable of patience when he chose to exercise it. Young Oliver, having evidently decided to attempt to act upon her advice, had approached him on several occasions, asking shyly to have this or that matter explained to him. Since the young man's interest was peripatetic at best, his approach was not methodical, but Meriden bore up well.

Dolly, encouraged by her aunt to join the others when they paid duty calls at Enderby Hall and Bennett Manor and to examine the monthly ladies' magazines with her when they arrived, began to show signs of behaving more civilly too. And when she discovered that Emily did not despise her more romantic choice of reading material, she became more approachable. Emily could not but wish, however, that her elder niece would begin to think occasionally of someone other than herself.

With Melanie she made no headway whatever. Indeed, she rarely saw the little girl, and when she did, their conversations were distressingly one-sided. Emily persevered, giving the child a blue silk ribbon for her hair and inviting her to walk in the garden with her whenever the opportunity arose. After one of these occasions, upon meeting Meriden in the hall afterward, she described her walk to him.

"I prattled like a magpie, I promise you, but I never got more than a single word at a time out of her."

"She just needs more time," he said.

"Well, she seems to enjoy hearing stories about my family, about my childhood, you know. Indeed, today—once—I am very nearly sure I almost made her laugh."

"Telling about one of your many childish scrapes, no doubt."

"How did you know?"

He smiled. "I have no doubt that your childhood was filled with such incidents. Will you tell me it was not?"

"No, for I was certainly a mischievous child. Fortunately, with so many brothers and sisters to look out for me, I rarely came to grief."

"And you spent most of your time winding them all round your little thumb, I make no doubt."

She favored him with a look of wide-eyed innocence. "I cannot think what gave you such a notion."

"Merely the fact that you seem so confident, even here and now, of being always able to make everyone march to your drumming. Take care that you do not stumble up against something or someone who will not leap to your command."

Fortunately for the state of their truce, Emily chose not to take offense, thinking only that he must have been indulged a good deal himself as a child. He was the last of eight children, Sabrina had told her, with his two elder brothers and one sister dying in an epidemic before his birth. How his parents and elder sisters must have doted on and cherished the precious heir to Meriden, she thought. No doubt, even now, his lordship believed he had only to decide upon a course of action and those about him would follow obediently along behind him.

Matters went smoothly between them for a time,

however, and the arrival of Oliver's friends, Alban
Saint Just and Harry Enderby, at the end of the week,
provided diversion without causing ructions. Ted
Bennett had left their company at Helmsley, but
Enderby, who stopped at Staithes only long enough to
deliver Saint Just before continuing to his own home,
proved to be a cheerful young man with a snub nose,
rounded cheeks, twinkling blue eys, and an unpre-
possessing demeanor. He dressed fashionably but con-
servatively and earned Emily's respect from the outset
with his open countenance and excellent manners.

Saint Just, with his reddish-blond hair, brown eyes,
long-oval face, and excellent figure, proved to be handsome, charming, even witty. He was welcomed by
everyone, particularly by Oliver and Dolly. He was
taller than Oliver, two years older, and though he
claimed to be one of the dandy set, Emily privately
thought him a fop, for his clothing was as colorful as
Oliver's. He prided himself, he said, on being unafraid
to experiment with hue and tint. Not for Mr. Saint Just
were the pale yellow pantaloons, dark coats, and snow-
white, well-starched linens that were currently enjoying
favor among the London dandy set.

"Unenterprising and dull," he pronounced flatly
when asked about that fashion over dinner the evening
of his arrival.

Dolly giggled. "Oh, Mr. Saint Just," she said, "you
must know so very much about London. Do tell us."

Mr. Saint Just airily admitted having spent some
weeks in the capital, acquiring polish. "Town bronze,
they call it," he said, and willingly went on to describe
various sights to his audience, two of whom were
particularly fascinated. But since his descriptions
included only such clubs, gaming hells, and sporting
events as he had visited, Emily soon found herself
looking to the earl, also present at the table that
evening, in expectation of having the conversation
directed into more acceptable channels.

Meriden only grinned at her. It was Miss Lavinia who
squelched Saint Just. "Didn't encourage you to spout

stuff about cockfights to ladies in the metropolis, did
they, young man? Learnt that much all on your own-
some, I daresay.''

Impaled upon the basilisk stare emanating from
behind Miss Lavinia's wire-rimmed spectacles, Saint
Just flushed deeply, having clearly been so caught up in
his narrative that he had forgotten his audience. "Beg
pardon, ma'am. Meant no offense. 'Twas an amusing
story, was all.''

"I daresay," said Miss Lavinia, unimpressed. "You
one of the Saint Just lot out of Norfolkshire?''

"I have that honor, ma'am.''

"Thought so." Miss Lavinia returned her attention to
her dinner.

The rest of the meal and the two days that followed
passed uneventfully except for Emily's second
experience of a Sunday service at Mr. Scopwick's little
church, where the very rafters vibrated with the vicar's
extensive periods. It amused her, as it had the week
before, to watch her sister sitting in rapt concentration,
her brow furrowed as she tried to follow the sense of
what was being bellowed at them. Emily, who considered devotion to be a private matter and who had
never had the least desire to bellow at God, was rather
startled to discover that her uppermost emotion was
amusement.

The ladies' escort that morning had been provided by
Oliver and Mr. Saint Just, but the Meriden pew was
directly across the aisle from the Staithes', and the gates
were low enough for her to see that it was occupied. The
single occupant looked up just then and she saw her
amusement reflected in his gray eyes. Blushing, she
turned her gaze virtuously to her prayer book.

Mr. Scopwick was holding forth at that moment on
the wicked treatment suffered by the French prisoners
of war in England, and Emily's attention was soon
drawn by his words. She was shocked, not amused at
all, to learn that there were upwards of twelve thousand
such prisoners in camps throughout the country.

"So distressing," Sabrina said on the way back to the

Priory. "One cannot help but feel for them, but I cannot agree that we should look to their needs before those of our own, try as I might."

"Of course not," agreed Emily, walking at her side along the path that led from the chapel and vicarage to the road through the home wood. Miss Lavinia walked ahead of them, while Oliver, Dolly, and Mr. Saint Just, enjoying their own conversation, followed some distance behind. After a moment's pause, Emily added, "By all accounts, the French treat our people much worse than we treat theirs."

Miss Lavinia, clicking her tongue, said over her shoulder, "Saw in the *Times* last week that they wouldn't let poor Lady Lavice enter France to visit her husband in that detention camp at Verdun. Foolishness, that's what it is."

"Well, but we don't let Frenchwomen into England either," Emily pointed out.

"Spies," declared Miss Lavinia flatly. "We couldn't trust one among the lot of them. A proper English lady wouldn't stoop to such nasty deeds."

"On Wednesday evening it was the deserving poor," Sabrina said musingly, wrapped in her own thoughts. "Do you know, I have never known how to tell the difference between the deserving and the undeserving poor. Unless it's children, of course. Perhaps that is what he meant."

Emily smiled. "Was Mr. Scopwick so fierce about our obligation to the poor?"

"Oh, dear me, yes," Sabrina replied. "He is always fierce."

"Always has been," put in Miss Lavinia. "Takes things to heart, Eustace does."

"Well, his heart must be a large one if it matches the rest of him," said Emily, thinking her sister's description of the man as a Goliath had hit the mark. He didn't dwarf Meriden, but the earl did look somewhat reduced in size standing next to the massive dark-haired, fiery-eyed vicar.

They didn't see any more of Meriden that day, but he

was on hand Monday afternoon when a large, lumbering traveling carriage drew up at the front entrance of Staithes Priory to deposit a burly man of medium height and a sturdy boy of thirteen with tousled light-brown curls and a surly look of defiance in his light-blue eyes.

Emily and Sabrina, observing the arrival from the drawing-room window, hurried down to greet them, joining Meriden, who saluted Giles's companion with smiling affability. "Well done, Harbottle. I knew I might depend upon you. Any trouble?"

Emily noted the quick, challenging look in the boy's eyes and the reassuring wink from Harbottle.

"Naught to mention, m'lord," said the latter. "We changed teams often enough to make good time, think on, and I'll warrant the lad and me rubbed along tolerable well, all told."

"Good man. Well, Giles?"

"How do you do, sir?"

"Very well, thank you," replied the earl, favoring him with a look of sardonic amusement. "You and I will talk later. You may make your bow now, if you please, to your mama and your Aunt Emily."

Giles obliged with more grace than might, under the circumstances, have been expected of him. The look in his eyes when his gaze encountered Emily's was shy and mischievous at one and the same time. "How do you do, ma'am?" he said. "You didn't half give me fits with that letter, you know. I didn't realize females could read Latin."

"I can't, you wretched brat, but my brother Ned translated the whole, and when we discovered what you had done, we decided to serve you up some of your own sauce."

"Served is right," Giles said, grimacing. "My tutor saw the thing and made me translate every word. It took me two full evenings and made me muck up some of my other work, besides."

"Poor boy," said Emily, grinning at him. "No wonder you never deigned to reply."

Giles grinned back, unabashed. "I should say not."

Meriden had been listening to the exchange with interest. He said, "The letter must have been a very long one to have occupied two evenings in translation."

Giles favored him with a chilly look. "I daresay you could have done the thing in a trice, sir, but Latin is not my favorite subject."

"Nor is any other, by the look of your school reports," the earl observed evenly. "Get your traps inside, lad, and take some time to get your bearings. I will see you in the library at three o'clock. I have a number of things to say to you."

Giles did not look as though he expected to enjoy their interview, but he went obediently into the house with Sabrina on his heels, and Emily soon found herself alone on the front drive with Meriden. He had lingered to issue orders to his servant and to the coachman, and she had lingered, hoping to make his forthcoming interview with Giles a little easier on the boy.

When the coach had gone, Meriden looked down at her with the same touch of sardonic amusement she had noted earlier. "You would do better to spare your breath," he said gently.

"I wanted only to remind you, sir, that Giles is merely a little boy and deserves—"

"We won't discuss what he deserves," Meriden said, cutting her off abruptly. "You have not been privileged to see the very impertinent letter he wrote to me, so you can have little understanding—"

"I know he wrote to tell Sabrina that he didn't care for the tone of your letter to him," Emily said, interrupting him in turn, "so I can well imagine what he must have written to you, but in this instance, sir, you must certainly concede that I have more experience with boys than you—"

"*What*?" He glared at her. "What can you possibly know about boys?"

"I have brothers, sir, and you do not."

He grimaced. "As I happen to know that the youngest of your brothers is at least four years older than you are—"

"Five, actually," Emily said, "but that doesn't signify in the slightest, for—"

"The devil it doesn't signify," Meriden retorted. "If you mean to try to tell me that you ever had the least say in your brothers' upbringing, I won't believe you. Furthermore, I have no intention of prolonging this idiotic conversation. The reason I put young Giles off till three is that I have business at the estate office that will occupy me until then, so if you will be good enough to excuse me, I will take my leave."

A moment later she was alone on the drive, fuming. As she returned to the house, she replayed their discussion in her mind, and she had to admit she had made an error in making such casual reference to her brothers. One simply could not expect a man raised by doting parents and attentive sisters to comprehend how much an intelligent young woman could learn about the proper management of boys merely by observing what went on around her as she grew up and by paying heed to the reminiscences of those involved in raising three of the creatures. Really, she thought, Meriden had a good deal to learn. She had been prodigiously patient with him until now, but this last confrontation had sorely taxed the limits of her civility.

5

THAT EVENING, ONCE EMILY HAD CHANGED HER clothing for dinner and was discussing with Martha whether she would wear her plaits coiled atop her head or in loops behind her ears, Sabrina entered her room, clearly big with news and just as clearly unwilling to speak before the abigail.

"Pin them up quickly, Martha," Emily commanded, "and then leave us. Dear Sabrina, do sit down before you explode."

Sabrina strode to the window instead and waited only for the door to shut behind Martha before she turned and said, "I am sure we never had secrets from her when we were young, but I cannot think it right to speak of such things before her now. Emily, do you know what that wretched man has gone and done?"

"Tell me."

"He has arranged for Mr. Scopwick to tutor my poor little Giles!" Sabrina exclaimed. "Have you ever heard of anything so brutal as that in all your days? That terrifying man! Why, I just quaked the day he stormed the place to complain to Jack about those dreadful Runners. Putting everyone up in arms, he said. Saying they had accused even the villagers of wishing to steal Miss Lavinia's jewels and had demanded permission to search people, which they must know they cannot do."

Emily had not been privileged to witness the vicar's invasion of Staithes, but she had heard about it. "He was incensed because they accosted his housekeeper," she said calmly. "Questioning her was certainly a foolish thing for the Runners to have done, for she could have had nothing to do with what happened here. But I must agree that he is not the man to take charge of a sensitive boy like Giles. I will speak to Meriden directly after dinner—that is, if he dines here tonight."

"Oh, he does, but do you think that wise, my dear? It might be better to consider carefully first what you mean to say to him, to wait until morning—"

"I never put off that which can be accomplished with speed and resolution," Emily said firmly.

Once again Sabrina looked as though she had conjured up something she knew not how to control, but although she twittered a little and flung up her hands, she made no further objections.

Neither Giles nor Melanie was present at the dinner table, but in Mr. Saint Just's presence Emily did not believe it proper for her to initiate discussion of Giles's tutor or to debate the earl's decision when Miss Lavinia introduced the topic.

"Understand you've asked Eustace Scopwick to tutor young Giles," she said during a lull in the conversation.

"I have." Meriden glanced at Emily, but she kept her attention riveted to her plate. "He is an extremely well-educated man who comes from an excellent family."

"Oh, yes," agreed Miss Lavinia. "He had every benefit open to a younger son. Always surprised everyone—being so big, don't you know—that he didn't embrace a military career. And then when he chose the church, everyone expected him to advance quickly. His mama was convinced he'd become Archbishop of York at the very least." She smiled as if at a fond memory.

"But he ended up here instead," observed Emily, deciding that this portion of the conversation was harmless.

"Didn't end," contradicted Miss Lavinia. "Began. The living was free when he took his orders, and Meriden's papa very kindly awarded it to Eustace. That was more than twenty years ago. Says he likes the people hereabouts."

Emily looked at her sister. "Then you have known Mr. Scopwick for a very long time."

Sabrina flushed. "Not really. That is . . ." She glanced with embarrassment at the interested Mr. Saint Just, then added with a self-conscious gathering of dignity, "You see, we were so rarely at home, Emily, and Laurence didn't hold with . . . with . . ."

"With all that religious claptrap," put in Oliver helpfully. Then, catching Meriden's steady, disapproving gaze upon him, he added defensively, "Well, that is what Papa said. I heard him say so more than once."

"There is no need for you to repeat his words, however," the earl said gently.

The reprimand brought a flash of anger to Oliver's eyes. Looking first at Saint Just as though to draw courage from him, he turned back to Meriden defiantly.

Emily's mouth opened but before she could speak she

saw that intervention would be unnecessary. The earl had caught and held Oliver's angry gaze with his own, and the young man's defiance evaporated quickly. Painful color invaded his cheeks, and when Meriden finally looked away, Oliver did not so much as glance at Saint Just again.

Unaware of the byplay, Miss Lavinia said musingly, "Letitia had some odd notions of devotion, though I suppose I ought not to say so of my own sister." Having drawn their attention, she added, "Staithes Priory, you know—daresay she had some idea of bringing it back to whatever grandeur it enjoyed before Henry the Eighth rearranged such matters. Kept her own chaplain, of course—you will remember, my dear." She smiled at Sabrina.

"Oh, yes," Sabrina said, giving a dramatic shudder. She looked at Emily. "Although Laurence's papa had been dead nearly five years when we married—for, like poor Laurence, he died young—his mama lived some ten years longer, three of them here at the Priory before Laurence prevailed upon her to retire to the dower house near Harrogate. There were services every morning and every evening for all the servants and the family while she was here. Laurence hated them, and I must say they were very long and dull. How the servants ever managed to get their work finished between times, I am sure I do not know."

"But surely," Emily protested, "you must have gone to church, Sabrina. You did not stay away all those years."

"Oh, no," replied Sabrina, more flustered than ever. "I am persuaded that we very nearly always attended St. George's Chapel in Hanover Square on Sundays when we were in London, for everyone does so. And I daresay we attended any number of private services at winter house parties."

Emily, catching Mr. Saint Just's fascinated eye just then, hastily changed the subject to one more appropriate to the company. When Sabrina signed at last for the ladies to take their departure, leaving the gentlemen to their port, Emily said quietly to the earl, "Before you leave for Meriden Park, sir, I would be grateful for a private word with you."

He raised his eyebrows, but his tone was polite. "I am at your disposal now, ma'am. Shall we go along to the library?"

Sabrina looked wildly from one to the other. "Emily, perhaps you ought—"

"Thank you, my lord," said Emily, not hesitating to interrupt her. "The library will do excellently well."

Miss Lavinia smiled at her and turned away with a little shake of her head to say to Sabrina, "Come along to the drawing room, my dear. You promised to show me how to manage that intricate knotting pattern I admired on your French shawl. Dolly shall read to us for a spell until Emily returns."

Grateful for her assistance in calming Sabrina, Emily did her best to concentrate on what she would say to the earl. He was behind her as she descended the stairway, however, and she was absurdly conscious of his presence. Nerve endings all over her body stood on end, making her feel warm despite the chill of the large hall. The feeling made it hard for her to think, though he said nothing at all until they had entered the library.

Meriden shut the door. "Will you sit down, Emily?"

Nodding, she chose a leather armchair near the huge Chippendale library table in front of a tall window overlooking the lake. She noted as she sat down the elegance of dark-red curtains looped back with gilt cords and the pleasant smell of leather that permeated the room. Books and papers piled on the table as well as on a nearby leather sofa gave her to understand that he must have worked there after his interview with Giles.

Instead of taking the leather chair near the window behind the table, as she had expected him to do, Meriden simply pushed papers aside and sat on the table directly in front of her, his hands resting by his hips, his long fingers curled around the edge just above a carved festoon of flowers. "I trust you remember my warning," he said gently, looking down into her eyes.

He looked so big, so like a predator poised to spring, and once again he was too close for her comfort. She blinked up at him. "Warning?"

"About interfering. You wish to take me to task over my treatment of Giles today, I suppose. I have been expecting it, of course, so I will endeavor to contain my temper in patience."

Emily suddenly discovered that she was having difficulty restraining her own temper. Speaking with forced calm, she said, "You agreed to hear my opinions, sir."

"Not precisely. I acknowledged that I would find it well nigh impossible to prevent your voicing them. But for goodness' sake," he added hastily when she stiffened, "let us not haggle over whether I will listen. Say what you must and have done."

Emily opened her mouth and shut it again, forcing herself to count slowly and silently to ten as the estimable Miss Matthews had frequently counseled her to do during her formative years. Since she accomplished this feat only by not looking higher than his lordship's polished boot tops, it was with some surprise that she glanced up at last to find his eyes aglint with amusement.

"Finished counting?" he asked.

Stifling the urge to begin again, she said tightly, "It is a practice you might cultivate to some advantage, sir, if you know how to count."

She regretted the rider when he clicked his tongue and said chidingly, "Don't be childish, Emily. You don't really doubt the quality of my education, do you?"

"Of course not," she said, wishing he would rid himself of his habit of positioning himself so close to her when they talked. "You are being absurd, my lord, and we have strayed from the point of our conversation."

"I was afraid you would notice that," he murmured.

Exasperated and tired of feeling dwarfed, she stood, stepping back away from him as soon as she was able to do so, a little surprised, but grateful, too, when he did not also come to his feet. "The point is certainly Giles, sir."

"You agreed to call me Jack," he reminded her dulcetly.

"That has nothing to do with this discussion."

"But it is difficult for me to follow your reasoning," he complained, "if I must constantly be wondering whether you will next address me as 'sir' or 'my lord.' "

"Will you just once, for the love of heaven, listen to me? Why on earth did you choose that dreadful man to instruct poor Giles?" It was not, certainly, the way she had meant to begin. She had meant to lead up to the point with the utmost tact. But the man was infuriating. He had goaded her past any ability she had to command tact.

His reply was in keeping with all the rest. "I chose him," he said, shifting his weight and folding his arms across his broad chest, "because he is the right age for the task."

"I beg your pardon?"

"As well you might." He crossed one booted foot over the other. "I told you you might repose complete faith in my judgment. Surely you see now that I have done the best thing possible for all concerned."

"I see nothing of the sort," she informed him. "What possible importance can his age have with regard to anything? Indeed, I distinctly recall your mentioning that you had instituted a search for a young man to tutor him."

He shrugged. "I came to my senses, fortunately, before any damage had been done."

"I do not agree that there would have been any damage done at all," Emily said with dignity. "A young tutor would be entirely satisfactory, more able than Mr. Scopwick is to enter into those activities that Giles most enjoys."

"Dolly would certainly agree with you," he said pointedly, "but I do not, and I have enough on my plate already without adding complications from that direction."

Startled, she let her gaze meet his. "I see," she said slowly. "Yes, it was foolish of me not to have considered Dolly. You are very right, of course. Unless . . . perhaps you could manage to find an ugly young man."

He chuckled. "Do you think that would put her off? I do not. She practices her wiles on anything in breeches. Saint Just, Enderby, and Bennett no doubt, and even the grooms, I'm sorry to say, do not appear to be immune from her attention."

"Then age will not deter her either, so—"

"I do not think, however, that the estimable Scopwick will succumb to her wiles."

Instead of making her laugh, the image he drew stirred her temper instead. "The man is a brute," she said. "One has only to look at him, to listen to him, to know that much. How you can possibly consider giving a sensitive, innocent little child—"

"Look here, aren't we discussing Giles?"

She gritted her teeth. "Flippancy does not become you, my lord. You know perfectly well that Giles is no more than a mishievous little boy. To turn him over to a gruff, short-tempered, bellowing man like Vicar Scopwick simply is not to be thought of. You simply must find someone else, and that is all there is about it."

His eyes narrowed ominously. "You may express your opinion, Miss Wingrave, but do not, if you value a peaceful existence, endeavor to dictate to me."

But Emily no longer cared about peace. The more she thought about poor Giles under the vicar's huge thumb, the more incensed she became. "You expect Mr. Scopwick to use physical force," she said fiercely, "to beat and bellow learning into poor Giles."

"I expect him to set Master Giles on the straight-and-narrow path, certainly, but I doubt that Scopwick will do anything to the boy that he does not deserve." His tone was grim.

"He will bully Giles as he bullies everyone," Emily said, her hands on her hips. "You are simply taking the

easy route, sir, turning your own responsibility over to
Mr. Scopwick when with but a little effort you might
win the boy over by gentler means. If only you
would—''

"That will do," Meriden said curtly, rising to his feet.
"I have listened to all I wish to hear on this particular
subject."

"But I have not finished—"

"Oh, yes, you have. I agreed to hear your opinion,
but I never agreed to let you command the tune. I have
made my decision and I mean to abide by it. Moreover,
I will thank you to keep your long nose out of this affair
in future. I know I indicated willingness to listen to you,
but you are no more capable of offering a simple
opinion than you are of flying, so you will be wiser
henceforward to tend to your own business and leave
mine to me."

"Giles is my business," Emily said haughtily,
standing her ground in defiance when he stepped closer
to her again. "And I'll thank you, your lordship, to
refrain from making personal and disparaging remarks
about my features."

"About your long nose?" He grimaced. "You may
not like the description, Emmy love, but 'tis true
enough. You've a damned long, interfering nose,
and—"

His words ended in a gasp when Emily's right hand,
quick as light, flashed out and made sharp contact with
his left cheek, leaving a dark imprint in its wake.
Appalled by what she had done, Emily stepped quickly
back away from him, a little frightened by the look of
cold fury that leapt to his eyes.

Meriden rubbed his cheek without taking his gaze
from her. "You do realize what you deserve in
retaliation for that little display of bad manners, do you
not?"

"You provoked it." But she took another step away
from him.

"You deserve," he went on as though she had not

spoken, "to be put across my knee and soundly spanked." He took a step toward her. "Punishment in kind is my way, madam, whenever possible." He took another step toward her, then another.

She backed away step for step; then, eyeing him warily, she said, "You wouldn't dare."

"Do you truly believe that, Emmy love?" he asked softly, taking yet another step toward her.

Throwing dignity to the wind, Emily turned and fled, snatching at the door latch and flinging the door wide.

Meriden caught her in the great hall. "Not so fast, my little vixen," he said, his grip firm upon her shoulder as he forced her to turn and face him.

"Jack, be sensible." The words tumbled out. "Merritt, William, the other servants . . . You wouldn't. You can't."

He held her tightly with both hands now. "Look at me," he commanded.

Hoping to placate him, she obeyed instantly.

"Now, answer me this. Do you honestly believe I will not dare to punish you as you deserve?"

She bit her lower lip, unable to drag her gaze from his. But then she shook her head. She had no doubt whatever. "Please," she muttered, looking away at last, only to become more aware than ever of the presence not just of Merritt and the footman but also of a number of other interested servants. "Please, can we not go back into the library to finish this discussion?"

"No," he said, "that would be too easy. You chose to come out here, so you must accept the consequences. Now, look me in the eye and tell me how sorry you are to have behaved so badly."

His mocking tone served only to infuriate her the more, and though she looked straight at him as he had ordered, she had no intention of apologizing and every intention of describing his character to him in terms that she hoped would leave him limp. She uttered not a single word, however, for the moment she lifted her chin and opened her mouth, Meriden's right hand moved to cup the back of her head and he bent to stop her lips with his own.

Emily's mouth clamped shut as her whole body went rigid with shock, but a masculine chuckle originating from the direction of the baize door beneath the stairs brought her quickly and angrily to life. Both fists flailing, she beat at Meriden's arms and waist, but he only moved his left arm to embrace her, clasping her tightly against him, pinning her right arm between her body and his arm. Her left hand was still free, but it seemed to have no effect whatever upon him until her slim fingers curled into claws and moved toward his right cheek.

"Don't do it, love," he warned, his breath warm against her swollen lips. "If you do, you will get what I originally promised you, right here and right now." When her fingers relaxed and her hand dropped to her side, he murmured, "That's my good lass," and his lips claimed hers again.

Intending merely to suffer the indignity in silence until he had finished, Emily was dismayed to feel her body leaping in response to his touch. As his fingers moved in her hair and his other hand caressed her back and shoulders, unfamiliar sensations swept through her, bringing fiery heat to her cheeks and to other parts of her as well. Her lips began to move softly against his, and when he ran the tip of his tongue along her lower lip, she trembled, sighing with a sound in her throat that was perilously near a moan. Meriden's lips felt firm against hers, then soft and warm. The scent of him, of buckskin, leather, and lemons, was heady stuff. His tongue was gentle, pushing at last between her small white teeth to explore the interior of her mouth. She strained upward, against him. Then, suddenly, she was set free.

As she stumbled back, striving to regain her composure, he grinned at her. "Learned your lesson, or do you want more?"

"Ooh!" she exclaimed, her right hand rising almost

of its own accord to slap the grin from his face.

He caught her hand easily this time. "Naughty," he said, still grinning at her. "You don't seem to learn very quickly, but I can continue these lessons indefinitely if you like."

Emily drew a long breath, seeing from his expression that to persist in fighting him would be nothing less than foolhardy. "You may release my hand, sir," she said quietly. "We have provided the servants with gossip enough for a fortnight, I shouldn't wonder. I have no wish to entertain them further."

Meriden looked around then. "Good Lord," he said, grimacing comically, "we've drawn a large audience, have we not? Here, you lot, unless you belong in this hall, don't let me see your faces again today."

The hall cleared rapidly. Only the butler remained, his eyes carefully averted.

Meriden looked ruefully at Emily. "An outrageous thing to have done. You needn't tell me so. But I did warn you that when I lose my temper, I do outrageous things."

She wished more than anything just then to be able to tell him he ought to think shame to himself, to read him a lecture on the proper behavior expected of a gentleman toward a lady, but remembering what he had said about giving one's best ammunition to the opposition only to find it used against oneself, she held her tongue. Her behavior certainly had been nothing to claim as a standard. Moreover, her body was still playing games with her mind. Even more than she wanted to tell him how despicable his behavior had been did she want him to repeat it.

That last thought startled her, and without another word she turned on her heel and left him standing there staring at her retreating rigid back. She did not see the wide smile that lit his eyes and softened his countenance as she watched her go, for the simple reason that she did not look back.

Upstairs, she turned toward the corridor leading to her bedchamber, but the drawing-room door had been left ajar and Sabrina had heard her coming up the stairs. Popping her head out the door, she hissed, then gestured frantically, giving Emily little choice but to join the others inside.

Miss Lavinia and Dolly were there, but there was no sign of Oliver or Saint Just, and Emily found herself hoping they were not overindulging themselves in the port. She had little time to think about that, however, before Sabrina demanded to know if she had been successful in her mission.

"I have scarce been able to think of anything else!" Sabrina exclaimed, pulling Emily into the room and shutting the door. "Pray tell me that you have succeeded in changing Jack's mind and that you have not set up his back at one and the same time."

Emily, believing she had been mauled and pulled about entirely enough for one evening, gently withdrew her arm from her sister's grasp as she said stiffly, "I cannot tell you what you wish to hear, Sabrina, for the simple reason that the man is as stubborn as an ox and a mannerless oaf besides."

"Oh, dear, then you have vexed him again. Oh, Emily, why must you cross swords with him every time you speak to him, when you were used to handle Papa and the boys so easily? I do wish you could discuss matters civilly with Jack without always coming to cuffs with him."

Miss Lavinia snorted. "Impossible. No man discusses anything civilly. A man, by his very nature, sees only one side to any issue—his own. Surely you learned as much after nearly twenty years of marriage, Sabrina."

Sabrina's eyes welled with sudden tears. "I assure you, ma'am, that my beloved Laurence was never unreasonable."

When she searched unsuccessfully for her handkerchief, Emily handed her a lacy one, saying, "I am sure he was not, my dear, just as sure as I am that you never gave him cause to be."

"Very true," said Miss Lavinia. "Never went against him. Always agreed with everything he said, just as if he talked like a sensible man, which he didn't. A great mistake, I always thought. Men's heads are big enough, by and large, without any encouragement to grow bigger. Much better, in my opinion, to cut them down to size now and again. Assume you didn't accomplish that much tonight with Meriden, however.''

Emily shook her head. "He is a stubborn man."

Miss Lavinia shrugged. "Typical, that's all. So Eustace gets young Giles."

Sabrina covered her ears. "Please, I beg of you, Miss Lavinia, if you love me, do not speak as though an ogre is about to devour my precious child."

Miss Lavinia chuckled. "Stuff."

"Indeed, Sabrina," Emily said, "the situation cannot be so dire as that. In fact, it may be all to the good if Giles is a little frightened at first, for he may develop a healthier respect for his books as well as for his tutor."

She was not entirely convinced of that fact herself, but she was glad to see that her words had eased her sister's concern, and the next day when she saw Giles off to the vicarage in Harbottle's charge, she could discern no particular emotion in the boy's expression other than profound displeasure. While that was enough to remind her that she had a score to settle with Meriden, she could think of no punishment appropriate to the situation. Disconcertingly, whenever she attempted to ponder the matter, she found herself thinking instead about his kisses. It certainly had not been the first time she had been kissed, but she could remember no other kiss—even his own, at Christmas—that had had such lasting effects. Firmly she reminded herself that she intended never again to consider marriage, only to wonder afterward what stimulus had put such a thought into her head in the first place.

Intending to blow some fresh air through her mind, she took herself out into the garden, where she discovered that the day had warmed considerably. Espying Miss Lavinia at work in the knot garden, she went to join her there.

"Just hold those branches out of my way, will you?"

commanded that lady the moment she became aware of
Emily's presence. "Dratted gardeners can't tell a weed
from a yew. Lazy, the pack of them."

"Like all men," Emily said sympathetically.

Miss Lavinia grinned at her. "You got spunk, gel. I
like that. Don't seem missish like most. Sabrina said
you wasn't, but knowing Sabrina . . ." She let her voice
trail off as she efficiently plucked away some carnation
gillyflowers that had overgrown an area meant to be
dominated by great whites.

Emily had not closely examined the pattern of the
knot before, though it was clear evenf rom the top of
the lawn that it was a double heraldic device. "Is one of
those the Staithes crest?" she asked.

"The Priory's device," said Miss Lavinia, nodding
toward the pattern on her left. "By rights, the other's
not proper to display here. 'Tis the Haworth crest. My
grandfather was Marquess of Haworth. Title's gone off
to another branch of the family now, but I always liked
the crest.

Can you see the stag?"

Emily looked and admired, fascinated by the way the
outline of low boxwood and yew hedges bordering the
paths had been forced to wind and twist back upon itself, the way various colors had been woven throughout. The beds of flowers and aromatic herbs growing in
the spaces outlined by the hedges were raised. In a very
few of the spaces there was only sand or colored
pebbles, but all the others were filled with brilliant,
fragrant flowers.

Having stooped to help Miss Lavinia search for
nearly invisible weeds and watch her while she tidied
edges, Emily straightened at last and wiped her brow
with her handkerchief, looking longingly at the calm
blue waters of the lake.

"One might wish for a bathing machine," she murmured.

Miss Lavinia chuckled. "Thought you'd had your
swim for the week, but if you want to cool your feet,
there are steps into the water garden on the far side

before you cross the stone bridge, just where the path turns into the home wood. If you slip off your stockings and sandals, you can sit on the top step and cool yourself with no one being the wiser.''

"To tell you the truth of the matter, I was thinking of cooling more than my feet."

"Then you want to follow that path by the bridge straight into the wood," said Miss Lavinia, entirely unabashed at having this odd desire expressed to her. "The path follows the brook for about a quarter-mile, and then you'll come upon a pond where the brook's been dammed up. As the crow flies, the pond's not far from the road up the dale, of course, but it's private enough. The boys swim there from time to time. Do you want me to go along with you?"

"No, thank you. I think I will explore a little." She explained about her riverbank sanctum at home, adding, "I know one ought never to swim alone, but I have nearly always done so, so it doesn't seem the least odd to me."

"Never learned to swim, so I wouldn't be a particle of use to you that way if I did go," was the response. "Just thought you'd like the company."

Emily thanked her and wandered along the shore of the lake to the narrow trail beyond the bridge, which did indeed follow the course of the brook. As she entered the wood, she smelled damp earth and heard the birds chirping to one another. A slight breeze rustled leaves, as a black-and-yellow great tit took wing from a low branch just before her, and the brook sang its merry song as it tumbled over the rocks in its path. Though Emily reached the pond quickly, she was totally out of sight of the house and the lake when she did so. The only sounds she heard were those of the woods around her. Some small creature, a shrew or a little brown wren perhaps, scurried across a flat rock and disappeared into a dark crevice beyond.

Emily glanced around. The water in the pond looked most inviting. Did she dare? What if Oliver and Saint Just had the same notion? What if someone else came along? She was far enough from the road on the other side, she thought, so that no horseman ought to disturb her. And despite her walk through the shady wood, she was still uncomfortably hot.

Finally, casting caution to the wind, she unlaced the bodice of the sprigged-muslin round gown she was wearing and slipped out of it, quickly bending to remove her stockings and sandals. Clad only in her cotton shift, she waded carefully into the pond, shivering deliciously as the chilly water lapped at her calves, then her knees, her thighs, and then her hips. When it reached her waist, she took the plunge, swimming lazily at first, testing the depths beneath her as she went. The pond was deep. There were even, she discovered after successfully essaying a barefoot crossing of the rough dam, flat rocks suitable for diving.

At last, after swimming strenuously for a time, enjoying the sensation of stretching her muscles and trying her strength, she crawled out onto a rock in the sun near where she had left her gown, lay down flat upon her stomach, and let the sun and the breeze dry the back of her shift. The front was not completely dry when she began to feel nervous and to wonder just how long she could count on her privacy. Quickly, glancing about from time to time, she slipped her gown back on and laced the bodice. Her stockings came next, then her sandals. Only then did she begin to relax and even to feel a bit foolish for her worrying.

An idea came to her on the way back to the house, one that she thought might help matters at the Priory on one account at least. She hurried up the front steps and into the hall, intending to find Sabrina at once to discuss the notion.

6

EMILY DID NOT HAVE FAR TO LOOK. SHE ENCOUNTERED
Sabrina the moment she entered the hall, in the midst of
a tense argument with Dolly. Sabrina fell upon her in
relief. "Oh, thank goodness, perhaps you can explain to
this idiotish girl that she cannot attend an assembly in
York, that such a thing simply isn't to be thought of."

"Of course it is not," Emily said calmly. "What nonsense is this, Dolly?"

"It isn't nonsense," retorted Dolly fiercely. "I am
going. 'Tis the assembly following the York races, and
everyone will be there, and since I was not allowed to
have my come-out—"

"For you to attend such an assembly would be most
improper," Emily cut in. "Not only are you not out, my
dear, but you are in mourning, or had you forgotten
that fact?"

"Of course I have not forgotten. How could I forget
when everyone keeps recalling the stupid fact to my
mind?" Her voice rose alarmingly, causing Emily to
glance warily at the closed doors of the library.

"Lower your voice, Dolly. A lady does not shout."

"I'm not shouting. I'm *not*! Oh, grown-ups are all
the same. I might have known you would take Mama's
side."

"Yes, you certainly might, when your mama's
reasons are entirely right and proper and yours are
merely selfish."

"I am not selfish," wailed Dolly, her blue eyes filling
with tears, "but if no one else will ever consider my
feelings, then surely it is not odd when I try to make
them do so. You simply don't want to understand."

Emily had given up trying to make Dolly keep her

voice down, so she was not surprised when the library doors opened and Meriden appeared on the threshold, looking annoyed. "What's all the row?" he demanded.

"Oh!" exclaimed Sabrina nervously. " 'Tis the merest nothing, nothing at all to signify. Indeed, Jack, we are sorry to have disturbed you."

"*Nothing*?" shrieked Dolly. "Is that how you choose to describe an event that is of the utmost importance to me?"

"Please, Dolly," Emily begged, casting a quick glance at Meriden. She was not the least bit reassured by the ominous glint in his dark eyes. "Remember who you are, my dear, and try to speak in a more becoming fashion."

"I know who I am," snapped Dolly. "I am never allowed to forget that fact either, though what purpose it serves to know that I am the sister of Baron Staithes, I cannot tell you, for all that ever comes—"

"Stop that childish ranting and come nto the library at once," Meriden said, cutting Dolly off mid-sentence in a tone that brooked no disobedience.

She stared at him as if she had only just that moment taken note of his presence.

Sabrina twittered, "Oh, dear, I am persuaded we need not disturb you further, Jack. Indeed, we must not, for my carriage must be at the door. I distinctly told them three o'clock."

"You were going out, ma'am?"

"Only to pay a call at Bennett Manor. But Dolly was to go with me and, indeed, she is out of countenance now, so perhaps it ought not to be thought of, after all."

"Dolly will stay here," Meriden said calmly, "but you need not change your plans. Merritt, is her lady-ship's—"

"At the door, sir," the butler replied promptly. "And the horses are fresh, m'lord."

"Then we will not keep them standing," Meriden said.

"Oh, but—"

"No, Sabrina," Emily said, taking her tone from the earl. "I will look after Dolly. You go along to Helmsley."

"But I want to go too," Dolly said. "Lettie is expecting me to arrive with Mama."

"Then next time," Meriden said smoothly, "you will remember to control your emotions as a lady should. Now, say good-bye to your mama and come into the library. I wish to speak to you."

Emily gently pushed Sabrina out the door and into the care of her waiting footman, then turned to follow the others. Glancing up at Meriden, who stood patiently, holding the door open, she said, "I am glad to see that you did not think to exclude me from this interview."

"Not a chance," he said with a tired smile. "For once, I've a notion we may be allies."

She nodded, moved to take the leather chair she had sat in on her previous visit to the room, and waited to hear what he would say.

Dolly had not heard their exchange and was looking a little scared, but as soon as he had shut the door she said on a note of bravado, "You cannot wish me to be unhappy, Cousin Jack."

"No, Dolly," he said quietly.

"There, I knew it." Relaxing visibly, she smirked. "Then you will help me to convince Mama and Aunt Emily that there is nothing in the least amiss in my attending the York assembly after the race meeting."

Meriden was silent for a moment. "So that's the bone of contention," he said at last. "Sit down, Dolly, and do not be so foolish as to enact any tragedies for my benefit. You have certainly seen enough of me to know how I will respond to them."

"I won't," she said, smiling sunnily at him as she dragged a straight-backed chair closer to the library table, "but you will help me, won't you?"

"I will not." He sat on the edge of the table near Emily, but since he was looking at Dolly, his nearness didn't affect her the way it normally did. She was able to examine his profile, to decide she approved of his firm chin and the straight, aggressive line of his nose.

"You must help me," Dolly begged. "Mama will listen to you, and if you say I may, even Aunt Emily—"

"That's enough," he said sharply. "I will not allow you to ruin your reputation before you've even developed one. You are in mourning—"

"Six months is enough!" cried Dolly. "That's more time than I spent with Papa in my whole life. He never cared a fig for any of us, except perhaps for Oliver, on account of his being the heir, and I do not see why the rest of my life must be ruined just because he caught a cold and died of it!"

"You are being impertinent," Meriden said coldly, "and if I hear another word of that nature from your lips, you will find yourself confined to your bedchamber until I find it expedient to release you from it. You are not going to York, and that is the long and the short of it. If you cannot understand why you are expected to mourn your father's passing, then understand me when I say that I utterly forbid you to attend any parties or assemblies until your year of mourning is completed. If you disobey me, the consequences will not be pleasant."

Round-eyed, Dolly stared at him. "But that is not fair, Cousin Jack. Why, Lettie Bennett and her brother and Mr. Saint Just and Oliver are going to attend the assembly, and although Harry Enderby did say it would not be the thing for me to go, he did not say that Oliver must not, and if my own brother has agreed to take me with him—"

"Do not try my patience any further," Meriden warned her. "Such things are different for men, I'm afraid, but I will certainly speak to Oliver. He will not be going to York."

When Dolly subsided, scowling, Emily would have spoken up in an attempt to soothe her, had she not caught Meriden's steady gaze upon her just as she had opened her mouth.

He shook his head, then said sternly to Dolly, "You have behaved very badly, and I think that despite all your airs and complaints to me, you know that much perfectly well without my telling you. Among other things, you have upset your mother badly. I want you to go to your bedchamber now and think over the manner in which you have conducted yourself. I will expect you to apologize to your mama before dinner.''

Dolly looked at her hands from beneath beetled brows.

"And, Dolly"—he waited until she glanced up—"if you intend only to sulk, I suggest you seek out Miss Brittan and ask her to lend you a book describing the conduct expected of a gentlewoman, so that you may study it carefully. You may go now. I have said all I mean to say to you.''

Still glowering, Dolly got up and left the room.

Meriden looked at Emily, practically daring her to criticize his handling of the situation, but she smiled sympathetically instead, for she had no wish to stir his temper further. Not, in any case, before she had had a chance to speak to Oliver.

Learning from Merritt that the young man had gone out shooting on the moor with his friends Saint Just, Enderby, and Bennett, Emily was certain that she had at least an hour or more before she would have to look for him. Certain, too, as she was, that the earl would employ his usual heavy-handed methods in dealing with Oliver, she was determined to have a word with the young man before Meriden did, to show the earl that just as much good could be accomplished with sweet reason as with sternly issued commands. In order to accomplish her purpose, however, she knew she would have to intercept Oliver before he received Meriden's orders to attend him in the library.

In the meantime, she returned to her bedchamber, where she had promised to help Martha sort through a pile of clothing Sabrina had set aside for Mr. Scopwick's poor box. Items to be mended had to be sorted from those that needed cleaning. The task occupied half an hour. When they had finished, though she had not yet had an opportunity to broach to Sabrina the idea that had occurred to her earlier, she decided to speak to Melanie.

She found the little girl in the schoolroom with her governess, but they were not engaged in schoolwork. Miss Brittan, dressed in the plain stuff gown of her calling, was knitting a bright, varicolored woolen scarf while Melanie stitched a colorful floral border in crewel work on the hem of one of her white muslin frocks.

Emily greeted the governess and walked over to look at the pattern of Melanie's border. "What exquisite work, my dear," she said a moment later. "I particularly like the lavender roses and the way you have blended pink and yellow together in your daisies. The design reminds me of Miss Lavinia's knot garden."

Melanie looked up, pushed wisps of fine flaxen hair out of her eyes, and it seemed for a moment that she would smile.

"Reply to Miss Wingrave properly, Melanie," her governess said with quiet firmness.

"Thank you, Aunt Emily."

"If you have finished your schoolwork for the day," Emily said, "perhaps you would like to come out for a walk in the garden with me. I've taken a notion into my head that I should like very much to discuss with you."

Melanie glanced at Miss Brittan, who nodded, whereupon the child tied off and snipped a French knot, set her work aside, and followed Emily downstairs and out into the garden. She remained silent, and Emily did not attempt to make conversation until they had crossed the wooden footbridge and walked some distance along the lakeshore path.

"I was wondering," she said at last, speaking thoughtfully, "if you know how to swim, Melanie." She looked down in time to see the little girl's eyes widen as she turned her head to look up at her. "Well, do you?"

Melanie shook her head but continued to gaze expectantly at Emily.

"Would you like to learn?"

Melanie nodded, her eyes still wide. She looked down at the lake, then up at the house.

"Not here, goose. I have no wish for either of us to provide entertainment for the entire household. Do you know the pond in the home wood?"

Melanie nodded, but her eyebrows knitted together in a worried frown.

"Do the woods frighten you?" Emily asked. "I will be with you, you know."

The frown disappeared, and Melanie tucked a small, thin hand into Emily's.

Emily squeezed it. " 'Tis too late today, but we will begin tomorrow after your lessons are done. Would you like to walk to the pond now just to see how nice it is?"

Melanie nodded again and, without taking her hand from Emily's, walked beside her toward the stone bridge and the narrow path along the brook. Before they reached the path, however, two horsemen emerged from the woods on the road opposite them. Slowing their mounts at once, they waved, and Emily recognized Oliver and Saint Just. Remembering her intent to speak to the former, she waved back, gesturing for them to approach.

Obligingly the two young men clattered across the bridge. Both were laughing merrily.

"You look like a pair of schoolboys who've been up to mischief," Emily told them, responding to their laughter with a wide smile of her own.

"Too right, ma'am," Saint Just replied with a grin. "Dashed if it don't feel like I've returned to my schooldays at that."

Oliver regarded her with a look half of laughter, half of defiance. "You won't squeak beef on us, will you, Aunt Emily?"

"We'd never do such a shameful thing, would we, Melanie?"

The little girl shook her head.

"There, you see? Now, tell us, just what dreadful thing have you done?"

Oliver waved a pair of buckskin breeches, a shirt, and a top boot at her that he had been concealing on the off side of his horse. Saint Just, in turn, revealed a dark brown coat, a long white cloth, and a second boot.

For a long moment Emily stared from one young man to the other, bewildered. Then, glancing toward the woods, she gave a little gasp of comprehension. "You didn't!"

"We did," Oliver said smugly. "Cousin Jack likes to take a swim before dinner on the days he dines with us, and I remembered that little fact when we were riding through the wood just now. We left our horses and crept up on the pond as silently as a couple of poachers, and there he was, swimming back and forth, his clothes piled neatly and most temptingly on a nearby rock. He didn't so much as catch a glimpse of us."

"We thought about leaving him a horse," said Saint Just virtuously, "but after some small discussion, we decided that he would not properly appreciate such a handsome gesture."

"Afraid to risk it, I daresay," Emily said, thinking swiftly. "Look here, Mr. Saint Just, will you allow me a moment alone with Oliver? There is something of a private nature about which I must speak to him at once." When Saint Just nodded, she smiled down at Melanie. "We will see the pond tomorrow, dearest. I don't think that now is a good time to do so, after all."

Melanie actually smiled. "No, Aunt Emily," she said demurely.

Chuckling, Emily gave her a little hug. "You go along with Mr. Saint Just, my dear, like a proper lady with a proper gentleman escort. And, Mr. Saint Just," she added as that gentleman dismounted from his horse, "will you oblige me once more by giving Oliver those of the stolen garments that you retain in your keeping?"

As soon as Saint Just and Melanie had walked far enough away to preclude their overhearing him, Oliver said testily, "Look here, Aunt Emily, I hope you ain't meaning to tell me to put these clothes back, for I won't do it. Sure as check he's discovered they're missing by now, and I'd as lief not have to face him until he's had time enough to regain at least a small portion of his temper."

"Do hush, Oliver. I have no intention of forcing you to face your Cousin Jack or to confess this prank to him. But you ought to know at once that Dolly has informed him of your intention to attend the York assembly as well as your agreement to take her with you, so he is already displeased with you. The plan simply won't do, Oliver. Indeed, it will not."

Oliver flushed. "Dolly's tongue is a great deal too busy. She ought to have kept it tight behind her teeth."

"Oliver," Emily said quietly, "Dolly would be ruined if you were to allow such a thing. Not only by attending the assembly when she is expected to observe half-mourning for at least another five months, but for attending with only your escort and that of Mr. Saint Just. When she appears in public for the first time, it must be with her mama or with another suitable lady companion, not with—"

"With a couple of rag-mannered, half-baked fribbles?"

Emily grinned at him. "Exactly so, although I would never have described you so uncivilly."

"Daresay you wouldn't, but Harry Enderby ain't so nice in his notions as you are. Called me those things and worse while we was out shooting today. Called Dolly worse things, for that matter, when I told him that she and Saint Just had cooked the notion up between them. I shan't call Harry out for what he said, though. Practically my brother, Harry is, and he was in a flaming temper at the time. Luckily Saint Just and Bennett had ridden on ahead for a moment to speak to their loaders, although I doubt Harry'd do anything so improper as to take Saint Just to task over a thing like that."

"Mr. Enderby sounds like a sensible young man," said Emily. "I do hope—"

"Oh, I've already told Saint Just the scheme won't answer, and I mean to speak to Dolly too." He glanced unhappily toward the home wood. "Wish she'd had the sense to keep silent, though."

"Your cousin has expressed a desire to speak with

you," Emily said gently, "but I doubt that he will stay angry once he learns of the decision you have come to on your own. Nonetheless, I do think your conversation will march more smoothly if you do not confess this prank to him."

"Good God, I should think so!"

"Perhaps if you were to give me his clothes," Emily suggested, "I could take them back to the pond and explain that I found them where some unknown prankster dropped them."

"By Jupiter, that's the very thing," said Oliver approvingly. "Only, what if . . . that is, I mean, well, what if he should be . . . you know . . ." He paused delicately.

"What if he has got out of the pond?" Emily said helpfully.

Oliver nodded.

"I shall make a great deal of noise when I approach," she said firmly.

The buckskins and coat alone were heavy enough to be cumbersome, and there were also his boots, shirt, neckcloth, and small clothes. Emily felt weighted down as she made her way along the narrow trail beside the brook, and since her load prevented her from seeing the ground directly beneath her feet, it was as well that she had no objection to announcing her approach. Even so, as she neared the dam at the end of the pond, she called out, "Jack, where are you?"

"Behind you," came the grim response, easily audible above the noise of the water as it spilled in streams of varied widths through the small openings in the rock-and-log dam and tumbled onto the rocks below.

Emily froze. "Are you . . . that is—"

"Don't turn around unless you have a strong desire to become better acquainted with the finer points of male anatomy," he replied, still grim. "What made you change your mind about this little prank of yours, anyway?"

"Of mine?"

"Oh, surely you won't deny it. I'll confess my first thought was that Giles had come along on his way back from the vicarage—"

"He returned to the Priory some time ago, I believe."

"I know, so that leaves you." His voice was soft when he added, "Did you act too impulsively, my dear, and forget until afterward that I make it a practice to retaliate in kind?"

A frisson of fear raced up her spine. "I brought your clothes back to you, Jack. I didn't take them."

"Then who did?"

She swallowed. "I . . . I found them."

"Don't take me for a fool, Emily. You expect me to believe that you found a pile of men's clothes, knew they were mine, and knew exactly where to find me? You called my name, you know, so you couldn't have been searching for some unknown owner."

She wanted to turn around. She needed time to think. Determined though she was not to give Oliver away, she had come to know Jack well enough to believe him entirely capable of the most outrageous behavior. If he decided to punish her, she had not the least doubt that she would fervently wish he hadn't. Striving to keep her voice calm, she said, "If you don't want your clothes, I can simply take them away again."

"And how far do you suppose you would get?"

She was standing near the dam, and she was sure she could run across to the other side. She had crossed it barefoot safely enough, and although she wasn't sure her sandals wouldn't betray her, she doubted that Jack would really chase her through the woods in all his no doubt splendid masculine glory.

In order to get a better idea of how close he was, she said, "Couldn't we call a truce?"

"Seems, from your point of view, to be a good time to do that, does it?" He was not too close, but she knew he could close the distance quickly if he were not first somehow diverted. "Put my clothes down, Emily," he said sternly. "We will discuss this matter more thoroughly once I've dressed."

"Very well." She took two steps nearer the dam; then, scarcely pausing to draw breath, she flung the armful of clothing as far as she could fling it into the pond, snatched up her skirts, and ran. The bellow of rage behind her lent wings to her feet, and they scarcely seemed to touch the rocks and logs of the dam as she sped across. She nearly slipped once just before she reached the other side, but fear that Meriden was right behind her held her upright and she made it safely to the other shore, dodging past trees and through shrubbery as she pelted for the road. She didn't stop running, however, until she reached the gardens in front of the house.

Breathless, she looked back over her shoulder, half-expecting to see a large naked man erupting in fury from the woods. But the landscape was reassuringly devoid of human life.

Tempted to order her dinner served in the safety of her bedchamber, Emily hurried up the drive and into the house. The first person she encountered, in the empty hall where he had clearly been waiting for her, was Oliver.

"Did you find him?" he demanded. "Did you give his clothes back?"

"He thought I took them," she gasped, still breathless. "He wouldn't believe I just found them."

"Oh, Lord." Oliver clapped a hand to his artfully tousled head. "What did he say? No, don't tell me. I can guess."

"I daresay you can; however, it was not what he said but what he was going to do to me that frightened me silly," Emily told him frankly. "I had to throw his clothes into the pond in order to get away from him."

"You what?"

"I thought he would care more just then for his boots than for revenge," she explained.

"You threw everything—" Words failing him, Oliver looked at her in awe. Then suddenly, as they stared at one another, the whole thing struck them as funny. Sabrina, appearing by the gallery railing at the top of the stairs a moment later, demanded to know what on earth had cast the pair of them into conniption fits.

Containing herself with difficulty, Emily looked up at her and gasped, "It is nothing, love, only a foolish joke." Looking back at Oliver, she added on another choke of laughter, "It's the second pair of boots. What a rage he will be in!"

"If he should come to dinner . . ." Oliver could not continue. Gales of merriment overcame him once again.

"Emily," Sabrina said tartly, "if you do not intend to explain this odd behavior to me, then I suggest that you tidy yourself. You've got branches caught in your hair." So saying, she turned away and disappeared into the drawing room.

Ruefully Emily reached up and pulled a small leafy twig from her curls. When Oliver chuckled again, she wrinkled her nose at him. "Odious boy. This is all your doing. I shall expect exemplary behavior from you in future. And I hope you will provide a handsome wreath for me after your cousin catches me. Roses for my tombstone, and perhaps—"

"Unless he comes to dinner," Oliver said, still chuckling, "you needn't fear so tragic an end. If he'd caught you at once, of course . . ." He raised his gaze expressively to heaven, then shook his head, adding, "But once the first heat of his anger has passed, he will do no more than shout a bit, I daresay."

"You can have no notion how much your words comfort me," Emily said wryly. "What you mean to say is that unless he storms this house in search of me within the hour, I've got only sound and fury to endure. Is that it?"

"Something like." Oliver grinned at her.

With a final, expressive grimace, Emily went upstairs to her bedchamber to find Martha waiting for her. The tirewoman clicked her tongue in disapproval of her mistress's appearance, particularly when a rent was discovered in her gown, but Emily's hair required no more than a good brushing, and once her face had been washed, her gown and sandals changed, and her pearl necklace clasped around her neck, she was able to repair to the dining room the very picture of a young lady of fashion.

She had not thought again about the advisability of ordering a tray carried to her bedchamber, having decided that she would not seek the coward's way out. Nonetheless, she did not scorn to breathe a sigh of relief when Meriden did not appear at the dinner table.

"Inconsiderate of him not to have told us," Miss Lavinia observed. "Like them all. Did think he might be a cut above the rest, but I expect that would have been asking too much."

Sabrina expressed her belief that something must have occurred to keep him away. This was followed by a vaguely worded hope that he had not met with an accident.

Dolly grimaced but didn't say anything, and Oliver winked at Emily, who attempted to frown him down while struggling with suppressed mirth. She carefully avoided his gaze for some moments thereafter and was exceedingly grateful when Mr. Saint Just introduced a perfectly harmless topic of conversation. The rest of the evening passed uneventfully.

7

THE FOLLOWING MORNING, IN THE BREAKFAST PARLOR, Sabrina informed Emily in a tone of distress that Mr. Tickhill was annoying the servants again.

"Mr. Tickhill?" Emily's bewilderment lasted only a moment before she remembered. "One of your Bow Street Runners. What does he want?"

"He is not *my* Bow Street Runner," Sabrina said indignantly. "Jack foisted him upon us, and all he will say when anyone complains to him—as many people have, Emily, for Mr. Tickhill and Mr. Earswick bring chaos and upheaval wherever they go, and if my servants leave, I shall take to my bed, and so I promise you—but all Jack will say is that since he has not got time to search for Miss Lavina's baubles, the Runners must do so.'' She blinked. ''Do you suppose you could talk to him, my dear? I simply cannot, but those dreadful men . . .'' Her voice trailed away, and she stared at Emily hopefully.

Emily grimaced. ''Not today, Sabrina, I beg of you. I mean to keep well out of Meriden's way today.''

''Oh, dear,'' Sabrina said, ''then you have vexed him again. I do wish you would not, Emily, for you are really the only person who can stand up to him, and who will help me if you cannot?''

''My standing up to him is what vexes him,'' Emily said with a smile. ''He does not like anyone running counter to his lead.''

Sabrina sighed. ''Very true. What did you do to vex him this time?''

Emily's eyes gleamed reminiscently. ''Let us just say that he no longer owes me a new gown and leave it at that. I fear the tale is not one that he would be pleased to hear noised about.''

''As if I would!'' Sabrina regarded her steadily, but when Emily remained silent, she shrugged. ''Oh, very well, then. I daresay Oliver knows all about it and that is what the two of you were in such whoops about yesterday. And no doubt he will tell Mr. Saint Just and Dolly, but if you wish to keep silent, all I will say is that if you have made Jack look foolish, I don't wish to know the details, and I think you are very wise to play least in sight for a day or two.''

Emily intended to do that very thing. Although she agreed with Oliver that once Meriden's temper cooled she would have little to fear, she had no wish to hear her character described to her in unflattering terms or stentorian accents. Thus, after her late breakfast and some desultory conversation with Sabrina, she returned to her bedchamber, intending to use the time to finish the book Miss Lavinia had lent her.

Although Martha had been there earlier, when Emily entered the room it was empty. Remembering that she had left the book, with her page marked, upon her dressing table, she went to fetch it, noting absently that the satin-lined box in which she kept the few pieces of jewelry she had brought with her was open. The box was also empty.

Quickly she moved to the bell and rang for Martha. A full ten minutes passed before the woman arrived, and in the meantime Emily searched through her drawers and her other belongings. "Martha," she said crisply when the abigail entered, "have you moved my jewelry?"

"Why would I do such a thing as that when it's safe in its very own—" She broke off when her gaze was caught by the empty case. "Lord-a-mercy, Miss Emily, the lovely China pearls your father gave you!"

"Not to mention my gold bracelet and the amethyst earbobs Ned gave me when I turned eighteen. Is Mr. Tickhill still somewhere about the house?"

"Aye," Martha answered sourly, "but the man's a right menace if you ask me, poking and prying and asking fool questions."

"Go and find him," Emily ordered, thinking fast, "and tell him I will see him in the little parlor next to the morning room. My sister will be in the drawing room now, and I do not want to distress her."

"You'd best tell Lord Meriden about this," Martha said.

"No, not just yet. He will only tell me to report it to the Runners, so I shall do that before I speak to him."

Mr. Tickhill kept her waiting only a few moments. A burly man with narrowed eyes, round cheeks, and a pugnacious chin, he reminded Emily of a bull terrier one of her neighbors in Wiltshire had owned. The dog, she recalled, was neither as fierce nor as intelligent as he looked.

"Yer wooman tells me ye've lost yer jewels, mum."

"That is correct," Emily replied. She did not ask him to sit, nor did he move to do so. She described the missing pieces, adding, "Trumpery stuff mostly, and of little value, except for the pearls, of course, but they mean a great deal to me."

The man wrote in his black occurrence book for several moments before he looked up from under beetling brows and said, "That wooman . . . what's 'er name? Martha Cooling? Knowed 'er long, mum?"

"Martha? Goodness, you cannot suspect Martha! That is too absurd, Mr. Tickhill. She would never steal from anyone."

"Been known to 'appen, mum. Could be she's took a likin' to them baubs over time and just now decided ter lift 'em."

"Well, I will not listen to such nonsense," Emily said angrily. "It is obvious to the meanest intelligence that my pieces were taken by the same thief who stole Miss Arncliffe's jewelry. Martha wasn't even here then."

"Nor yet were young Master Giles," said Tickhill with a shrug, "but you won't cozen me into believin' as this ain't precisely the sort o' mischief as would suit that young scamp down ter the ground."

"Giles? Martha?" Emily's hold on her temper snapped. "You stupid man, you put me all out of patience. No wonder everyone is so out of reason cross with his lordship for inflicting you and your ilk upon them. To suspect Giles or Martha when the thief has very likely been right under your nose is as ridiculous as if I were to accuse you of the thefts. More ridiculous, in fact, for you were the only stranger in the house today when my things were taken."

"Now, lookee 'ere, mum, that Harbottle feller—"

"No, you look. I won't listen to another word of this foolishness. Moreover, I intend to tell his lordship precisely what I think of your conduct and your capabilities."

"Slow and thorough does the job, mum."

"Oh, get out of my way," Emily snapped, pushing past him and hurrying down the stairs to the hall.

The doors to the library were closed, but she did not hesitate. The confrontation by the pond was forgotten, and she wanted only to tell the earl precisely what she thought of his Bow Street Runners. Pushing open the doors without ceremony, she stormed into the room, only to be brought to a stupefied halt by the sight of Meriden seated in his leather chair behind the library table with little Melanie standing white-faced before him, her small hands held out, palms down, in front of her. As Emily watched in speechless horror, the earl rapped the little girl's knuckles soundly with a heavy ruler.

Paying no heed whatever to the interruption, Meriden dealt two more sharp blows to the back of each small hand, then said sternly, "If you ever do such a thing again, Melanie, your punishment will be far more severe than this. Do you understand what I say to you?"

Sobbing quietly, Melanie lowered her hands and nodded without looking at him.

"I prefer to hear your voice," he said in that same implacable tone.

"Yes, sir," murmured the child, "I understand." Despite the gentle sobs, her words came dully, evenly, as though they were part of a lesson learned for recitation.

"You may go back to the schoolroom now. Whether you decide to tell your mama or Miss Brittan about this is your own affair."

Without another word but with tears streaming down her cheeks and her fists clenched tightly into the folds of her white muslin skirt, Melanie hurried from the room, passing Emily without looking at her.

Emily waited only long enough to shut the door behind the child before she rounded in fury on the earl. "Have you lost your mind, my lord?" she demanded. "Have you taken to ripping the wings off butterflies for your amusement? How could you use that poor child so? I could scarce believe my eyes. 'Twas a wicked, wicked thing to do!"

Instead of firing up at once as she expected him to do, he looked defensive. It suddenly seemed to occur to him that he ought to stand up. But as he came to his feet, Emily angrily waved him back.

"For once, have the goodness just to sit down, sir. I want answers to my questions, and I do not want you looming over me while you provide them."

To her surprise, he sat down again at once, saying heavily, "You have every right and reason to wonder what devil possessed me. I am not entirely sure of the answer myself. The fact is that I simply didn't know what else to do."

He was truly distressed, and both his tone and his attitude were uncharacteristic enough to mitigate Emily's wrath. She stepped nearer the table, saying more calmly, "What happened, Jack?"

He looked at her, searching her face for a long moment before he said, "I still don't know the whole of it, and what little I do know will sound crazy."

"Tell me." She pulled the leather chair close to the table and sat down opposite him.

He nodded, leaning back in his chair with a sigh as he said, "I sent my bailiff from the park into the village this morning to settle some trifling accounts. He rode over here an hour ago to tell me that Melanie has, eleven times over the past three months, borrowed small sums from Hayworth, the chandler, telling him each time that she had other purchases to make and wanted to have everything on one account. Hayworth knows her, of course, and she gave my name as surety. He told my man that he knew that although we have our candles sent up from London, sooner or later someone would settle the account. My man checked. Melanie made purchases at no other shop. When I asked her what the devil she thought she was about, she said only that she needed the money—hardly an acceptable explanation, you will agree."

"No," Emily said, "but surely there was more."

He shook his head. "When I scolded her, told her it was the same thing as stealing, she just stared woodenly into the distance beyond my shoulder until I finished, as though she were refusing to hear a word I said. I could think of no other way to get her attention, to make her understand that I won't tolerate such behavior."

"Well, for heaven's sake," Emily said, "if you were going to be so brutal with her, why didn't you get to the bottom of things while you were about it?"

"I beg your pardon?" He leaned forward in his chair, glaring at her.

"It sounds to me," she said, "as though you still have not got the least notion why the child needed money. Surely you do not believe her to be a thief. She must have had a good reason for what she did."

"I gave her ample opportunity to explain her reasons to me, and she refused to do so," Meriden said with forced patience. Making a visible effort to relax, he pushed his chair away from the table and leaned back again, tilting the chair onto its hind legs and rocking gently back and forth as he added grimly, "I am sorry for what I was forced to do. Believe me when I tell you that I felt every inch the brute you've named me. But the plain fact of the matter is that Melanie took money without permission and had to be taught never to do such a thing again."

"The plain fact," Emily retorted in sharper tones as she leaned forward and shook her finger at him, "is that you were a fool not to discover what she was about."

Meriden's jaw tightened, and his eyes narrowed ominously, but before he spoke, he drew a deep breath. Then, as though to show her how much in control of himself he was, how truly relaxed, he folded his hands across his stomach, tilted farther back, and propped first one booted foot, then the other, upon the tabletop, crossing them at the ankles. "Perhaps you ought to talk to Melanie," he said in a musing tone. "If you think your efforts will serve better than mine, you may certainly do what you can to learn the truth of the matter from her."

"I can hardly do worse than you have done, sir," Emily said through her teeth, watching him. His casual, not to say unmannerly, attitude was affecting her temper nearly as much as his earlier behavior had done.

"I will certainly talk to Melanie, for you will come to see your own error much more clearly when she has explained the matter in a perfectly unexceptionable way, as I am persuaded she can."

"I hope she does," he replied, still fixed in his casual position. The look in his eyes was not so casual, however, when he added, "Make no mistake, Emily. My threat to that child was not an idle one. If she obtains money by this method again, I will make her very sorry for it. You will be doing her no favor if you fail to make that point clear to her."

"If that isn't just like you," Emily said scornfully, "to employ threats and force where gentle words and a loving hand would serve so much better."

He did not reply. Instead, he regarded her steadily from beneath his brows, clearly expecting her to acknowledge her understanding that he meant what he had said and did not mean to be deterred by her disapproval.

After a moment of this treatment, Emily growled through her teeth and rose swiftly to her feet. "You make me so angry," she said, leaning over the table to return his look with a fierce glare. "You deserve that someone should set you right. I only wish I were big enough and strong enough to be that someone."

"Did you know," he inquired gently and with a glimmer of amusement in his eyes, "that your dimples show when you're angry? They are fascinating to watch."

With a shriek of fury, Emily grabbed his booted feet with both her hands and heaved upward; and, since his chair was still balanced on only its hind legs, the earl went over backward with an ease that astonished her.

Shock registered briefly on Meriden's face as he attempted unsuccessfully to regain his balance. Grabbing wildly for something to break his fall, he snatched at the curtains behind him, but his weight proved to be too great for the rods and with a clamor of noise satisfying only to Emily's ears, down he crashed, the curtains and rod collapsing atop him.

As Emily hurried from the room, his muffled curses followed her, but she managed to walk with dignity, telling herself firmly that there was nothing he could do to her, that he deserved rough treatment after such insolence and after what he had done to poor Melanie. As she neared the stairway, her memory chose to remind her of their confrontation the day before, and she moved more quickly, hoping to find sanctuary with either Sabrina or Miss Lavinia in the drawing room. She reached the landing at the head of the central stair before his voice stopped her.

"Emily, don't run away. You are not such a coward as that."

She looked back over her shoulder, surprised by his calm. He stood upon the library threshold, looking more tousled than usual, watching her. The amusement in his eyes was unmistakable now. "If you expect an apology," she said stiffly, "you will have to wait for it. I daresay I behaved badly—in fact, I know perfectly well that I did—but I am still too angry with you to apologize."

"I know that, so go put on your riding habit instead. I've got business at the park this morning, but if you ride over with me, we can talk on the way and my housekeeper will give us a meal before we ride back. We'll take a groom with us too, so the proprieties will be observed and so you needn't fear I'll murder you. It is past time to declare a truce. We need to talk."

She regarded him warily. "You aren't angry?"

"Not at the moment, so you would be wise to take advantage of the fact. After the turn you served me yesterday and that nursery stunt you pulled just now, only consider what I might feel justified in doing to you. I think you will agree that a ride to Meriden Park is preferable."

Attempting to ignore the tremor that shot up and down her spine at the images his words had created in

her mind, Emily nodded and hurried to obey him. Their
horses were waiting at the front entrance when she
rejoined him in the hall, dressed in an elegant habit, the
color of which matched her eyes.

"I like that hat," he told her with a grin. "Have you
any notion how seductively that blue feather curls on
your cheek?" He reached out a finger to touch the
feather, but Emily, blushing, stepped away from him
and straightened her hat. He shook his head and
indicated with a bow of exaggerated gallantry that she
should precede him.

Convinced that the earl could not be as composed as
he pretended to be, Emily wondered if she was making a
mistake by accompanying him to his house. Perhaps,
she thought, he merely wished to get her away from the
safety of Staithes Priory in order to wreak his vengeance
upon her in a place where no one would dare to
interfere. At the top of the steps, she looked back to
find him smiling at her. Her fears vanished, and without
really stopping to consider why she did so, she smiled
back.

As he cupped his hand beneath her elbow, a rider on a
sleek chestnut hack hove into view and cantered up the
drive. By the time Meriden and Emily had reached the
bottom step, Mr. Enderby had jumped lightly down
from his saddle and tossed his reins to the grinning
stableboy who held Meriden's gelding.

Harry doffed his beaver hat and said cheerfully,
"Dashed fine day. M' mother sends her regards, Miss
Wingrave." He glanced at the house. "Trust Ollie and
his great gun ain't shoved off already."

"No, indeed," Emily told him after a brief struggle
with herself. "In point of fact, you will find the pair of
them lingering in the breakfast parlor. They played
piquet rather late last night, I believe."

"Sluggards," Mr. Enderby said. "Been up for hours
m'self. Uh, suppose I ought first to pay my respects to
her ladyship. She about?"

Emily smiled, nearly as certain as she could be after

her short time at Staithes that he had not come to see Sabrina. "She and Dolly are in the drawing room, sir."

Meriden cut in impatiently, "Just run along up and tell Merritt your business. He will point you in whatever direction you choose to go."

"Dashed good notion," said Mr. Enderby, replacing his hat and running up the steps without futher ado.

Meriden watched him. "Fop," he said disparagingly.

"You wrong him, sir," Emily said. "He is a dandy, perhaps, but not a fop. Only consider the difference between Mr. Saint Just's appearance and Mr. Enderby's."

"Look here," said Meriden, appalled, "do you like that sort of thing? Everything starched and twisted about, and a man's shirt points so high and his coats so tight he can't breathe?"

Smiling, she cast a quick glance over him. He had clearly been able, without the least difficulty or assistance from his valet, to shrug his dark gray coat on over his pale-biscuit-colored buckskins. The breeches fitted his muscled form to a nicety, however, she noted approvingly. His neckcloth was snowy white, but it lacked the stiffness demanded by the sartorial smarts, and it was simply tied. His shirt points were moderate, and his topboots, though well-polished, were certainly not so shiny as to make other gentlemen demand to know his recipe for blacking. "I believe," she said gently, "that men who expend so much thought on their attire can have little time left to think about anything else."

Apparently satisfied with her response, he tossed her up onto her saddle, ordered the boy to take Mr. Enderby's hack around to the stables, and told Emily's groom to follow without crowding them. When he swung into his own saddle, the gelding sidled and danced, but Meriden let him do so for only a moment before firmly drawing him in next to Emily's mare.

They rode in silence through the shady wood until they had reached the first fork in the road, when Emily, glancing sideways at him, said, "You did say you wished to converse with me, did you not? Where does that road lead?"

"Up onto the moor and beyond to the village," he said. "The next turning leads to the vicarage, as you know, and the next after that goes to Meriden." He looked serious again. "I was trying to think how to begin what I wish to say to you."

"How to begin tactfully, do you mean? That will take too long." Seeing by his quick, flashing grin that the shaft had gone home, she said, "I suppose I ought to apologize for throwing your clothes into the pond."

He winced. "If you had the least notion of how much I paid for that jacket or those boots—"

"Well, I do have a pretty good notion," she said ruefully, "for despite what you seem to think, sir, my brothers—graybeards that they are—do talk, and complaining about how much Weston demands for a coat or Hoby for a pair of good boots is a favorite pastime of theirs. You frightened me, you see, and I didn't know what else to do. It was an infamous thing to have done, however, and I know you were vexed—"

"A little," he admitted, smiling at her again. "You need not dance around the point, you know. Oliver told me the whole tale this morning."

"He did?"

Meriden nodded. "He's got more bottom than I thought. I couldn't tell you with Enderby standing there, but the real reason he was late to breakfast was that before Harbottle took young Giles to the vicarage, I sent him to roust Oliver out of bed. I'm afraid I was rather unpleasant to the lad."

"No, were you?" she retorted sweetly. "What a busy morning you have had, to be sure."

"Mind your tongue," he said. "Oliver heard me out without a whimper and then told me he had already spoken to his friend and to Dolly. Then, without so much as drawing breath, he informed me that I had misunderstood certain things about yesterday's incident at the pond."

"Goodness," said Emily, impressed, "but he never said a word about this to me. The breakfast-parlor door was open when I passed it on my way to change into my habit, and I called a greeting to him, but he didn't even mention having seen you."

"I asked him not to do so."

"But why?"

He grinned. "I wanted to punish you, of course, for ruining another expensive coat and a second pair of boots. I hoped you would employ the extra time in sober consideration of what I might be planning to do to you in retaliation."

"But I've explained to you why I did that," she said, glaring at him when she remembered her fears. "Indeed, you must have known why at the time, and since you now know that I was not the one who took your clothes, surely now you will apologize for frightening me so."

"I will," said the earl, turning to gaze directly at her, "if you can tell me honestly that had you chanced to arrive at the pond before Oliver did, you would not have taken my clothes."

Emily bit her lower lip, refusing for some moments even to look at him. When she did so at last, her eyes brimmed with laughter. "You are quite the most abominable man I have ever encountered. Surely you must know that I had considered and rejected any number of plans to repay you for kissing me in the great hall that day. I doubt I would have overlooked an opportunity that simply presented itself, and Melanie and I were walking to the pond when we met Oliver and Mr. Saint Just and they told us about their prank."

"Why didn't you leave matters as you found them?" he asked.

"Why, because once I discovered what they had done, I thought only of extricating Oliver from the tangle he had got himself into. I knew he would be able to explain the York-assembly nonsense to your satisfaction, but I was afraid that if you guessed he was responsible for taking your clothes, you wouldn't listen to anything else he said to you."

Jack shrugged ruefully. "I am sometimes a trifle impatient, I suppose."

Emily choked on the rising gurgle of laughter in her throat.

He grinned again. "Look here, why have I never seen this side of you before? I thought I understood the reason for your unmarried state, but now I am not so sure. Some man ought to have seen beneath that cool exterior to the laughter and passion before now. Don't tell me none has ever done so."

"There have been several," she replied, growing serious at once. "Even one gentleman whom I rather favored." She paused, adding with some difficulty, "That was during my first Season, when I was not so cool or confident as perhaps I appear to be now. But Mr. Campion married a girl with a larger portion. 'Tis the way of the *beau monde*, is it not?" She glanced at him to see that his lips had hardened into a straight line. Then, because she was afraid he would ask more pressing questions about that dreadful time, she asked quickly, "What did you mean before, about thinking you knew why I am unmarried?"

For a moment she thought he would not answer. Then he said gently, "In London and at Woburn you were always so controlled, so sure of yourself, so damned cool. Even when I kissed you at Christmas—and I know I made you angry—you just froze up, looked at me as though I were muck beneath your feet, and then became more chillingly polite than ever. That sort of behavior puts a man off, lass. But, knowing you as I do now, I cannot believe you didn't want to see my head summarily removed from my shoulders, at the very least, for what I did to you that night."

Emily's color heightened at the memory, but staring straight ahead, she said calmly, "I prided myself then on my ability to control my temper. I never could do so as a child, you see, and unkind people had told me that my temper was as much a cause as my lack of a large portion for Ste . . . for Mr. Campion's having chosen another lady to wed. I am ashamed to say that my temper was very nearly a joke in my family, except that no one ever laughed when I got angry. Instead, they did whatever they could to placate me. I daresay I grew to be a trifle spoilt as a result.'' She looked at him. ''Did you say something?''

Meriden shook his head, his lips pressed more tightly together than ever.

''Then perhaps you coughed.'' When he made no reply, she said, ''Well, in any event, I also grew to be a trifle stubborn in my ways, so—''

Unable to control himself any longer, Jack shouted with laughter, ''Enough, you wretched woman! Don't do this to me. A trifle spoilt? A trifle stubborn? Why, you must have been the most outrageously spoilt and mule-headed little demon in Wiltshire, and how you ever learned to hide it behind that prime-and-proper mask of yours is more than I shall ever know. Good Lord, you must have wanted to murder me at Woburn.''

''Very nearly,'' she admitted, ''but then afterward— immediately afterward, that is—I was so proud of my-self, proud that I had not so much as boxed your ears, you see, that instead I had behaved as a proper lady of quality ought to behave.''

''How long before the reaction set in?'' he asked dryly as they turned onto an uphill track.

She made a face at him. ''By that night I was regretting my lost opportunity. You were so smug, so cock-o'-the-walk pleased at having won your wager. The worst of it is that I have thought so often of the incident since then, always wishing I had succumbed to the urge to slap that smugness off our face. Usually, once I've lost my temper, I forget about the incident, but I've relived that night a hundred times over in my mind, always behaving more as I wish I had behaved toward you. When I arrived here and Sabrina told me that you were the Cousin Jack she had mentioned in her letters, when she even hinted that the gossips had dared to link my name with yours after Christmas—well, I suppose I reached the limit of what my temper would stand. So when you goaded me at the table that first night, I simply reacted." She sent him another sidelong glance. "I certainly never expected you to respond as you did."

He grimaced. "This nonsense has got to stop, Emily. I realized that much while I was trying to extricate myself from those damned curtains. I was in a blazing rage at first—our tempers are too much alike, I think, too quick to flare. You are fortunate I could not catch you at once. What saved your skin was that I realized how ridiculous I would look if one of the servants chanced to walk in just then. Instead of making me angrier, it made me want to laugh. I saw then how absurd our behavior has been. We descended to nursery tactics that very first night and we haven't ever progressed beyond them."

To her shock, she thought about when he had kissed her, and color darkened her cheeks as she said carefully, "What do you think we can do about it? I cannot help getting angry; it just happens. And even though I'm nearly always sorry afterward, that doesn't help what's gone before. I thought I had learned to control it, but I don't seem able to do so around you."

"You needn't tell me that," he said with a chuckle. "I react the same way to you, as you know to your cost. In point of fact, it might help you to restrain your impulsive nature if you can contrive to remember that I still owe you a trifle on account for my ruined clothes, for making me walk this distance yesterday in sodden boots and buckskins, for the curtain trick, and for my injured pride."

"Why did you walk home in wet buckskins yesterday?" she asked. "That other time you borrowed something to wear from one of the men in the stables, did you not?"

"I did, but nothing in this world would have dragged me back there a second time in a like condition. I'd never have heard the end of it. And it's as well for you, my lass," he added grimly, "that I didn't go near the house. To say that I was in a rage is to understate the case. My temper works as yours does, remember. If I lose it, I quickly forget the cause. But though the first heat cools with time, if I must restrain myself for long, if I am not allowed to forget, but am further provoked . . . Do I need to explain this any more clearly?"

"No," Emily replied, "but if your answer to our problem is merely to say that I must not provoke you, I cannot see that we are any farther forward, because—"

"I didn't say that." He gestured toward an opening in the trees ahead of them. "There is the house now. We can continue this discussion later."

8

MERIDEN PARK HOUSE, NEARLY TWICE AS LARGE AS the Priory and a good deal older, had been augmented over the centuries until it was a sprawling pile with little symmetry in its design. Emily thought it beautiful nonetheless. For the most part it was constructed of the rose-colored brick so common throughout Yorkshire, and its setting high on the edge of the wooded escarpment, overlooking the lush dale below and the broad, rolling moors beyond to the east, provided a remarkable view.

Inside the house, Meriden turned her over to the care of his housekeeper, Mrs. Kelby, while he attended to his business. When they met later for the promised nuncheon, there was no chance for private discussion because of the hovering servants.

"Your house is beautiful," Emily said as she accepted a serving of sliced fruit. "Mrs. Kelby very kindly showed me over the central block."

"No time to see much else," he said, smiling. "I still get lost from time to time, but this warren used to afford me the most wonderful opportunities to lead my sisters a merry chase."

She chuckled. "When I think of the rude things you said about my childhood—"

"True, every one. Can you deny them?"

"No, though I wish I could. Since meeting you, I find I have wished on numerous occasions that I had led a saintly life, just so I could tell you to your face what a sad case you are."

"Tell me anyway," he invited.

She shook her head. "Having pointed out to me how very unequal the score is between us, 'tis ungentlemanly of you to bait me now," she said. "I confess to feeling some sympathy for your sisters, however. Mrs. Kelby told me you expect one of them to pay you a visit soon."

He nodded. "My sister Janet, Lady Filey, is coming next week from Richmond with my mother."

"I am surprised Lady Meriden does not live here."

He laughed. "She much prefers the household at Richmond, for she and Filey's mama are great cronies. I'd have to import a poor relation to bear her company here, and she wouldn't like that nearly as well as being with Janet, her children, and old Lady Filey."

When they stood together on the front terrace later, looking out over the vast gentle landscape, Emily said, "I thought the moors were more barren, bleaker. I didn't expect to see so much color everywhere."

"It's the heather coming into bloom, mostly," he said, "but the longer one looks upon the moor, the more one sees." He put his arm around her shoulders and added quietly, " 'Everywhere peace, everywhere serenity, and a marvelous freedom from the tumult of the world.' The abbot of Rievaulx Abbey, which is near here, wrote those words over four and a half centuries ago, but they provide as apt a description now as they did then."

Emily had gone very still the moment he touched her.

She did not want to move, but she wished he would take his arm away. If only his embrace did not make her feel so warm, so safe, she thought. This was a new Jack, one she was not certain she could handle. Accordingly, she greeted the arrival of her groom, leading their horses, with a sigh of relief.

They rode silently for a time. Then Jack said suddenly, "I think I was wrong about Oliver."

"Perhaps," she agreed. "I thought at first you were right about him, but I find I like him in spite of his faults."

"What do you think of Saint Just?"

She shrugged. "I don't like him as well, but that may be only because Harry Enderby doesn't like him and I like Harry. Moreover, Mr. Saint Just is not my nephew. He certainly puts himself out to charm, however."

"Miss Lavinia doesn't like him either."

"Miss Lavinia doesn't like men," she pointed out. "Oliver did say that Mr. Saint Just and Dolly had joined forces to convince him that the York scheme was a good one."

"I think Oliver has been accustomed to follow Saint Just's lead for some time now," Jack said. "I recognize the man's type. You heard him yourself, rattling on about gaming hells and vast sums lost at the track. When there are no ladies at hand, he talks mostly of game little bits of muslin and birds of paradise. More talk than action, probably, but I shouldn't be at all surprised to learn that he's here on a repairing lease."

"Harry Enderby suggested the same thing once, I believe," Emily told him. "Of course, he tends to disparage anything of which Dolly approves, so I paid him little heed at the time."

Another silence fell. Then he said abruptly, "I may have been wrong in the way I dealt with Melanie too."

"You know you were," she said flatly.

He looked at her. "I don't know it for a fact, but I won't argue the point with you now. We've got to declare a truce between us, and I think one way to achieve one is if you leave Giles and Oliver strictly to me

and I leave you to do your possible with Melanie and
Dolly. I scarcely heed Dolly's megrims anyway unless
she forces them upon my attention, and perhaps you
can persuade Melanie to confide in you.''

"You will truly leave her to me?''

His jaw tightened. ''Don't mistake truce for
surrender, Emily. I still don't make idle threats. If
Melanie arranges any more of her odd little 'loans,' she
will have to answer to me, and I promise you, I won't
spare her. Until such a thing occurs, however, you may
do what you can to draw her out. That is all I can agree
to allow, I'm afraid. Why did you burst in upon us
today, anyway?''

Accepting the change of subject in order to avoid
heated debate, she explained about her missing jewelry,
deleting her opinion of the Bow Street Runner and
telling him only that she had reported her loss. When
another silence followed, she commented casually, ''I
have offered to teach Melanie to swim, Jack. The pond
is a good place to talk, if we can be assured of our
privacy.''

"I'll see to that,'' he said. '' 'Tis a good notion, lass.
Perhaps you can induce her to trust you.''

Emily was certain she would succeed in that
endeavor, but Melanie confounded her. Though the
child proved to be a willing, even an enthusiastic pupil
in the days that followed, not one word would she speak
about her own affairs. At first Emily tried subtlety,
attempting to approach the subject obliquely. When
that failed, she tried more direct methods.

"I have been meaning to apologize to you, Melanie,''
she said on the third day of their late-afternoon lessons
when she and the child had sprawled next to each other
on a flat, sunny rock to dry their shifts before donning
their clothes.

Melanie looked at her curiously but did not speak.

"For entering the library without warning the other
day,'' Emily explained gently. ''I ought not to have
done such a thing, but I acted without giving thought to
the fact that your Cousin Jack might not be alone.''

Melanie flushed deeply and looked away.

"Why did he punish you, Melanie?"

"You know." The reply was nearly inaudible.

"Only what he told me," Emily said, "and he did not explain why you needed money. Does he not give you a generous allowance?"

Melanie nodded.

"But you required more?" Emily prompted.

Melanie nodded again.

"Why?"

After a long silence Melanie looked at her. "I am sorry I made Cousin Jack angry, Aunt Emily. I didn't mean to do so."

"No, darling, of course you didn't," Emily said, adding with a conspiratorial grin, "Nobody in her right mind would make Cousin Jack angry on purpose."

Melanie smiled wanly, then said, "My shift is dry now, Aunt Emily. Ought we not to put on our dresses again?"

"Tell me first why you needed the money, Melanie."

But that Melanie would not do. There were tears in her eyes when she shook her head, and Emily forbore to press her. Instead, once they had returned to the house and Melanie had been turned over to Molly, the upstairs chambermaid, to dry her hair, Emily went directly to the schoolroom.

"Miss Brittan," she said, finding that lady reading a French novel by a cheery fire, "I must speak to you about Melanie. Has she told you about her recent confrontation with Lord Meriden?"

Miss Brittan marked her page and set aside her book. Then, indicating a second chair by the hearth, she said, speaking in her precise way, "Pray sit down, Miss Wingrave. Certainly you have seen by now that Melanie confides in no one. Was the confrontation one of which I ought to have been made aware?"

Emily, sitting, shook her head. "Meriden said she needn't tell you if she didn't wish to do so, but I am convinced that there is more to the incident than we know. In the short time since my arrival, Melanie has lost weight. Her color is pale, and she has dark hollows under her eyes, as though she does not sleep well. But she will tell us nothing about what distresses her. It is not my custom to break a confidence, but because I believe we must put our heads together in order to help her, I will tell you what happened. Please understand, however, that Melanie has already been punished."

Miss Brittan promising to keep faith, Emily explained as much as she knew about Melanie's visits to the village and Meriden's discovery of the method by which the child had been obtaining money.

Looking aghast and not a little displeased, Miss Brittan exclaimed, "I know not what to say, Miss Wingrave! I must be at fault, for I had no idea that anything of this sort had occurred. I can assure you that while she is under my eye, Melanie has no opportunity to do such things; however, I do have my half-day on Wednesday afternoons, when I visit a friend, whose coachman drives me home at nine o'clock. Hitherto I have given Melanie but light tasks to accomplish in my absence, but I promise you that that will no longer be the case. I will be breaking no confidences of yours if I inform her that I have discovered that she is frequently away from the house during my absence. Indeed, a brief conversation with Merritt should suffice to provide me with what little information I require. In any event, I shall speak sternly to her and provide her with more work to do during those afternoons. Of a certainty, the nonsense will stop."

Despite such reassurance, Emily could not rest easily, for she did not believe that the governess understood that the problem rested not with keeping Melanie out of trouble but with discovering why she had behaved as she had. Understandably, Miss Brittan was concerned that she would be blamed for Melanie's peccadilloes, but neither did it reassure Emily to recall that although she had attempted to elicit a promise from Melanie never to obtain money by such methods again, the child had never actually said she would not. Indeed, all she would say on the subject was that she was sorry to have vexed Cousin Jack.

Accordingly, the following Wednesday afternoon Emily waited only until she knew Miss Brittan had departed to visit her friend before taking herself off through the home wood to the fork leading up to the moor and beyond to the village. Concealing herself in the shrubbery, she had not long to wait before Melanie appeared, walking quickly and keeping her eyes firmly fixed upon the road ahead of her, as though she was afraid of what she might see if she looked to one side or the other.

Once the little girl was well ahead of her, Emily emerged from her hiding place and followed her uphill through the woods and across the open moor into the village. Melanie went, just as Emily had expected her to, along the cobbled street and into one of the village shops. It was not the chandler's, but that with the sign of the apothecary; yet Emily had no doubt that the child was spinning him the same tale that she had used before.

Stepping quickly into the mercer's, she waited until Melanie had returned to the road before following her again. The child walked more slowly now and twice glanced about her, and though she did not actually turn around, the openness of the moorland made it necessary for Emily to fall well behind her until she turned downhill into the woods again. Hurrying to catch up, Emily snatched up her skirts and ran, but despite her haste, she rounded a curve in the road barely in time to see Melanie hand something to a stooped and elderly woman, who then turned away and vanished into the thick shrubbery.

Melanie hurried homeward, and Emily, making no attempt now to conceal her presence, sped after the old woman. Discovering the direction she had taken was not difficult, for there was a clear, though narrow path leading through the shrubbery. Emily followed it, taking care in her haste only to avoid those branches that threatened her face and eyes. Once she thought she caught a glimpse of the old woman's gray gown just ahead, but though she moved as quickly as she could, she saw no more.

Coming to a small clearing, she paused. The path had disappeared altogether, and she was uncertain of which direction to take. The sound of a footfall directly behind her startled her so that she cried out in alarm as she began to turn toward the sound, but her cry was cut off abruptly when, with a sharp explosion of pain in the back of her head, she collapsed to the hard leaf-strewn ground.

"Aunt Emily, Aunt Emily, oh, please wake up!"

Small hands smoothed hair from her face and touched her shoulders, pressing but not shaking her. Emily became aware of a chill in the air and the prickling of leaves, sharp pebbles, and dried twigs beneath that side of her body upon which she was lying. Only when she tried to move did the sharp, pounding ache in her head make itself felt.

"Be still, Aunt Emily," said the anxious voice from behind her. "Oh, I was so afraid she had killed you. Are you badly hurt? Shall I run for help?"

"Melanie?"

"Yes, it's me." The little girl moved around to squat down where Emily could see her. There were tearstains on her cheeks.

"You came back," Emily said dully.

"I was afraid she would kill you," Melanie said, her voice shaking now. "I could not just walk home without knowing."

"You saw me?" Emily tried to sit up, got as far as propping her elbow beneath her, then stopped, too dizzy to do more.

Melanie was nodding. "In the village and again on the moor. You fell behind, though, and so she didn't see you. I never thought you would follow her. When I heard you cry out . . ." She stopped, her voice catching in her throat.

"Who was she?"

Melanie looked away. "Just an old woman."

"Oh, Melanie, did you give her the money you got in the village? Have you been trying to help her for some reason?"

"Can you get up?" Melanie asked.

Emily managed to sit up, holding her head in a vain attempt to stop the pounding. "I think I will be steady enough to stand in a minute or two," she said, "but tell me about that old woman, Melanie. Did you give her the money? It will not do to prevaricate, you know. You must have got some in the village, for you have no other reason to visit the apothecary. Moreover, I saw you give her something."

"I bought some pennyroyal for Mama's tea," the child said, holding out a small brown paper packet. "She has been complaining of feeling bilious after she dines. I thought the tea would soothe her."

"I have no doubt that it will," Emily said, trying to look stern, "but you gave that woman something. What was it?"

"Will you tell Cousin Jack?" Melanie asked.

Emily hesitated, wondering if fear of punishment would induce Melanie to confide in her. "I certainly ought to do so," she said slowly.

Melanie stood up, squaring her thin shoulders. "I expect it is your duty to tell him."

Trying not to jar her aching head, Emily moved back a little so that she could lean against a tree trunk. Looking up even so short a distance was painful, and she knew she dared not attempt to stand just yet. "Look here, Melanie," she said quietly, "I am no tale bearer, but neither am I a fool. I won't have to tell Cousin Jack a thing if you mean to go on getting money in the village. He will find out for himself soon enough, and it won't take him months to do so this time, either. You know what will happen then, do you not?"

Melanie nodded, biting her lip.

"You cannot want him to punish you."

This time Melanie shook her head, but though tension showed clearly in her face, still she said nothing.

Repressing a sudden urge to shake the child until her teeth rattled in her head, Emily said, "The very best thing you can do now is to tell him yourself what you have done. He will be angry, but if you will tell him why you did it, I am persuaded he will not punish you severely."

Looking down at the ground, Melanie shook her head again.

"Are you afraid to tell him?"

She nodded.

Emily sighed. "He only wants to help you, darling. I promise you, it will be much better to explain the whole to him before he discovers for himself that you have done it again. I will go with you if you like. Cousin Jack will help that old woman if she needs help. Indeed, I am sure that he can fix whatever is wrong if you will but place your trust in him."

Melanie shook her head again, her lips pressed tightly together. Then she said, "Can you get up now, Aunt Emily? I don't like it here."

Emily gave up. Her head was hurting too much to allow her to think clearly, and all she wanted to do was to find a soft pillow upon which to rest it. Discovering that she could get to her feet, she still had all she could do to make it back to the house. She felt dizzy and nauseated, and when Melanie said in a small voice as they were making their way up the drive, "You won't tell him, then?" Emily would have liked very much to snap at her, but she didn't have the strength to do so. Instead, with an effort she managed to utter just one word:

"No."

Melanie gave an audible sigh of relief, only to gasp a moment later when the front doors flew wide and a tall, muscular figure ran down the steps and across the drive to meet them.

"Emily!" Jack put a strong arm around her shoulders. "I saw you from the library window. Good God, what happened?"

She managed to smile. "Do I look as though I've

been dragged through a bush backward? I promise you, I feel worse than that."

"You look as though it hurts you to walk," he said grimly, drawing her to a halt and making her look up at him.

The effort was too much. No sooner did she tilt her head back than the dizziness overcame her. She didn't swoon, but neither did she protest when he scooped her up into his arms. Settling her head against his shoulder, she was just thinking about how much more comfortable she was when she heard him demand that Melanie tell him what had happened to her.

Speaking quickly, Emily said, "Someone attacked me from behind as I passed through the woods on my way home from the village. If Melanie hadn't heard me cry out and run to find me, I should no doubt be lying there yet."

"In the woods? The home wood?"

Not wishing to nod, she murmured, "Yes, Jack, and I've got the very devil of a headache, so would you pray be so kind as to stop bellowing in my ear?"

She thought he growled, but he didn't say anything more until he had laid her down upon the sofa in the library and shouted for a servant to bring him some cold cloths to lay upon her head.

"When you're feeling more the thing," he said, "I'll carry you up to your own bed. Did you see who it was who struck you?"

"No," she answered, glad she was telling the truth, since his gaze was singularly penetrating.

"Did Melanie see anyone?"

"Ask her," Emily suggested, but the little girl had taken the first opportunity to slip away. When Jack turned as though to shout for her, Emily added casually, "I daresay she would have told me before if she had seen anyone."

Miss Lavinia hurried in just then with a basin of cold water and some cloths. "Said you'd been hit on the head," she said briskly, wringing out a cloth and placing it upon Emily's brow. "Told Cook to prepare a tisane for you. My own recipe. Never failed me. We'll have you feeling stout again in the twinkling of a bed-post. Be best if you was in your own bed though.''

"I'll carry her up," Jack said.

"I can walk," Emily told him, smiling.

"I saw you walk. I'll carry you."

Understanding from his implacable tone that further argument would be useless, she suggested that the sooner he did so, the better it would be. "We shall have Sabrina down upon us if you don't, and I'd as lief talk to her without having to move my head. My own bed and about a dozen pillows would suffice for heaven just now."

"Blasphemy," murmured Jack. "Don't let the vicar hear you say such stuff. My bellowing is nothing compared to his, you know." He scooped her up again, careful not to dislodge the cloth, and carried her up-stairs.

Martha, having learned in the servants' room of her mistress's accident, was awaiting them. "What this world's coming to, I don't know," she muttered. "Just you set her down in that armchair, m'lord. I've ordered a hot bath, and the lads will be bringing the water straightaway."

"Martha," Emily said, "I don't want a bath. I just want to go to bed."

"What you want and what you'll get are two different things, missy," said her abigail tartly. "You've torn your frock and scraped your face and your elbow, and you've dirt and whatnot all over you. And that's just the part I can see. Get between clean sheets like that you will not. Not while I've breath in my body to prevent you. First we'll have a look to see how bad you hurt yourself. What manner of villain strikes a lady down in broad daylight, I should like to know."

Emily glared at Jack, daring him so much as to smile at seeing her thus reduced to nursery status.

He patted her hand. "Mrs. Cooling is right, my lass. You just sit quietly here while I hurry the lads with the water."

Emily gritted her teeth. "I am perfectly capable of washing my face and hands at the basin. I do not need a bath. All I want to do is to get into bed."

Jack smiled at Martha and said gently, "Perhaps I ought to remain here to assist you, ma'am. It appears that your charge is prepared to be recalcitrant."

"You will do no such thing," snapped Miss Lavinia from the doorway behind him before Emily could voice her outrage. "You just run along downstairs, young man, and leave poor Emily to her tirewoman. Here is the tisane I promised you, my dear," she added, taking it from Molly, who entered just then. "You drink this up and have your bath, and you will feel much more the thing. Meriden, you still here?" she demanded. "Shoo!"

Jack fled, leaving Emily feeling somewhat bereft. For all his teasing and his concern for her injury, he didn't seem compelled to fuss over her, and she enjoyed his banter. Not that she would tell him so, of course.

When he and Miss Lavinia had gone and the tub was full, she allowed Martha and Molly to help her out of her clothes, and she had to admit that the bath felt better than she had expected it to. She had a few scrapes and incipient bruises from her fall, but only her head gave her any pain to speak of.

Once Emily was out of the tub, Martha insisted upon brushing her hair and plaiting it as she normally did for bed.

"You'll be more comfortable so," she said, and Emily didn't argue with her, knowing she would not be comfortable with her hair pinned up or with it hanging loose. Nevertheless, the brushing was an ordeal, and by the time she was tucked up in bed with the last drop of Miss Lavinia's herbal tisane inside her, all she wanted to do was to sleep.

To her astonishment, she slept the whole night through, not waking until the following morning was well advanced. Her curtains had not been opened, and Martha was sitting in a chair drawn up by the bed, her hands folded serenely in her lap.

Emily smiled at her. "I hope you have not sat there the whole night long," she said.

"That I have not," said her abigail, rising and moving to open the curtains. "Molly and one of the other maids sat here, turn by turn, after I went to my bed. I came in this morning at my usual time. Seemed a pity to wake you, though, when you was sleeping so peacefully."

"But why did anyone sit with me? My injury was not so bad as that. Indeed, barring some soreness where I was struck, I feel as fresh as a daisy this morning."

"You was unconscious afterward," Martha said, "so his lordship insisted on someone staying by you through the night."

"His lordship? Good gracious, Martha, you do not take your orders from Meriden."

"No, Miss Emily, that I don't, but happened I agreed with him. And you needn't take that high tone with me, or with him neither, for you owe him your thanks if for nothing more than keeping Miss Sabrina from wringing her hands over you all the whole night long. Wanted to come along up and waken you just to hear with her own ears that you wasn't perched ready to go aloft with the angels. His lordship put a stop to that right quick."

Emily chuckled. "Then, truly, I am grateful to him, and so I shall tell him. May I get up and go to breakfast with the family, or do you intend to keep me tied by the heels in my bed the whole day long?"

"I am sure that must be your own decision, Miss Emily. It is not my place to be telling you what to do."

"No, it certainly is not, you wicked woman, and what you were about to be giving me orders yesterday like you did, and in front of Meriden, at that, I cannot think." Emily grinned. "I will wear the pomona-green sprigged muslin and the green sandals. And I think," she added with a small grimace, "that I shall wear my hair in a net."

"It still has to be brushed if you're meaning to show your face outside this room," Martha said firmly, "but

I can contrive to arrange it in a coil at the back of your neck without hurting you too much, I expect.''

Though the hour was more advanced than usual when she went downstairs, Emily found Sabrina and Miss Lavinia still seated at the table in the breakfast parlor. Oliver and Mr. Saint Just were likewise present, and the latter appeared to be attempting to conceal amusement.

Sabrina, who had been talking when Emily entered, broke off to demand to know how she fared. ''For although Jack assured us that you would mend quickly, I could not help but think you had simply lost consciousness again, you know, and weren't asleep at all, but he wouldn't let anyone waken you. He said so long as your breathing was even, it was foolish to disturb you. Wouldn't let me send for Dr. Prescott either.''

''I am perfectly stout, thank you,'' Emily said, nodding to the two young gentlemen, who had got to their feet, then moving to peer beneath the lids of the dishes on the sideboard. ''I'll have some sliced beef,'' she said to the maidservant, ''also some bread and butter, and a dish of that fruit. Oh, and a fresh pot of tea, Anna.''

''Ordered raspberry tea for you already,'' Miss Lavina said. ''Soothing. Body's had a shock, don't you know. Raspberry tea's just the thing.''

''Very well, ma'am, I've no objection, certainly.'' Emily took her seat, peering at her sister. ''What's amiss, Sabrina? I heard you chattering like a magpie as I came in. You sounded most distressed.''

Oliver chuckled, earning himself a glare from his mama. ''If all you and Mr. Saint Just can do is to laugh, then I'll thank you to take yourselves elsewhere,'' Sabrina said severely. ''You won't think it so funny when our neighbors descend upon us in a fury, one after the other.''

''Good gracious!'' Emily looked from one to another. Miss Lavina's thin lips were twisted wryly. ''What is it?''

''The Runners,'' Oliver said, carefully straight-faced, ''have organized a horse patrol.''

"They couldn't get a proper Bow Street horse patrol up from London on such short notice," Mr. Saint Just added in an explanatory tone, "so they are using local lads."

"But why—"

Sabrina wailed, "They are trampling the woods, the moors, and no doubt every farm and garden for miles around. I shan't be able to show my face for weeks! Everyone will complain. Only think how angry Mr. Scopwick became when they did no more than question his housekeeper. His kitchen garden is his pride and joy! If he even thinks—"

Both young men were laughing now, and when Sabrina turned on them angrily, Emily looked to Miss Lavinia for explanation.

"Meriden told that Tickhill person that you was attacked in the home wood. Fool man leapt to the notion that your assailant was the same villain as stole our jewels. He and Earswick went round collecting lads with horses, and then this morning young Oliver and Mr. Saint Just, when they were out riding, came upon a group of them clattering to and fro in the woods."

"Said they were searching for the man who struck you down," Oliver said, chuckling. "Even a nodcock like Tickhill ought to know the fellow wouldn't hang about overnight to be caught. Gave us a good laugh, I can tell you."

"I hope your cousin is also laughing," Emily said slowly. "Is he about?"

"Aye," Oliver said, "been here nearly an hour. He is in the library reading over the household accounts. Dull stuff, I should say. Bound to have put him in a bleak humor. I wouldn't disturb him just now."

"Well, I shall certainly finish my breakfast first," Emily told him, taking a tentative sip from the cup the maidservant placed before her. "This tea is good, Miss Lavinia."

"Don't matter a whit if it's good or not, so long as it does the job," was the tart response.

Emily grinned at her, but her mind was racing.

Though she knew Sabrina was probably right in saying that an uproar would be caused by this recent turn of events, she couldn't imagine what could be done to prevent it.

9

WHEN EMILY HAD FINISHED HER BREAKFAST, SHE WENT down to the hall, debating with herself over whether she would disturb Jack before noon. The decision was made for her, however, before she had reached the bottom step of the grand stair. Merritt turned sharply toward her, and William, who was the footman on duty in the hall just then, straightened with the same startled air, for their attention had been firmly riveted upon the library doors and they had failed at first to note her approach. Emily could scarcely blame them, however, for the racket penetrating the closed doors of the library would have distracted anyone.

She had no difficulty recognizing the source of the noise. Having now been in Yorkshire for some weeks, she could not fail to recognize Mr. Scopwick's stentorian accents.

"How long has he been here, William?"

"Half an hour, sithee, miss. Happen his lungs'll wear out soon, think on."

"I doubt that. Is it the Runners again?"

"Aye. Searched through his kitchen garden this time. Told him they had orders from that Mr. Tickhill, sithee, to search every nook and cranny of the woods and surrounding countryside. Near as we can tell, the vicar wants his lordship should either hang both them Runners or send 'em back to Lunnon, post."

"If they've destroyed his kitchen garden, no one can blame him for being a trifle put out," Emily said fairly.

"Nay, miss." Both Merritt and William grinned at the understatement, but neither man offered further comment.

Emily regarded the library doors thoughtfully. Scopwick had neither run out of breath nor lowered his volume. Deciding that Jack had heard enough shouting for one morning, she took a deep breath and moved purposefully toward the doors.

"Tha' must not go in, miss," said William quickly. "He said they wasna to be disturbed."

"Who said? His lordship or Mr. Scopwick?"

"The vicar, miss."

"Open the doors, William, and stand back."

Grinning now, the footman did as she told him, and Emily, chin high, sailed past him into the library.

"Good morning, my lord," she said briskly. "Good morning, Mr. Scopwick. How nice to see you, sir. My sister was saying only yesterday that we see too little of you these days. Perhaps you would honor us by dining with us one evening soon."

Mr. Scopwick, having been interrupted mid-bellow, straightened and turned on her, his anger unmistakable, and for a moment Emily feared the man would continue where he had left off. She was amazed as always to see how large he was. Jack was sitting in his chair behind the library table, more or less as though he had been pinned there, and when she entered, the vicar had been leaning across the table glaring at him, words pouring forth from his mouth like a river in full spate. At her entrance he had whirled indignantly to face the door, and it was clear from his expression that he intended to deal short shrift to whoever had dared to interrupt his discussion with Meriden. Fortunately, he recollected himself at once. Instead of sharp words, he executed a curt bow and waited impatiently to hear what she would say. Her words had clearly astounded him.

Behind him, Jack was grinning, his relief at seeing her as self-evident as the vicar's dismay.

Mr. Scopwick, dark blue eyes flashing, shoved a ham-like hand through his curly black hair and regarded Emily doubtfully. "I should be honored to receive an invitation to sup with you ladies at any time," he said, striving to achieve a proper note of politeness. "However, perhaps you . . . that is, I have some trifling business just now with his lordship—"

"Oh, my dear sir," Emily said, stepping forward with her hand held out to him, "I heard of the damage done to your garden, and I cannot tell you how sorry I am. Sabrina has told me what a wonderful garden it is, and Miss Lavinia too, for you must know that she simply adores gardening, and so she is quite an authority on the subject." Dazed, the vicar took her hand, and she rattled on quickly, "Both of them are so very distressed over what happened, and I was hoping you would be able to tell us that the damage was not so severe after all, but clearly that is not to be. Sabrina is beside herself to think that the attack on me should have stirred Mr. Tickhill to such extravagant action. Indeed, my trifling hurts should not be considered at all, for as you see, I am quite restored to my customary good health, except for a slight headache, which I am persuaded will pass off before long. You must not consider me. Certainly not."

She raised a hand to her brow and allowed herself to sway a little, glaring at Meriden when he moved quickly, as though to come to her aid, and with a deep sigh of gratitude accepted Mr. Scopwick's strong arm when that gentleman moved to assist her. "Oh, thank you, sir. So kind," she murmured, letting him seat her gently in a nearby chair. Meriden's eyes were hooded now.

"My dear Miss Wingrave," said the vicar loudly, shoving his hand through his dark curls again, "indeed you must not believe for one moment that I am not fully conscious of your injuries. Nor would I deny anyone the least opportunity to lay the villain who assaulted you by the heels."

"Oh, you are very kind," said Emily faintly, not daring to look at Jack. "But your poor garden. I have heard that it was completely destroyed." Indeed, she had heard that much through the doors while she stood in the hall.

"'Twas not so bad as that," he assured her. "No, I daresay that with a careful hand, a good many of the plants might be rescued. Not that it was necessary for those louts to ride their horses right through it, for it wasn't. A clear lack of consideration, that's what it was, for they might have seen perfectly clearly that no one was hiding there. Invasion of my privacy, that's what it was. That fool Tickhill—"

"Indeed," Emily cut in gently, her voice in clear contrast to the vicar's, "Mr. Tickhill is most assiduous in performing his duties. He is—"

"He is a damned officious scoundrel," Mr. Scopwick interjected, building up a new head of steam. "Those men had no business to be doing what they were doing, and if Meriden don't mean to send them about their business, I'll make it my business to write directly to the chief magistrate at Bow Street. We'll just see what Mr. James Read has to say about his people destroying valuable property."

"I will speak to Tickhill," Meriden said quietly when the vicar paused for breath. "You may write your letter to Mr. Read if you wish to do so, of course, for I certainly agree that Tickhill's searchers overstepped their bounds. But they are not trained men, Scopwick, nor are they Read's men. They are merely local lads who wanted to help."

"Oh, yes," agreed Emily, leaning forward in her chair and striving to sound breathless, "and how kind it was of them, too. Surely, Mr. Scopwick, you would not be so cruel as to blame them for searching too hard to find the man who knocked me down!"

"Not at all, ma'am. Furthest thought from my mind." The vicar regarded her ruefully. "You mustn't think that I don't want to catch the villain as badly as anyone does, for I'd soon teach him better manners, I can promise you. Well, Meriden," he added, turning back to the earl, "I suppose I've said more than enough. I still cannot approve of your having brought that Tickhill fellow down upon us all, but I don't wish to be accused of putting a rub in the way of finding Miss Wingrave's assailant. Trust you to keep an eye on your man, though."

"I'll do that," Jack replied, getting to his feet. When the vicar had gone, he looked at Emily and shook his head in mock reproof. "My dear Miss Wingrave, you ought to be thoroughly ashamed of yourself for deceiving a man of God like that."

"I suppose I ought to have let you manage alone," she said sweetly. "You were doing so well with him before I came in."

"I was having my character described to me in terms that I'd as lief never hear again," he said shortly, taking his seat once more and propping his feet up on the table. Then, realizing what he had done, he eyed her warily. "I say, you are planning to sit there in that chair for a time, are you not?"

She grinned at him. "Coward. If there is any finish left on that table, I shall be amazed. Do you treat your own furniture so sadly, or only the things at Staithes?"

"I like to be comfortable," he said, returning her grin, "and my boots don't touch the finish. The blotter will have to be replaced soon, however. In case I have failed to make my gratitude clear, may I express my thanks to you now for a timely rescue? That man is a menace."

"At least he only bellows," Emily said. "Consider what might happen if he were the physically violent sort."

Jack's mouth twisted. "Do you mean to imply that I would be bested by that fellow? Me? You cannot know my reputation for fisticuffs, swordplay, and the like."

"Bragging, my lord?"

He chuckled. "No, but I don't fear Scopwick either. Even if he were the physical sort, big men like that are generally slow movers. I think I could hold my own

against him. Verbally it's another matter, however."
His expression became serious. "Emily, I may have
made a bad mistake."

"Several, I would imagine, but which one in
particular has raised its head to distress you, sir?"

"Scopwick, of course. I knew he was loud, but I'd no
idea the man had such an outrageous temper."

"But we told—"

"Don't say you told me so," he said sharply, "for
you didn't say that at all. You merely complained about
the fact that he bellows at people. Giles can do with
some bellowing. But now that I've seen Scopwick lose
his temper—twice, actually—I begin to wonder if I was
as wise as I thought in turning that boy over to him to
tutor."

Although she made no attempt just then to debate the
earl's statement, believing it would do him no harm to
doubt for once the rightness of his actions, Emily found
herself thinking more and more about Giles's situation as
the day went on. She realized she had seen no sign whatsoever that the boy feared his mentor, and many signs to
indicate that he was taking an uncharacteristic interest in
his studies. Several times she had actually seen him
curled up in a chair reading long after his allotted study
time had ended for the day. And although he had twice
begged to be allowed to stay at home in order to
accompany Oliver and his friends when they took their
guns out to the moors for a day's shooting, he had put
up little argument when his request had been denied.

For the most part, Emily had been pleasantly surprised by Giles's behavior. The scowling, churlish boy
whom Harbottle had delivered to the doorstep seemed
to have turned into a cheerful, though rather inwardly
focused young man. Indeed, the change in Giles had
been remarkable enough that, had they not all been
distracted by other events, it must have been noted by
everyone.

Deciding to find out just what was going on, Emily
set out that very afternoon to visit the vicarage. Upon
leaving the house, she recalled the events of the previous

day and nearly asked William to accompany her, but she changed her mind at once, silently stigmatizing herself for a coward. It was but a step through the wood, after all, to reach the path leading to the vicarage and the little chapel. And she could be in no danger so close to home, particularly since she was firmly convinced, as she told herself more than once after entering the wood, that her assailant had been either the old woman or an accomplice.

It was, nevertheless, a trifle daunting to discover upon her arrival at the two-story stone cottage that served as the vicarage that neither Mr. Scopwick nor his charge was there.

"Gone fishing, they have," the vicar's housekeeper informed Emily at the door, dusting her hands on her apron as she spoke.

"Fishing! How shall I find them?"

"Happen they be a mile or so up the dale from yonder dam, Miss Wingrave. Vicar's favorite spot, that be. Just tha' follow the brook, sithee, and happen tha'll find them afore long."

Following the woman's directions, Emily soon found herself in the thickest part of the wood, some distance from the road. The merrily rushing brook sang to her as she carefully made her way along a deer trail, between trees and through shrubbery that clung to her skirts and scratched at her bare arms. The mile or so described by the vicar's housekeeper seemed much longer.

Finally, when she stopped to disentangle her skirt from a blackberry bush, she heard a shout of laughter ahead that carried well above the babble of the water. Scopwick's voice was easily recognizable. As she drew closer, she heard Giles too.

"I've caught another!" he shrieked. "He's a foot long if he's an inch."

" 'A man may fish with the worm that hath eat of a king, and eat of the fish that hath fed of that worm,' " pronounced Mr. Scopwick in his customary accents.

Emily was close enough now to see them through the shrubbery. Both were nearly hip-deep in the waters of the brook, and Giles was leaning back, his rod bending forward with the weight of the trout that leapt and danced in the sparkling water beyond. Emily watched, fascinated, but the boy's mind appeared to be only half on his sport.

"I know that one!" he cried. "It's from *Hamlet*, the third act, I think. Part of that devilish silly stuff he puffs off to the king when the king wants to know where Polonius is and Hamlet don't want to say he's killed him. I didn't understand the half of it when I read it."

" 'I am glad of it,' " said Scopwick. " 'A knavish speech sleeps in a foolish ear.' " He plowed forward through the water with the net.

Giles chuckled. "That's from the same place. Rosenkrantz tells Hamlet he don't understand him, and that's Hamlet's reply." He peered into the net. "A good big one, just as I said. Now, sir, 'bait the hook well; the next fish will bite.' "

"Misquoted," retorted Scopwick with a chuckle, "but 'tis from *Much Ado About Nothing*. You'll not catch me with one so simple as that, laddie."

" 'Thou deboshed fish thou,' " quoth a third voice from across the brook, a voice that Emily had least expected to hear in such a setting as this. Looking in the direction from which it had come, she espied Miss Lavinia in a heavy green jersey and an ancient, well-worn stuff skirt, perched upon a boulder and nearly hidden in the overhanging branches of a huge weeping willow tree. Her rod was propped up in a pile of stones beside her, its line disappearing into the water some yards downstream from her, and she had a book propped open on her lap.

Scopwick's laughter startled Emily, and she looked back at him. "You never had that line out of Shakespeare, Lavinia."

Miss Lavinia favored him with a look down her thin nose. " 'Thou liest, most ignorant monster,' " she said sweetly. " 'I am in case to justle a constable. Wilt thou tell a monstrous lie, being but half a fish and half a monster?' "

"By Jupiter, she's right, sir!" Giles exclaimed, chortling with glee. "It's from *The Tempest*. I don't know which act."

Scopwick bowed to Miss Lavinia, and then just to show that he had recognized the source at last, he added, " 'Lo, how he mocks me! Wilt thou let him, madam?' "

Miss Lavinia chuckled. "You've misquoted that one, Eustace. Caliban calls Trinculo his lord, not madam."

"You'd not have thanked me for following suit, Lavinia, so 'keep a good tongue in your head.' "

Realizing belatedly that none of the anglers had noted her presence, Emily started guiltily and moved to show herself. Just at that moment, however, a muscular arm snaked around her body from behind and a large hand clapped tightly over her mouth. Though she struggled, her strength was as nothing compared to that of her captor, and the noise of the brook covered the sound of her efforts. Not one of the three fishermen so much as glanced in her direction.

Kicking wildly now with both feet, she tried at the same time to bite the hand over her mouth. When her heel connected soundly with her assailant's right knee, a familiar voice muttered furiously in her ear, "Dammit, Emily, if you do that again, I'll drop you on your backside right here and now." She ceased struggling at once, and a moment later, well away from the fishermen, Jack set her on her feet again.

She whirled to face him. "Whatever possessed you to do such a thing, you idiotish man? You scared the liver and lights right out of me." She raised her hand. "I ought to—"

"If you're going to do it," he said gently, putting his fists on his hips and smiling down at her in a way that could only be described as challenging, "you'd better get it done. Just be very sure it is truly what you want to do."

Glaring at him, Emily lowered her hand to her side. "You deserve that I should," she said. "You frightened me witless."

"Impossible. 'To be furious is to be frightened out of fear.' Good God, it's contagious!" He looked over his shoulder, then shook his head and turned back to her. "Don't, for the love of heaven, ask me where that quotation comes from. I haven't the least idea. I'm not even altogether certain it's Shakespeare, only I never memorized much by anyone else, barring pages and pages of Latin, of course, so it's bound to be. That's why I grabbed you before you made your presence known. Can you imagine what a fool I'd have looked if Scopwick had asked us to join that ridiculous game of theirs?"

"It is not a ridiculous game," Emily said. "Only consider how much Giles must have read and studied to be able to keep up with the vicar like that. No one else has ever stirred him to study at all before. And what a memory he must have! I am certain I could never remember so much, no matter how hard I tried. And," she added, giving him a searching look, "I don't believe you would be put so much out of countenance as you claim you would by an invitation to join their game, sir."

"Well, you're out there," he replied. "I don't want to join the game. I wasn't looking for a party, only for you."

"Me? Is anything wrong?" Thoughts of Melanie and Sabrina flashed through her mind, bringing a worried frown to her face.

"Nothing's amiss," he said, though he looked more serious now, "except for your having come into these woods unattended. Do you think that was wise, lass, after what happened yesterday?"

"Now, look here, Jack," she began, forgetting her own brief fears earlier, "don't you start—"

"Don't rip up at me, you little shrew. I was concerned about your safety, nothing more."

"Well, you needn't concern yourself. I am a full-grown woman, and I am well able—"

"To take care of yourself? Like yesterday? By rights, you probably ought to be still laid down upon your bed, and that's precisely where you'll soon find yourself if you . . ."

"If I what?" she demanded when he broke off.

He grinned ruefully. "I don't think I would be altogether wise to say what I was about to say."

"Say it."

"No. Look here, Emily—"

"Say it, Meriden. You were going to threaten to send me back to bed if I don't do as you tell me to do, weren't you?"

"Something to that effect," he admitted, "but I didn't say it, and that ought to count for something. Oughtn't it?"

"I don't know," she said, pretending to take the matter under consideration. "So quick a reaction, the involuntary nature of your words, the fact that you thought such a thing at all—" Her own words ended in a shriek of laughter when Meriden grabbed her by the shoulders and proceeded to shake her. "Stop it, Jack! You will make my head ache again!"

"You deserve that your head should ache," he muttered grimly, and although he did stop shaking her, he did not take his hands from her shoulders. "Have you got any idea what sort of thoughts passed through my mind when William told me you had walked out alone? Have you?"

She looked up at him from beneath her lashes. "No, I don't. Tell me."

Jack's hands tightened with bruising strength upon her shoulders. "Don't tempt me, Emily. Oh, damn you, Emmy love, you'll drive me—" Where she would drive him she never heard, for instead of finishing his sentence, he pulled her into a crushing embrace, bent his head, and pressed his lips to hers.

Emily made no attempt to evade his kiss. Indeed, she had seen his intent perhaps even before he knew himself what he meant to do, and she had waited with bated breath, wanting him to kiss her more than she could remember wanting anything before in her life. Her breath came raggedly now, and the feelings she remembered from the last time he had kissed her coursed through her body anew, making it tingle with vibrant energy. His hands moved over her, exploring the contours of her figure as though they would memorize every line, every curve.

When his tongue sought entrance into her mouth, she sighed with longing, moving her hands to his waist and upward, standing on her tiptoes, responding instantly with a passion to match his own. After several moments Jack set her back upon her heels and looked searchingly down into her eyes, not speaking for a long moment. When he did, his voice rasped deep in his throat.

"I hope you don't expect an apology for that, because you won't get one. I am not at all sorry. In fact, I should very much like to do it again."

Emily looked at him, scarcely knowing what to say. Her body was still aflame with the sensations his caresses had stirred to life, but lifelong training kept her from telling him so. She, too, wanted him to do it again, all of it, for she had not known that a man's touch could be so electric, so stimulating to one's nerves. Indeed, the way he was looking at her now made her feel as though he still touched her. Her body strained beneath her gown, inviting further caresses. Her fingertips itched to do to him what he had done to her. His gaze held hers. At last he reached toward her, his hand feeling gentle upon her arm.

"Emily?" His voice was mild, curious.

She blinked. "I don't want your apology," she said. "I think I would cry if you apologized. And don't mock me, Meriden, or I shan't be responsible for my actions. I don't understand the things I'm feeling just now. Perhaps I had better go back to the house. Indeed, we should not be here alone like this."

His gaze was still searching but gentle, and he did not reply at once. When she moved to turn away, his hold on her arm tightened. "Don't go back," he said. "We'll walk a little until you have recovered your composure."

"There's nothing amiss with my composure," she said tartly. When she looked pointedly at his hand upon her arm, he released her. She lifted her chin. "You think too highly of your charms, my lord, if you think a simple kiss can disconcert me."

He grinned at her. "The same old Emily. That was no simple kiss, and you know it. There were sparks enough to light a blaze between us. You cannot say one minute that you will weep if I apologize and then tell me I underrate my kisses. I've a strong fancy to prove you wrong on that last point just for the sake of feeling those sparks again, but I shall bow to my gentlemanly instincts and resist temptation. Unless, of course, you are afraid to walk with me." He paused, raising his eyebrows.

Emily made a rude noise. "I don't fear you," she said, "though I doubt you've a gentlemanly instinct in the whole of your body." Blushing as she found herself thinking thoughts about his body that no lady ought to think, she turned quickly away. "We can walk if you like. It is a fine day for walking."

"Aye," he said amiably, falling into step beside her, "or for any other activity that might tempt us."

Shooting him a speaking look, she found herself unable to look away again and would have stumbled over a raised root in her path had he not steadied her with a firm hand beneath her elbow. After that, she did not look at him again, but she was unnaturally aware of his presence beside her, and the tingling in her body did not decrease for some time.

Finally, as though he were fully aware of the unfamiliar thoughts and feelings creating a tumult in her mind, Jack began to speak calmly about Giles and the vicar. "It appears to me that we both underrated Scopwick," he said. "The man seems to have a gift for dealing with that young scamp. Imagine Giles spouting Shakespeare. I'd have laughed to scorn anyone who had suggested a fortnight ago that he would ever do such a thing."

Emily remained silent, but she was grateful for his conversation. Her emotions were settling down at last, and when he began to tell her tales of his youth, of adventures he had had in the woods then, she soon found herself laughing, comfortable again. By the time they returned to the house, the incident by the brook was, if not forgotten, put into a clearer perspective for her.

She had, she decided, overreacted. She had allowed Jack to stir her body and thus her mind with his practiced charms. Heaven knew, she told her reflection as she prepared for dinner that evening, that he had known precisely what he was doing to her. No doubt he had meant to teach her a lesson, to have some sort of revenge upon her for her lack of response to his attentions at Christmas or for all she had done to him since. Certainly he had said nothing to indicate that his interest in her now was anything more. He had often called her cool, even chilly. He had once told her that such an attitude put a man off. Surely his behavior today had been meant only to warm her up. He had been vexed with her for going into the woods without an attendant, worried that she might be assaulted again. Perhaps he had wished to punish her a little. She had been refining too much upon his ability to stir her senses. No doubt any man of experience could stir any woman just by wishing to do so. She would not give him the satisfaction of seeing that she had set any great store by his actions or by her own response to them.

If a kind of sadness colored her thoughts once she had reached these conclusions, she ignored it, telling herself that to pay heed to such feelings would only be to play into Jack's hands. Probably he was bored—a little bored, at any rate. There was no personable female around to practice his wiles upon, only herself. Dolly was too young and impressionable, and he was responsible for her.

Emily knew how the game was played. She knew the rules set down by the *beau monde* for such flirtations, and so, she decided, Jack probably trusted her not to read too much into his actions. Very well, she told herself firmly as she shook out her skirts and prepared to join the family, she would take his attentions as he

meant them to be taken. She would ignore the little
voice deep inside her that insisted she wanted those
attentions to mean more, because even to consider such
a thing was to lay herself open to another heartache
such as the one she had suffered when Stephen Campion
had chosen to wed a lady other than herself.

When the evening meal passed as others before it had
passed, without so much as a teasing remark from
Meriden to Emily, she was certain she had read him
correctly. To show him she understood his intent, she
was as coolly polite to him as ever, confining most of
her conversation to Miss Lavinia and Sabrina. When
she glanced up once to find his gaze upon her, his
expression one of slight mockery, she flushed and
looked away, annoyed with herself for giving him such
an opportunity. He left for Meriden Park directly after
the meal, and Emily told herself she was glad he had
done so.

10

WHEN JACK DID NOT APPEAR AT STAITHES THE
following day, Emily decided that he had been called
away upon business of one sort or another, but she
refused to ask about him, and no one offered a reason
for his absence. The day after that, however, when he
still did not appear, when there was not so much as a
note from him to explain his absence, she could not
stand it any longer. Seeking out Miss Lavinia in the knot
garden while she waited for Melanie to join her for their
swimming lesson, she got directly to the point.

"I cannot think where Meriden has been these two
days past, ma'am. Surely he has not deserted us
entirely."

Miss Lavinia looked up from her weeding. "I thought you knew," she said. "Annabel . . . that is, his mama, and his sister Lady Filey arrived yesterday from Richmond. I am persuaded that they will claim his attention for several days yet to come, for he has not clapped eyes upon either one these seven months and more."

"Good gracious, I quite forgot," Emily said, looking back toward the house as she felt warmth creeping into her cheeks. "He did tell me that Lady Meriden was expected, and Lady Filey too. I just never thought about it again. Indeed, I am surprised he did not mention the other evening that they were arriving so soon. We ought to invite them to dine, surely."

"I expect they will invite us," Miss Lavinia said comfortably, getting to her feet and reaching back to rub the small of her back. "It is Annabel's place, after all, since dear Sabrina is still in mourning and cannot be expected to entertain. We shall see them at the services tomorrow in any event."

Her prophecies were entirely accurate, for the very next day the ladies of Staithes were invited to join Lady Meriden and her daughter for a nuncheon on Monday afternoon. Thus it was that Sabrina, Emily, Miss Lavinia, and Dolly, the latter excited at being included and dressed in her best white muslin, set out in Sabrina's carriage shortly before noon.

"But I am tired of dark ribbons and sashes," Dolly protested when Emily complimented her upon her appearance. "I long to wear pink and bright yellow again."

Regarding her speculatively, Emily said, "Yes, pink would become you, I think, but not yellow, Dolly. It takes a particularly brilliant complexion to wear yellow, you know, and yours is so delicate, I daresay it would look a trifle insipid. Lavender would be better, or pale blue."

"Ought to think of something more than her appearance, is what I say," declared Miss Lavinia.

"Oh, dear," Sabrina said, fluttering anxiously as she

settled herself against the comfortable squabs of the carriage. "I am sure you are right, ma'am, but do not scold her just now, I beg of you. I am persuaded, dearest Dolly, that you would look charmingly no matter what you chose to wear."

"Tell me about the dowager countess, Miss Lavinia," Emily said quickly. "I know nothing about her. Indeed, though I am very nearly certain I have met Lady Filey somewhere or other, I cannot recollect her mama, and Meriden has said little about her other than that she enjoys living at Richmond."

"Annabel don't go about much," said Miss Lavinia obligingly. She and Dolly occupied the forward seat, and she glanced at the girl as she spoke, as though she expected another comment from her. But Dolly remained silent, looking out the window at the passing scenery. Miss Lavinia looked again at Emily. "Never was one for cutting a dash, Annabel wasn't. Fortunate, since Meriden's papa was pretty well content to spend the entire year at the Park. They turned their daughters off in style, of course. Did the required Seasons in London, but that would have been a good while before you was there yourself, my dear. Filey and Janet are more fashionable about such stuff. Most of the year they spend here in Yorkshire, but they generally spend February through May in town. Daresay you'll like Annabel. Comfortable soul, to my way of thinking."

"Mama don't think so," Dolly said with a chuckle, turning to look at Sabrina.

Her mother bristled. "I am sure I have never said such a thing, Dolly. What can you mean?"

"Well, Lady Meriden always scolds you for one thing or another," Dolly said. "You told me just before the carriage arrived that you wondered what she would find amiss this time."

"Well, you shouldn't say so, at all events," Sabrina retorted. Looking defensively first at Emily and then at Miss Lavinia, she added, "I am sure you cannot wonder at it if I am a trifle nervous. Lady Meriden says whatever comes into her head to say, and you know that perfectly well, Miss Lavinia, if Emily does not. I assure you, she can be a tartar when the mood strikes her. *Comfortable* is not how I would describe her."

Miss Lavinia said reflectively, "Daresay you don't find comfort in uncomplicated conversation, but I do. Annabel don't mash her thoughts up in fool attempts to be tactful. One need never guess at what she means, for she says what she means. I find that exceedingly comfortable after years of conversing with mealy-mouthed women who think the worst thing they can say is whatever they are thinking."

"I hope," said Sabrina, offended, "that you do not think me mealymouthed, Miss Lavinia."

"Never said so, did I?" Miss Lavinia looked at her with a hint of a smile on her thin lips. "Daresay you don't always say what you think, Sabrina, but you never wrap insults in sugar coating like some I can call to mind. You do try to find good things to say about people, but I doubt you ever say things you don't believe to be true."

Mollified, Sabrina said to Dolly, "I hope you will have the good sense to refrain from telling Lady Meriden that she makes me uncomfortable. Perhaps I do find her a trifle too outspoken for my own tastes, but I like Janet exceedingly well."

"Oh, so do I," Dolly agreed. "So cheerful, always, and such a merry laugh. It would be great fun to know her better."

Almost immediately upon being introduced to Lady Filey in the elegant blue drawing room at Meriden Park, Emily found herself in full agreement with her niece.

"Oh, I remember you!" Janet exclaimed, squeezing her hand. "The most beautiful creature. I remarked upon it to Filey at the time, you know, telling him I would snap his nose off if he so much as mentioned your name to me later. I was so envious of your flaxen hair, for mine looks like it came straight off a mouse, and I have no countenance and no figure. And there you were, looking so absurdly young, with a shape like a willow, eyes like blue saucers, and hair I would kill to possess. You wore white muslin, of course, but it was trimmed with elaborate white silk embroidery—flowers all round the hem, with the pattern repeated on the edging of the sleeves and on the sash. It was a particularly wide sash, as I recall, tied right up under your breasts, and you wore pearls in your hair. Ravishing!''

"I remember that dress," Emily said, smiling. "It was one of my favorites during my first Season. I wore it often, despite my sisters' apostrophizing me for a dowdy."

"Impossible," said Jack, who stood beside his mother, a slender, elegant woman with iron-gray hair and his own gray eyes. "No one could ever have called you such a thing."

"Sabrina did," Emily said, rewarding him with a cool smile.

"Well, but no one would blame me," Sabrina said. "You had more dresses than you could count, Emily. There was no need to wear any one of them more than once, twice at the most. You only wore that one because Stephen Campion was partial to it, and when he decided he could no longer tolerate your temper tantrums and offered for Melinda Harcourt, you never wore that dress again."

"It wasn't my temper," said Emily hotly. "Stephen wanted Lady Melinda's money."

"Nonsense," retorted Sabrina.

"I was wrong, Sabrina," Miss Lavinia murmured when Emily, flushing deeply, glanced at Jack, then away again. "You don't always look for good things to say to people. Annabel, how have you been keeping yourself?"

"I am quite fit, thank you," said Lady Meriden, taking her seat in a high-backed wing chair near the hearth. "Do sit down, everyone. They will call us when our meal has been served. Janet, stop flitting about and sit down."

"I thought Sabrina would like a cushion," Lady Filey said. "Her chair is not as comfortable as some of the others."

"She provides her own cushion," the older woman said, adding with a critical look at Sabrina, who was still attempting to recover her composure after Miss Lavinia's reproof, "I declare, you get plumper every time I see you, Sabrina. You really ought to exercise more and eat less. Young Dolly takes all the shine out of you these days, though you were thought to be quite as much a beauty as Emily in your younger days."

Since Sabrina was as incapable of responding to this severe speech as she had been of responding to Miss Lavinia, Emily, taking pity on her, said calmly, "I was never so beautiful as Sabrina, ma'am, though I thank you for your kind words. I daresay Dolly will contrive to make the *beau monde* forget she ever had a mother or any aunts."

"If I ever get to London," Dolly said pettishly.

Meriden's lips tightened. He had taken a seat near his mother but had said very little.

Lady Meriden looked at Dolly. "You are a good deal prettier without that scowl, but I daresay you know that, my dear. You will no doubt go to London next year."

"I wanted to go this year so as to make my come-out at the same time as my friend Lettie Bennett," Dolly said, careful not to scowl, "but Cousin Jack would not permit it."

"Certainly not," the dowager said. "I am sure that you would not wish people to think more about your improper behavior than about your beauty."

"No," said Dolly doubtfully.

"You will be the belle of the Season when you do go," Janet said brightly. "Why, I daresay that all the young men will be clamoring for just one hint of your favor, my dear. I must insist that Filey take me to London in February so as not to miss a single moment of your come-out. No doubt Jack will want to give a ball for you at Meriden House."

"No doubt," said her brother dryly. "No, Dolly, we are not going to begin planning it this moment, though if you can contrive to behave yourself until then, something of that nature might well come to pass."

Dolly's eyes were shining now, and she looked toward her mama to see if Sabrina had heard the good news. But Sabrina appeared still to be lost in thoughts of her own, and revived only when, at the table, Janet demanded to know if it was not she who had promised to send her a recipe for damson-plum cake.

"Why, I daresay I did, for Cook prides herself upon her cake and I was used to serve it often in London. We have not had one this age and more, however, and I do not recall promising to send you the recipe."

"But I am certain I asked you for it," Janet said, "for I can remember that it just melted in one's mouth. Have you ever tasted it, Jack?"

The earl disclaimed any knowledge of damson-plum cake, but Sabrina assured Janet that she would send her the recipe just as soon as she could persuade Cook to write it out for her.

The following day, when Sabrina announced self-consciously that she meant to walk to Meriden Park to deliver the cake recipe to Janet with her own hands, it occurred to no one to try to stop her. Nor did anyone suggest that she might simply send it to the Park with Jack, who had come to the Priory as usual. Emily, remembering the dowager countess's unkind words regarding Sabrina's weight, did not have to tax her mind to understand Sabrina's reasons, and all Jack said was that she must take her maid with her, since she would be walking through the woods.

No one expected trouble, so it was with a great deal of shock that the household greeted her return, for she was escorted home by a furious Vicar Scopwick, who demanded at the top of his lungs that someone send at once for Meriden so that he could do something about the grievous trouble he had caused.

When Emily arrived upon the scene, she discovered that Scopwick had escorted her sister into the library

and was kneeling beside the leather sofa where Sabrina
reclined, coaxing her in a voice that Emily scarcely
recognized as his own to take just a sip from the glass he
was holding to her lips. William, Merritt, and the maid
Anna hovered over the pair of them. Emily signed to the
servants to leave, saying to the butler as they turned
away, "You have sent for his lordship?"

"Yes, miss. Immediately upon their arrival."

"Good. Leave us now." She turned back to the vicar,
who had made no attempt to rise, his whole attention
being focused upon Sabrina. "What happened, sir? Is
she injured?"

"Oh, Emily," Sabrina moaned. "Those awful men
attacked me."

Emily stared at her. "What men? Where?"

"Wait until Meriden arrives," Scopwick said curtly in
his usual tone. "There is no need for her ladyship to
repeat this dreadful tale. Here, ma'am," he added,
"you must drink this. It will make you feel a good deal
better."

"But I don't like spirits," Sabrina protested weakly,
"and you are making my head ache, Mr. Scopwick. Do
try to talk more softly if you can."

"I am talking softly," he said indignantly. "Now,
don't argue with me. Just drink this up. I promise you,
you will feel much more the thing when you do. I'm a
man of God, ain't I? Would I advise you to drink
brandy if I didn't think it would do you good?"

"Oh, I cannot. I mustn't."

"Tilt it down her throat if you want her to have it,
man," recommended Meriden from the threshold, "but
don't coax her. She'll only mutter and moan some
more. What's occurred here?"

Scopwick started at hearing the earl's voice and in-
advertently did just as he had suggested. Sabrina sat
upright quickly, choking on the brandy, which
necessitated the vicar's administering a few sharp blows
to her back to aid her in regaining her composure. Thus,
Meriden had time to perch himself on the edge of the

library table before Scopwick turned on him again. The look of amusement on the earl's face faded abruptly, however, when the vicar demanded to know what he meant by subjecting Lady Staithes to such wicked treatment.

"Me! What the devil had I to do with anything? You tried to drown her in brandy, man, and as for what happened before, I've been here at the house all day, just as I usually am. And where's her maid, I should like to know? Didn't you take your woman with you, Sabrina? I certainly told you to do so."

"Well, of course she did," Scopwick retorted without giving Sabrina a chance to reply, "but the fool wench tripped over something in the road halfway back from Meriden Park and twisted her ankle, leaving her lady-ship to run to seek help, and what happened next is that those two fool Runners of yours jumped out of the bushes at her and flung her to the ground. If I hadn't heard her screams, God knows what they'd have done to her next."

"Nonsense," said Meriden calmly.

"Nonsense, is it? I'll show you nonsense." The vicar straightened to his full height and took two steps toward the library table before Emily leapt to stop him.

When her hand on his arm had no effect whatsoever upon him, she shouted his name, demanding, "What are you about, sir?" When he looked down at her much as he would look at a pesky fly, she added more calmly, "His lordship is perfectly right. It is nonsense to think that Mr. Tickhill or Mr. Earswick would ravish any woman, let alone Sabrina, whom they both know very well. Indeed, I cannot think how they came to attack her at all, when they must have recognized her at once even if the woods were dark, which they cannot have been at such an hour."

A small involuntary guilty cry from Sabrina drew their attention. Finding herself the focus of all eyes, she made a halfhearted gesture as though she would wave them all away, but Meriden had had enough.

"Well, madam, your sister makes an excellent point. How is it that such a thing came to pass, if indeed it did?"

"Oh, it did," she moaned, pressing a hand to her brow. "Truly, it did, and it was dreadful. I thought they would murder me. Indeed, if Mr. Scopwick had not heard my screams and come to my rescue, I do not know—"

"Are you attempting to tell me that Tickhill and Earswick did not recognize you?" Jack demanded.

"Well, not at first," she said wretchedly. "I was all alone in those awful woods, you see, and all I could think about was poor Emily being attacked as she was the other day, and so I was hurrying, you know—"

"No matter how fast you were walking, they must have seen you quite clearly," Jack said sternly.

"But they couldn't see me clearly at all, for I had pulled my shawl up over my head so I wouldn't have to be looking about me all the time, you know. All I wanted to do was to get to the vicarage to get help, but all of a sudden there I was on the ground with those two rough men on top of me, shouting that they'd caught me. And I was screaming and fighting, and my wretched shawl got all tangled about my face. I think Mr. Scopwick must have grabbed the Runners just as I got my face uncovered, for I am quite certain that the very first thing I saw was the two of them sort of dangling from his fists, looking frightened and dismayed, while he was shaking them like rag dolls. I must have fainted, I suppose, for I don't remember anything after that. The next thing I knew, Mr. Scopwick was carrying me up the drive toward the Priory."

"And the maid?" Jack asked. He had an odd look on his face, and Emily, controlling her own amusement with difficulty, decided it would be better if she did not look at him again until she had regained control of her sense of the ridiculous.

Scopwick snorted. "What, do you think I left the fool wench lying on the ground somewhere halfway between

Meriden and the Priory? Not but that it would have served her right, tripping herself up like that when her lady depended upon her. I shouted for young Giles, who was already coming to find out what all the row was about, meaning, you know, to send him for help, but then I realized those dam . . . those dratted Runners were coming to their senses—they had fainted or something just after her ladyship swooned," he added hastily when Jack looked about to ask a question. "Daresay they won't remember anything about it."

The earl's eyebrows shot upward, and Emily clapped a hand over her mouth, not daring to look now at anyone.

"Mr. Scopwick," Sabrina said, regarding the vicar with awe, "did you . . . that is, those Runners, did you . . . ?"

"Sorry if you think I ought to have sent a couple of servants back to assist your woman instead of turning her over to their tender mercies," he said, his dignity returning. Emily was certain he was purposely misunderstanding Sabrina. He added firmly, "She will take no hurt from them. I am as certain of that as I am that the sun will rise at dawn tomorrow."

"I am persuaded," said Meriden carefully, "that your woman will be perfectly safe, Sabrina. No doubt she has even now been returned to the house and is having her hurts attended to."

"Of course she's safe," said Scopwick impatiently. "Didn't I just say so? But now that you are feeling more the thing, my lady," he added, turning to Sabrina, "I want to know just what you were about, to be walking through those woods with naught but a scatterbrained wench to bear you company." When Sabrina fluttered her hands and turned her scarlet face to the sofa cushions, he glared at Meriden. "You will not tell me, sir, that there is no carriage available for her ladyship's use."

"No, of course I will tell you no such thing. The decision to walk to Meriden Park was Sabrina's alone. I did not object, so long as she took her maid, though I did assume that my mother would offer to send her back in our carriage.''

Nodding, the vicar turned back to Sabrina, who covered her face with her hands.

Chuckling now, Emily said, "You had better tell him, you know, Sabrina, before he accuses us all of having had a part in your mishap.''

"I cannot," Sabrina wailed behind her fingers.

"Then I shall do so. The man is concerned for your safety, for goodness' sake. He don't care a pin for your figure.''

"Her figure!" Scopwick stared at Sabrina, then grinned, the grin changing his rough features, softening them and bringing a twinkle to his eyes. "You're out, there, Miss Wingrave," he said in a much more gentle tone. "Lady Staithes has a magnificent figure, worthy of great care. Don't tell me, ma'am, that you were exerting yourself for the foolish purpose of reducing a single perfect curve of it.''

Sabrina's hands fell, and her eyes were wide. "Lady Meriden said I was too plump. Indeed, and so did Emily.''

"Lady Meriden is a fool," retorted the vicar, "and so is Miss Wingrave. So now that that is settled, I trust you will do no more unnecessary walking about these grounds until they can be made perfectly safe again. If you must go out, take a good strong footman with you. Do you understand me, madam?''

Sabrina nodded, still shaken and looking rather dazed.

Jack got to his feet. "Well, sir, now that everything is under control again—''

"Much you would like to think so," growled the vicar, turning back to face him directly, "but there remains yet one matter that is of grave concern to me.''

Jack sighed. "The Runners. Look here, Mr. Scopwick, I have already talked to Tickhill, but they are just trying to do their duty. Jewels have gone missing, not only Miss Lavinia's but also Miss Wingrave's. Unless you can think of a better way to find the items or the thief who took them, the Runners will remain.''

"You'd do better to hire a thieftaker to find the jewels alone,'' Scopwick said sourly. "Offer a large enough reward, man, and those baubles will turn up quick enough. Catching the thief is another matter.''

"I cannot do that,'' Jack said quietly. "The jewels were taken right here in the house at times when there were no strangers about. Therefore, someone in the house is guilty, or someone from the neighborhood who could provide an excuse for being present if he or she were caught inside. Getting the jewelry back without finding the thief would let him think he can get away with the same trick whenever it pleases him to attempt it. I won't do that.''

"Well, I won't tolerate having my garden overrun, my housekeeper scared out of her wits, or young women assaulted on my very doorstep. I believe I have convinced those two nodcocks of yours that there is nothing good to be gained from showing their faces in my vicinity again, but I'd prefer to send them packing altogether. As for strangers, what about that Saint Just fellow young Oliver's got visiting him? Don't wish to cast aspersions—''

"Wouldn't do any good if you did,'' Meriden told him. "Saint Just was still at Cambridge when Miss Lavinia's things were taken. I won't send Tickhill and Earswick back to London, Mr. Scopwick, but I will order them to confine their efforts to Staithes—no, that won't do, will it? The best I can do is to ask them to lie low until they have good reason to move. They have been running to and fro as a result of the attack on Miss Wingrave, you know, thinking their man and her assailant were one and the same. I can think of no reason to believe that to be the case. No doubt she merely startled a poacher in the woods.''

Emily opened her mouth to contradict him but shut it again when she realized that a debate on that subject would likely lead to questions she had no wish to answer. Though the notion of poachers roaming the home wood in broad daylight was plain ludicrous, she was just as certain in her mind as Meriden was in his that she had not been attacked by the jewel thief.

Mr. Scopwick agreed to the earl's suggestion, albeit with obvious reluctance. "Said all along those two was a pair of fools," he said acidly. "Still think you ought to pack them back to London, where they can do no further harm, but I'll say no more about it if you can manage to keep them out of my sight. Miss Wingrave," he added, turning to Emily, "you'd best see her ladyship up to her bed. She's endured quite a shock, and I don't think she ought to exert herself any more today."

Sabrina offered no protest, meekly thanking the vicar again for coming to her rescue and allowing Emily to lend her the support of her arm up the stairway. When Emily returned to the library, Jack was alone, seated in his chair, perusing the topmost of a pile of papers on the table in front of him.

Smiling, he got to his feet. "See the damsel safe to bed?"

"I did, and she seems to have conquered some of her fears, at least. I don't mean to stay, for I know you must have work to do. I came only to see if the heroic dragon slayer had been seen safely off the premises."

"He has." Jack chuckled. "I can just imagine poor Sabrina dashing through the woods with her shawl pulled over her head."

"She must have been terrified, poor dear. It really is fortunate that Mr. Scopwick heard her cries. The Runners would not have known what to do with her when they realized their error. And those poor men! I don't think, from the sound of it, that Mr. Scopwick can have treated them gently, do you?"

Jack grimaced. "I just hope he left a piece of them for me, for I can tell you that I don't mean to treat them gently either. At the moment, the only thing they have to be grateful for is that no one else is about to stir my temper more than it's already been stirred. I kept expecting Miss Lavinia to pop in, or Oliver and his foppish friend, or even Dolly. Where the devil is everyone, anyway? This place is as quiet as a tomb."

"Miss Lavinia and Dolly drove into Hemmsley to visit Mrs. Bennett, and I daresay Oliver and Mr. Saint Just may very well have accompanied them," Emily said. "Mr. Saint Just has been casting sheep's eyes at Dolly all week."

"Probably the man is bored," Meriden said brutally. "Just keeping his hand in, so as not to lose his touch before he returns to the company of his London friends. He still means to leave for York in a week, you know, so I doubt that he's seriously interested in attaching Dolly's affections."

Emily sighed, thinking, in view of her earlier thoughts on the same subject, that the notion of dalliance as a cure for boredom had come rather rapidly to the earl's mind. She kept her countenance, however, and said calmly, "No doubt you are right, sir. Her portion cannot be nearly large enough to tempt him."

Jack gave her a direct look. "It is entirely possible that some man may care for her, not only for her portion."

"Don't be foolish," Emily retorted. Then, finding her gaze held by his, she lifted her chin and added, "A woman's portion is of utmost import to any man who is attracted to her, sir. And a man in Saint Just's position—you said yourself that he is no doubt retrenching—will consider only the amount she can bring to his coffers, nothing more."

"You may be right about Saint Just's motives," Jack said, his look more penetrating than ever, "but I heard what Sabrina said to you yesterday. Are you certain that Stephen Campion turned to Lady Melinda Harcourt only for her larger portion and for no other reason? As I recall, her father was doing some retrenching himself at that time. Is it not possible—"

Emily turned on her heel and left the room.

Halfway up the stairs, she looked back, fully expecting to see Jack striding after her, but there was no one in the hall except William, holding a tin of brass

polish in one hand while he polished a wall sconce with a
rag held in the other. He glanced at her over his
shoulder, but when Emily did not speak, he turned back
to his work. Uncertain whether to be grateful or sorry
that the earl had made no attempt to follow her, she
strode up the stairs and directly to her bedchamber, glad
that Sabrina was napping and that Miss Lavinia and the
others were not in the house to plague her.

11

BY THE TIME EMILY REACHED HER BEDCHAMBER, SHE
knew she was angry and spoiling for a fight, but she
wanted one she could win, and she had an unhappy
notion that Jack would best her easily in any discussion
of her relationship with Stephen Campion. For one
thing, that wound was still unhealed. For another, often
though she had assured herself that it was Melinda Harcourt's money and nothing else that had captivated
Stephen, she had never entirely managed to convince
herself of that fact, so Jack's comment about Melinda's
father's difficulties had hit near the bone. If he had
dared to suggest Emily's temper as the probable reason
for Stephen's betrayal, as he had clearly been about to
do, she was certain she would have thrown something at
him.

Slamming her door, she was disconcerted to find
Martha seated in a chair by the window, a small pile of
poor-box mending resting upon a stool beside her.

"Good gracious, Miss Emily, mind that door! You'll
have it off its hinges, banging it like that."

"Go away, Martha. I don't wish to talk to anyone."

"My, we have pretty manners today," Martha said,
gathering her mending. "I shall return in a half-hour,

for it will then be time to dress for dinner, will it not?''

"I'm not dressing. You may ask Molly to bring a tray up."

"Someone," said Martha gently, "ought to have smacked you long ago, miss, for indulging in such sulks."

"How dare you!" Emily glared at the woman, but when Martha only returned the glare with a steady look of her own, she turned away, color flooding her face. "You are right, of course," she said wretchedly. "I am behaving badly, and I don't even know why. Don't be angry. I'll ring when I am ready to dress."

Martha's expression softened as she left the room, leaving her mistress feeling thoroughly ashamed of herself. Despite what she had said to the contrary, Emily did not have to think overlong to recognize the full cause for her surge of temper. Having suspected earlier that Meriden's interest in her was a fleeting one at best, she now believed her suspicion confirmed by the quick and easy way in which he had recognized Saint Just's transitory attraction to Dolly. Both men were being forced to live for a time out of the world they knew best, and Meriden had done so even longer than Saint Just, for the earl had been tied by the heels to Staithes Priory since the first of the year.

Saint Just had had his school friends and no doubt more than one bolt to town, as the young man called their jaunts to London, to amuse him. And if the earl thought Saint Just bored, could it be for any reason other than recognition of his own boredom in the younger man? And what better cure for ennui than a brief dalliance with an attractive, conveniently handy young woman? Indeed, Emily had amused herself in fashionable flirtations to cure her own boredom more than once, knowing that since she was no great prize on the Marriage Mart, there was little possibility of anyone being hurt. She knew the rules and she abided by them.

The problem now was that the rules didn't apply. She cared too much about the Earl of Meriden for her own peace of mind, and knew that he could hurt her much

more than Stephen Campion had done if she but gave
him the opportunity to do so. One kiss from Jack had
sent her senses reeling, had turned her to wax in his
hands. Though he must know she would not stoop to
become any man's mistress, for him to realize that he
could stir her passions so easily must, she told herself,
provide a tremendous boost to his self-esteem. Playing
with her sensibilities no doubt amused him, would—if
she but gave him the chance to do as he wished—even
provide him with an opportunity to punish her whenever he decided she deserved punishment. And the worst
of it was that she wasn't by any means certain she could
resist him even if he put his mind to seducing her. No
doubt, sooner or later, someone would notice his
interest in her and make him a wager. That, she decided
miserably, would be that.

By the time Martha returned, Emily had managed to
regain her customary composure. She apologized for
her earlier behavior and then turned her attention to the
important matter of deciding what to wear to dinner.
Forty minutes later, neatly attired in a pale-rose silk
gown decorated with embroidered chains of dark-pink
flowers along the hem, and a dark-pink sash, the ends
of which trailed to the hemline from a bow tied just
beneath her bosom, she descended the stairs to the
gallery to discover Dolly and Harry Enderby engaged in
hot-tempered conversation.

Mr. Enderby, precise to a pin in proper evening attire,
was remonstrating with Dolly, who wore a low-necked
bright-blue silk evening dress with a demitrain. Pink silk
roses, fastened with true lovers' knots, decked the skirt
and bodice, and a nosegay of roses was tucked into
Dolly's plunging décolletage. She wore pink satin
slippers, a brilliant diamond necklace, and a number of
bracelets clinked on both of her white-gloved arms.

Emily assumed that, in his usual fashion, Mr.
Enderby was taking her niece to task—and quite rightly,
too, she thought—for her dashing but most inappro-
priate appearance, and interrupted their conversation
without a qualm.

"Dolly, where did you get that appalling gown?"

Dolly flashed a glance at her. "From Lettie Bennett," she said. "Her mama wouldn't let her wear it after her godmother very kindly sent it to her all the way from London, so she gave it to me today. Is it not beautiful?" She turned, preening.

"Ought to be ashamed of yourself," muttered Mr. Enderby.

"Well, I'm not," snapped Dolly, turning on him, "and I am not dressed up like Christmas beef, either, and I do not think it was at all gentlemanly of you to say such a thing to me."

"Dolly," Emily said gently, hoping her calmer tone would provide an example for the girl, whose voice had risen, as was its wont when she was displeased. "Please, Dolly, you must know that that dress is not the thing for you to wear. Mr. Enderby is quite right to point that out to you."

"Well, if you must know, he never said a word about the dress," Dolly retorted. "He is vexed because he says I am always trying to attract Mr. Saint Just's attention. He says it is not at all the thing for me to do. But I have not tried to attract Mr. Saint Just, Aunt Emily. I don't have to try, so it is most unfair of Harry to say so. Indeed, I had rather he tell me the dress is unbecoming than accuse me of such stupid things."

"I like the dress," said Mr. Enderby simply.

Emily hid a smile. "Whether you like it or not, sir, it is not the thing for a young girl to be wearing in company. Nor should you be wearing that necklace, Dolly. Your mother will have a fit when she sees you."

"I don't think she means to come down to dinner tonight."

"Well, Miss Lavinia will be here, and Meriden will no doubt be here as well, for he had a pile of work on the library table when last I saw him."

Dolly shrugged. "I doubt that even Cousin Jack will send me from the table for wearing this dress, Aunt Emily. It is so pretty, and it does become me, whatever you say."

"Mind your manners, my girl," Mr. Enderby said sternly. "Not the thing to talk to your aunt that way."

"No," agreed Emily, "it certainly is not." She could say no more, however, for Oliver and Saint Just chose that moment to join them, and their enthusiasm for Dolly's attire silenced both Emily and Mr. Enderby.

Miss Lavinia was already in the drawing room when they entered, seated with her tatting by the fire, and Meriden entered the room several moments later. When his gaze lit upon Dolly's gown, he stopped where he was and raised his quizzing glass to his right eye.

Emily held her breath.

Dolly, seeing him and rightly guessing his opinion, glared back at him but said not a word, and both she and her aunt breathed a sigh of relief when he lowered the glass without comment and moved to exchange pleasantries with Mr. Enderby. Sabrina, to everyone's surprise, entered the room just before the butler announced that dinner had been served.

"I could not stay upstairs," she said lightly, "once I heard that Mr. Enderby had accepted dear Oliver's invitation to dine."

Harry bowed, but Oliver said with a laugh that she was mistaken. "Harry met us on the road. Said two gentlemen were not enough to protect Miss Lavinia and Dolly from footpads and that he would ride along to help us out. The truth of the matter is that Lady Enderby's cook has gone to care for an ailing sister, and Harry knew he'd dine better here than at home."

"Oh, dear, perhaps we ought to have sent her ladyship an invitation to join us too, ma'am," Sabrina said to Miss Lavinia.

Chuckling, Miss Lavinia informed her that Lady Enderby was perfectly content with her undercook. "Told me last time I spoke with her that the man likes making every decision himself and don't even trouble her to look over the menus."

Sabrina's countenance when she saw her daughter's dress was as revealing as Meriden's had been, but she, too, held her tongue, clearly unwilling to take Dolly to task before their guests. When the ladies had left the gentlemen to their port, however, she was not so reticent.

"You go straight up to your bedchamber, Dorothy Rivington," she said in an angry undertone the moment William had shut the dining-room door behind them, "and don't you dare to show your face again tonight. I have never been so angry with you. How you dared to wear that dreadful gown or my diamond necklace in company, I do not know, but I daresay you have vexed Cousin Jack again, and I would not have had you do so for the world."

Dolly began to protest but soon realized she was wasting her breath when both Emily and Miss Lavinia added their remonstrances to her mother's. Finally, in tears, she turned away, saying pitifully, "I do not know why everyone is so unkind to me."

Firmly suppressing a strong desire to shake her niece, Emily followed the others into the drawing room, wondering how long it would be before the gentlemen joined them there. She thought perhaps Jack would wish to speak to her, for he had sat opposite her throughout dinner, and although she had been perfectly civil, she had avoided his eye and, ignoring the fact that everyone else had talked across the table at will, had punctiliously confined her conversation to Mr. Enderby, seated at her right, and to Miss Lavinia, at her left.

Half an hour later, Oliver, Saint Just, and Mr. Enderby entered the drawing room, but Jack was not with them and none of the three remained long once it was explained to them that Dolly had retired. Emily told herself firmly that since she had no wish to continue her earlier conversation with the earl, she was not the least bit disappointed by his absence.

The following morning, when Emily went downstairs, Jack was leaning against the library doorjamb, his arms folded across his chest. He straightened when he saw her.

"I've nothing of importance on my plate today," he

said, "so I thought perhaps you would like to go riding with me."

"No, thank you, sir," she said calmly. "I have promised to help Miss Lavinia in the garden this morning."

"She won't miss you," he said, moving toward her. "You are only trying to avoid further conversation with me."

Eyeing him warily, she said, "I cannot think why I should do so, sir."

He stopped directly in front of her, much too close for her comfort. "Look here, Emily," he demanded, "are you still vexed with me for what I said about Campion?"

"Why should I be vexed, sir? I simply have no time for games of the sort that seem to amuse you at the moment."

He was silent for a moment, looking sternly down at her. "What games?"

"Need you ask?" she said, proud that her tone of voice gave no indication of the thrill of fear that raced up and down her spine as a result of the way he was looking at her. "I am no fool, Meriden, nor am I a woman with whose sentiments a man may lightly trifle. You had a wish to indulge yourself, to set your boredom at bay with a little light dalliance. I had no objection at first, but I have been otherwise engaged these past days and expect to be so engaged in days to come, so you would do better to choose another pastime." For a moment, when his expression hardened and his color heightened, she thought she had gone too far. She had seen that look before and knew he was angry.

"I do not trifle with anyone's sensibilities," he said at last, grimly.

The absurdity of the remark brought involuntary laughter to her lips, and her eyes glinted with mockery. "That statement is so patently untrue that I wonder you don't turn to stone on the spot, sir. I have watched you trifle any number of times in the past, and I recognize your motivation now just as easily as you recognized that of Mr. Saint Just in his dealings with Dolly.''

He reached for her with a purposeful look in his eye, but Emily had anticipated such a move and evaded his hand. "Do you dare to deny what I say, Meriden?" she demanded.

"Damn you, Emily, you ought to know what I meant when I said I wasn't trifling. If you think turning yourself into a pillar of ice will alter anything between us, you will soon come to recognize your error, I promise you."

" 'Tis you who have made the error, my lord, by thinking I would be so easily ensnared by your charm. Your words yesterday proved that you hold none of the tenderer feelings for me. Did you not learn anything about me last Christmas? Or has there now been some new wager made of which I have not been told?"

With a snarl of fury, Meriden turned from her and strode back into the library, slamming the door shut behind him.

Emily waited for a sense of triumph to surface within her, but it didn't come. Unhappily, belatedly, she realized that the last thing she had wanted to do was to enrage him. She simply hadn't known what else to do to keep him from toying with her feelings, nor did she know now.

The following days passed with constraint like a wall between them. The only happy moments for her were those spent with Lady Filey and her mama on Friday afternoon when they drove over to Staithes to return Sabrina's call. When they had gone, Emily's good spirits went with them. Leaving Sabrina and Miss Lavinia in the drawing room to discuss at their leisure the gossip imparted to them by their guests, she sought her bedchamber in order to reflect upon the ills of her situation.

Her chilly attitude toward the earl had become daily more difficult to sustain, for she wanted to smooth away his anger with her and to share her laughter with him, as well as those same items of gossip related by Lady Filey and the dowager that had so fascinated Sabrina and Miss Lavinia. But Emily wanted to regain his friendship without laying herself open to the devastating effect of his charm upon her sensibilities.

Lady Filey had mentioned that very afternoon, yet again, the fact that the family had long since given up on Jack's ever marrying; and, since his sister knew his intentions if anyone did, Emily decided that it would be more than foolhardy to let the man know how much he affected her, how much she was coming to love him. It had been easier, she mused unhappily, when she had only wanted to fight with him.

Her reverie might have drifted on in this vein for some time had not her bedchamber door suddenly vibrated with the pounding of a fist on its panels. Giles's voice sounded on a note of panic from the other side. "Aunt Emily, are you there? Come quickly! Cousin Jack has sent for Melanie to go to him in the library, and he's as mad as fire about something. Oh, do come quick, ma'am, do!"

With Giles at her heels, Emily rushed downstairs to the main hall. Once there, however, she paused to collect herself, then turned, managing somehow to speak calmly to the boy.

"Giles, I believe you will do better to go for a walk until this is over and done."

"I want to help Melanie," he said stubbornly, standing his ground and giving her look for look. "She hardly ever talks to me anymore, but when I met her on the stair, she looked scared, so I asked her what was wrong. She just said Cousin Jack means to beat her, Aunt Emily. He won't do so, will he?"

"I don't know what he means to do, and I shan't know until I go into the library," she told him, "but neither he nor Melanie would thank me for bringing you into this business. That much I can tell you."

"You didn't bring me. I brought you."

"Yes, and I am grateful that you were able to find me, but now you are keeping me standing here in the hall. Do go for a walk, Giles, and tell no one else about what is transpiring between your cousin and Melanie.''

"But I don't know what's happening. I know only what Melanie said, that Cousin Jack is as mad as fire and means to punish her for something she has done. She wouldn't even tell me what it was, and I wish to know. I am her brother, after all—her elder brother, too, so I ought to know what's wrong, and I ought to be able to do something to help her.''

Emily laid a hand upon the boy's shoulder and smiled down at him. "Your concern for Melanie does you proud, Giles, but your good sense ought to tell you that you have done all you can by fetching me. Now, the sooner I get inside the library, the sooner I can help her. I don't mean to allow Meriden to punish her if I can stop him from doing so. Melanie can tell you all you wish to know later.''

Reluctantly the boy stepped away from her, and Emily rewarded him with another smile as she turned toward the library doors. The hall was empty of servants for once, so she opened the doors without ceremony and walked in. To her surprise, there were not two people in the room but three.

Meriden stood in front of the library table. He was dressed in his riding breeches and coat, and held his whip and gloves in his right hand as though he had just come into the house. Beside him stood the maid Molly, wringing her hands in her white cambric apron, her mobcap sitting askew atop her brown curls. Facing them, her back to the door, was Melanie. Beneath her white muslin frock her spine was ramrod straight, and every line of her body shouted indignation. She turned belatedly, as though she had just become aware of Emily's entrance.

Emily shut the door and moved toward the child, only to be stopped in her tracks by Meriden's crisp voice.

"You intrude, Miss Wingrave. This matter is a private one.''

With difficulty Emily held her temper in check. She even managed a haughty lift of her right eyebrow as she replied, "So private, in fact, that you include a servant, sir?"

In answer, Meriden set his whip and gloves on the table and held up her missing amethyst earbobs and her gold bracelet. "You should thank Molly for the return of these baubles. I regret that your pearls were not with the rest of the things she found, but no doubt we will soon discover their location, so if you will be good enough—"

"Don't be absurd, Jack. Are you daring to tell me that you suspect Melanie, *Melanie*, of taking Miss Lavinia's jewels and mine as well? You must be all about in your head, sir." With that, she strode decisively forward and placed a protective arm about the little girl's shoulders.

Melanie stiffened.

"You see," Jack said sardonically, "she does not welcome your championship. Her guilt no doubt makes it difficult for her to thank you for such undeserved compassion."

"I didn't take Aunt Emily's jewels," Melanie said in a lifeless voice.

"Of course she did not," Emily said heatedly. "Molly, did you dare to accuse Miss Melanie of such a thing?"

"Now, look here, Em—"

"No, miss," said Molly at the same moment, "I did no such of a thing. His lordship said we was to tell him if anything that was lost was found, so I come here to tell him that I found them things in Miss Melanie's bedchamber because I doesn't want nobody thinking I knowed where they was and didn't say, as anyone would think who was to find them later on. I'm a right good cleaner, I am, and none as knows me would believe them things was in Miss Melanie's room without me knowing. But as for saying that young lassie took anything, well, I never, and that's the truth."

Meriden looked as he might have looked had an oak tree talked back to him, but he recovered rapidly. Fixing the maidservant with a basilisk stare, he said in cold tones, "That will do, Molly. I know how many days make a week, and the facts speak for themselves."

"Well, sir, if tha'll not take offense at me saying so, they don't." Molly returned his look, clearly knowing she was stepping beyond her place but just as clearly determined to say her piece. "Miss Melanie don't hide her treasures under her wardrobe, and that's a fact." She smiled at Melanie. "Aught she wants to keep hid out of sight, she puts in a wee recess back o' the headboard of her bed, and no one don't touch such."

Emily glanced at Melanie, but the little girl's face was devoid of expression. She stared straight ahead of her, making no attempt to respond to the maidservant's words.

Meriden also looked at the child. Then he turned back to the maid and said in measured tones, "You may go now, Molly."

Molly held her ground. "Tha' don't still be thinking—"

"I said, you may leave. And be so good as to take Miss Wingrave with you. I wish to be private now with Miss Melanie."

The maid opened her mouth; then, with an appealing look at Emily, she closed it again and walked quickly out the door, shutting it firmly behind her without having so much as looked to see if Emily were following her.

Emily stood where she was, waiting only for the sound of the door's snapping to before demanding to know if Meriden had lost his mind. "Melanie is no thief, sir, as you ought to know by looking at her. Someone put my things where Molly found them."

"Yes, someone did," he replied caustically. "Melanie did."

"Didn't," muttered Melanie.

"Then," Jack said, turning to face her, "perhaps you will explain how and why they came to be found in your room."

Melanie said nothing.

"Meriden," Emily said, "you are handling this

matter all wrong. You would do much better—"

"Now, see here," he said grimly, "I told you once to leave, and I insist now that you do so. This matter is strictly between Melanie and me. We have no need of your assistance, and I have no desire to hear any more of your opinions. There is a good deal more to this than you know—is there not, Melanie?—so if you will just for once do as you are told—"

"I am staying right here, and nothing you say will make me do otherwise," Emily told him defiantly, "so you might as well get on with whatever you have to say to Melanie."

Exasperated, Jack said, "Dashed if I don't understand perfectly now why young Campion refused to come up to scratch. In my opinion, the man showed a great deal of sense in not taking such an ill-tempered shrew for his wife." He glared at Emily, but for once his words had no power to hurt her and she simply glared back. Goaded, he snapped, "If you must know, madam, I intend to do more than just talk to Melanie this time, and if you are wise, you won't tempt me to deal you similar treatment. Indeed, if you don't wish to be picked up and thrust bodily out of this room, you will go quietly and at once."

"I won't," Emily said flatly, adding hastily when he took a step toward her, "and if you touch me I will scream the house down. I won't leave you alone to inflict your brutality upon poor Melanie. You are making much more of this great discovery of Molly's than it deserves, you know. You heard her yourself. Melanie wouldn't put something she meant to hide from everyone else under her wardrobe. Nobody would do so who meant to keep her plunder hidden. For goodness' sake, Jack, even in a less-well-regulated house than this one is, the servants sweep under the furniture from time to time."

"Does it occur to you," he asked sarcastically, "that a nine-year-old child might fail to comprehend the ramifications of that fact?"

"No, it does not," she retorted. "Children think such things through, particularly when they wish to protect themselves, and they are more observant than adults, who tend to forget that their servants exist. We talk together in their presence just as we do in privacy, and never consider what they think about us. Children don't do that. When I was a child, I would never have been caught out in such a way by a servant, that I can tell you. One might have caught me, but only because some of them knew me better than my parents did. I would never have been found out through having my ill-gained bounty discovered."

"No doubt that much is true," he said grimly. "I would believe you capable of anything, but Molly does know where Melanie hides her treasures, so your argument won't hold in this case. Perhaps there simply wasn't room for anything more in the headboard recess and she was forced to look elsewhere, perhaps even to hide the things quickly, in a panic."

"Didn't hide them," Melanie said. "Didn't take them."

"Enough of that," Jack said sharply. "You certainly didn't appear surprised to have been summoned to the library."

Melanie's face grew wooden and her eyelids drooped, hooding the expression in her eyes.

"Jack, stop tormenting her," Emily said, moving close to the child again. "You must know she wouldn't steal—"

"I know nothing of the sort," he snapped. "Do I, Melanie?"

Melanie did not respond. If anything, Emily thought she relaxed a little.

"Answer me, Melanie," Jack said in a stern voice. "Were you surprised to receive my summons?"

"No." The single word was barely audible.

"Did you think, perhaps, that I wished to discuss another matter with you?"

There was silence.

"Open your eyes and look at me, Melanie."

The little girl obeyed the first part of his command, opening her eyes, but her gaze was unfocused, expressionless.

Emily stared at Jack. "What is this, sir? Why do you carp at her so? Surely, even suspecting what you do, you are being too harsh. A little gentleness, a modicum of under—"

"She has convinced the village apothecary to credit more of her so-called loans to the Priory account," he said brusquely without taking his eyes off Melanie. "I had just returned from a talk with my bailiff, who informed me that he had paid her reckoning, and I was about to send for Melanie to discuss the matter when Molly came to me with her news. Whether Melanie has stolen the jewels remains to be seen," he added, flicking Emily with a whiplike glance, "but I can tell you here and now that she has disobeyed me for the last time."

12

UNDERSTANDING NOW WHY JACK WAS SO ANGRY, Emily made no attempt to answer him at once, looking instead, with sympathy, at Melanie. to her surprise, the little girl showed no fear. Her attitude was still unresponsive, but she was watching Jack with a look of resignation on her face. It was, Emily thought, as though she believed her fate to be both preordained and inevitable, as though she just wanted to have the matter over and done as soon as possible.

Realizing that Emily was not going to say anything, Jack gave a nod of grim satisfaction, then turned back to Melanie. When he saw the child's expression, his own tightened and he took a step toward her, then stopped, visibly taking his temper in hand as he said, "I told you what would happen if you took money again, did I not? Surely you know me well enough by now to know that when I say a thing I mean it, so you cannot have expected such defiance to go unpunished."

Melanie stared at a point beyond his shoulder, her trembling lips the only sign that she had heard him.

Emily said quickly, "She didn't exactly—"

"She did," he retorted, watching the child for a moment longer before he cast Emily a brief glance. "If you insist upon remaining, you will oblige me by keeping silent and by not interfering any further. I know you disapprove of what I intend to do, but that cannot be helped. Now," he added, turning back to speak directly to Melanie, "will you please have the goodness to tell me why you still find it necessary to obtain money from the village shopkeepers?"

Melanie swallowed hard but did not speak.

"Well? I am waiting."

Her eyes shifted, but she did not look at him or at Emily.

Emily thought she detected fear in the little girl's expression, but so fleeting was the look that she could not be certain. Nor, she thought, could she blame Melanie if she was afraid. Jack was at his most formidable, and Emily could only be glad that his anger was not, for once, directed at herself.

He took another step toward Melanie. "Believe me when I say that, one way or another, you are going to tell me what is going on, and if you did take your aunt's jewels, you are also going to tell me where her pearls are. It will be a good deal easier for both of us if you simply tell the truth at once, for although you will still be punished, your punishment will be much less severe than if you continue to refuse to speak. It is clear that you have fancied yourself in need of money and have done whatever you could think of to obtain it, but why you would steal from a lady who has been only kind to you quite passes my understanding."

"I didn't."

"But you did lie to get money from the apothecary."

When Melanie's only response to this gambit was to bite her lower lip, Jack gave a growl of anger and turned toward the library table. At first Emily hoped that he would give up his attempt to force the issue and merely send Melanie up to her bedchamber to contemplate her sins, but that hope evaporated in a gasp of outrage when he turned back again, holding the whip in his hand.

"Jack, no!"

"Come here to me, Melanie," he said, ignoring Emily's cry.

Melanie did not move.

"You have misbehaved badly, and you will take your punishment," he said grimly. "Only if you decide at once to tell me why you took that money will punishment be delayed, but it will only be delayed, not forgotten."

"Please, Jack," Emily begged, "you cannot—"

"I told you to hold your tongue."

"I know you did, but I cannot remain silent when you are going to do such a dreadful thing."

"There is nothing dreadful about a thrashing," he snapped. "Children are thrashed all the time, and it is held by most people to be good for them. I daresay your father might have utilized such punishment to excellent effect."

"He did," she retorted, "but he never used a riding whip."

"Well then, he ought to have done so. If ever—"

"What Papa did or didn't do doesn't signify in the slightest anyway," she said abruptly, striving to remain calm. "Melanie is much too small and fragile. You will hurt her terribly."

"Nonsense," he said. Then, turning back to the child, he added sternly, "Do not make me come to you, Melanie."

Still with that expressionless, faraway look on her face, Melanie began to move slowly toward him. It was, her aunt thought, watching her, as though she were in some sort of trance.

Jack's mention of Emily's father had triggered

memories of certain anxious moments spent in Viscount Wingrave's study, but she could not remember a single such instance when she had not fought buckle and thong to convince her father that she had done nothing wrong. Even when she had known that any attempt to justify her actions must prove ineffectual, she had striven mightily to achieve the impossible. Never had she simply stood and waited, resigned, for the ax to fall.

When she realized that she had fallen into a momentary daze and that Jack was actually reaching for Melanie, Emily leapt forward, crying, "No, you shall not!" Grabbing his arm with one hand, she pushed Melanie away with the other and said tensely, "Jack, you dolt, you mustn't do this. Not, at least, until she has done her best to explain. You are angry because she won't obey you, because she won't just do what you tell her to do and behave as you want her to behave. You are accustomed to seeing people jump when you speak, my lord. If they don't, you declare them disobedient, ill-tempered, or wicked. But Melanie is none of those things, so something must be very wrong. Even you must see that much if you will but look at her, *really* look at her."

"I don't have to look at her," Jack snapped, "and if you think I am accustomed to seeing people jump when I tell them to do so, you cannot have been attending very closely these past weeks. Nobody jumps. Instead they either fight me tooth and nail with no good reason at all or they complain that things are no longer as they were when Laurence held the reins. They ought to be glad of that last fact, if only they knew. I have tried to make allowances, Emily. I have listened to you and I've tried to be patient. But enough is enough. Melanie has been given every opportunity to explain her actions, and she has refused to do so. The consequences are well known to her, and thus . . ."

But Emily was no longer listening to him. Having told him to look at Melanie, she had done so herself, only to discover that the little girl was staring at her as though she would send her a silent message. When Emily frowned, Melanie looked pointedly at Jack, then back at her again. Then she shook her head, only a little, but nothing more was needed to tell Emily that Melanie wanted her to desist, that she feared Emily was intentionally diverting the earl's wrath to herself. Struck by a sudden idea, Emily turned back to Jack and spoke sharply, well aware that she was interrupting him.

"You are talking utter nonsense, Meriden. If you would only think instead of prating on and on like a self-centered lunatic, you would realize that something evil is at work here, that someone who knows about Melanie's loans has attempted to lay the blame for the jewel thefts at her door. Anyone," she added in a voice dripping with scorn, "anyone with a single thought in his head for anything other than his own selfish pride would realize that much. But you have no thought for anyone else, only for yourself. Well, if you are going to blame poor Melanie for continuing to obtain money by her odd methods, then you must blame me as well, for I have known exactly what she was doing for more than a week and I had no intention of ever telling you."

"You *what*?" That his temper had reached its zenith was evident to the meanest intelligence, for his cheeks had grown crimson and his jaw was thrust out belligerently. His voice crackled with the two words he barked at her, and Emily could not doubt for a moment that she had gained his full attention.

"I knew," she said, lifting her chin and looking directly into his eyes, willing him to rise high enough above his fury to follow her lead. Making him angry was dangerous, but she knew no other way to accomplish her purpose. "I followed her into the village that day I was attacked in the woods. I saw her give the money she got to an old woman on the road, but I promised her I would say nothing to you. Indeed, I would say nothing now if I thought any other course would answer the purpose. But you must see," she added, piling fuel on what appeared to be a promising fire, "that that makes me quite as guilty as Melanie is. If you insist upon punishing her, sir, then you must punish me as well, and since you can scarcely take a riding whip to me—"

"The devil I can't," he snarled, reaching for her.

"Oh, no!" cried Melanie.

"Jack, no!"

But he held Emily's arm now in a relentless grip. Clutching the slim leather-bound whip, he paused, looking sternly at Melanie. "You see now what you have brought about by your disobedience? Your aunt did very wrong to try to protect you, and she deserves exactly the same punishment you deserve."

For a moment when he had first grabbed her, Emily thought Jack had not comprehended her objective, but these words, as well as the pause itself, restored her confidence. She relaxed, waiting for Melanie to speak up in her defense.

That Jack did not also wait came as an appalling shock to her. Before a cat could have licked its ear, he sat on the edge of the library table, hauled Emily across his knee, and awarded her firm backside one single fiery stroke of the whip. Struggling frantically but futilely, Emily shrieked at him to release her, to put her down at once. Her cries were mere echoes, however, of Melanie's.

"No, no!" the child screamed, rushing at him, clawing at his arms. "Don't hurt Aunt Emily. I'll tell you! I'll tell you everything!" Bursting into tears, she flung herself protectively across Emily, and Jack laid the whip back down upon the table and gently rested his large hand upon her flaxen head.

"Stand up, Melanie," he said quietly after a long moment. "Aunt Emily cannot get up until you do."

Slowly the child's head came up and she stared at him doubtfully as she straightened. "You won't hit her again?"

"No." He helped Emily up, and there was a glint of amusement in his eyes when she turned on him angrily.

"You didn't have to—"

"I did," he said, cutting her off abruptly. "We can talk about it later if you like, but right now Melanie has something important to tell us."

Melanie's cheeks were tearstained, but at Jack's words she straightened her shoulders and took a deep breath. "I promised never to tell," she said, the words coming forth with difficulty.

Emily moved to speak, but Jack put a restraining hand on his arm and said calmly, "You are going to tell us, Melanie, because you said you would do so. For a child to speak to the people who love her best when they insist that she do so is not a betrayal of confidence but a duty. Aunt Emily and I will both give you our solemn word that if the promise you gave was a true promise, given freely, we will not betray your confidence to anyone for any reason. Do you believe that you can trust us?"

Melanie sighed deeply and moved to place her small hand upon his knee. "It isn't that I don't trust you," she said. "Truly, sir, it is not that."

Emily said, "Then what is it, darling?"

"You will die."

The three words were spoken so matter-of-factly that neither Emily nor Jack responded at once. Both of them stared at Melanie. There were tears in her eyes again, threatening to spill down her pale cheeks.

Emily looked at Jack and saw that he was frowning. She looked back at Melanie. "Do you mean to say that you believe we really will die if you explain everything to us, or only that we will be so angry that you fear—"

"She said you will die," Melanie said without waiting for her to finish. "She said she would put a spell on anyone I told about her and that the spell would kill them dead. So you will both die if you make me tell you."

Jack caught his breath in an audible gasp, then looked sharply at Emily. "You said you saw her give the money to an old woman the day you were attacked in the woods?" When Emily nodded slowly, still digesting

Melanie's words, he said, "Then I suppose you tried to follow the old woman afterward, did you not?"

She looked directly at him. His eyes were narrowed, and she experienced sudden gratitude that he was more interested in getting to the truth at the moment than in discussing the wisdom of her behavior. She nodded again.

"You knew all along then that it was not the jewel thief who attacked you."

"Well," she said, hoping she was right about his present priority of interest, "I could not be certain, of course, but I did think it was probably the old woman or her accomplice who struck me down."

"You and I will talk more about that business later, as well," he said meaningfully, still frowning. Then he turned back to Melanie. "Is the old woman a witch, sweetheart? Is that what you are not supposed to tell us?"

Melanie nodded, biting her lip, the tears now spilling down her cheeks.

"Well, then, there you are," Jack said, spreading his hands and smiling at her. "You have nothing to trouble your head about, because you didn't tell us about her, did you? First Aunt Emily saw her, and just now we guessed the truth all by ourselves. Tell us why you gave her the money."

Melanie looked at him, searching his face as though to judge for herself whether his words held merit. Then, with another sigh, she nodded and brushed tears from her face with the back of her hand. "She told me to give her money."

Jack grimaced. "And you just gave it to her? When did this all happen? The first time, I mean."

Having begun, Melanie went on with an ease of speech that Emily had never before witnessed in her. Resting her right hand upon Jack's thigh, she said, "I was walking into the village. It was . . . " She paused, silently ticking weeks off on her fingers. ". . . . twelve weeks ago, I think. She came out of the shrubbery just before I reached the moor. First she just said she wanted money. I told her I had only a shilling and I meant to buy a small silk scarf that Miss Brittan and I had seen at the mercer's. She said I should give her the shilling instead if I didn't wish her to put a spell on my whole family.'' Melanie's voice broke on the last words, and she looked pathetically at Emily. ''She said the spell would make them all die by inches, one by one!''

Firmly repressing a shudder, Emily shook her head and said firmly, ''No witch is strong enough to kill off an entire family with one spell, darling. Only consider for a moment. Can you imagine a witch strong enough to affect Miss Lavinia? She would snap her fingers at any old witch's spell. As for me, I would dearly like to meet your witch face-to-face. I'd show her a spell or two of my own.''

''I too,'' muttered Jack. He gave himself a shake, then said more casually, ''Is that all, Melanie? She asked you for money and you gave it to her? How often did this happen?''

''Nearly every week,'' Melanie said, regarding him more warily now, as though something in his tone had made her think him not so casual as he would have her believe. ''At first I gave her my allowance because I usually hadn't spent any of it, but then she wanted more and more. When I told her I hadn't got any more, she said I'd better find a way to get it or I'd be sorry. I was afraid of her, Cousin Jack.'' Her small hand tightened visibly on his leg, and she added earnestly, ''I didn't know what else to do. Papa had said once that it was easier to pay one big bill than a host of small ones, so I thought if I said that to Mr. Hayworth—the chandler, you know—he wouldn't ask too many questions. When no one said anything right away, I didn't think anyone had asked him any questions and that the reckoning had been paid when the other accounts in the village were paid.''

''Had you gone to the mercer,'' Jack said, ''someone would have discovered much earlier what you had done, but since your mama insists upon burning wax candles in every room of this house, we order them sent up once a year from London rather than purchasing them bit by bit locally. Had you thought about what would happen to you once you were found out, Melanie?''

She nodded, looking down, then quickly up again, as though she would not have him think her a coward. ''I knew you would not like it. When you did find out, though, you didn't really ever ask me why I had done it. Well,'' she added defensively when he gave her a look, ''you didn't say I had to tell you. You were too angry with me because of *what* I had done. I don't think you really wanted to know *why* I had done it.''

''To my shame,'' Jack said quietly. He glanced at Emily. ''You were right to call me a fool, lass.''

''I wouldn't have told you then, anyway,'' Melanie said. ''I remember you were angry because I wouldn't look at you when you spoke to me, but I couldn't do so. I was afraid that if I began to talk at all, I would tell you about the witch. I couldn't do that, so I pretended not to hear you.''

Emily smiled at her. ''Cousin Jack doesn't like his speeches to be ignored. It makes him cross.''

Jack grimaced. ''You ought to know.''

This time when she looked at him, his gaze held hers for a long moment, and his expression brought warmth to her cheeks and a curious, unfamiliar tension to her midsection.

''Are you going to punish me now, Cousin Jack?''

When Jack looked down at Melanie, Emily experienced a sense of deep relief, feeling not unlike a rabbit released from a trap. His next words startled her.

''Did you give the jewels to the witch, Melanie?''

''I didn't take the jewels,'' Melanie said fiercely. ''I told you. I wouldn't do such a thing. That's stealing.''

''So is what you did,'' Jack replied.

''It isn't the same thing,'' she insisted.

''Perhaps it is not exactly the same thing, but it is still taking money that is not yours to take. I told you that before, did I not?''

Melanie nodded, chewing her lip again.

Emily said, "Jack, you—"

Silencing her with a gesture, he said, "It's all right. I only want to be certain she understands the gravity of what she has done. When you know that what you do is wrong, Melanie, someone else's commanding you to do it does not make you any the less responsible for your actions. I know you were frightened. I know you believed the witch could do dreadful things, but that meant only that to defy her required greater courage from you."

"But she said everyone I loved would die, and Oliver once told me witches could do anything. Oh, Cousin Jack, are you sure she cannot do it? I don't want anyone I love to die, and she said they would, every one! I thought she had killed Aunt Emily in the woods that day only because Aunt Emily had seen her!"

Once again, when Emily moved toward the child, Jack tried to motion her back, but this time she defied him, taking Melanie in her arms and hugging her tightly. "I didn't die," she said gently. "I fainted, and you very bravely came back to rescue me. Knowing now how terrified you must have been, I cannot doubt that you have the courage to help us stop that woman from doing such terrible things ever again. For we are going to stop her, are we not, Jack?"

"She's got to be stopped, certainly," he agreed.

"But how?" Melanie asked through her tears.

Jack smiled at last. "The way one catches any beast, little one. We shall lay a trap for her. I have been thinking, and I believe that that is much the best way. You can help us."

"Oh, no, I can't!" Melanie cried, panicking again. "You can't do that! She will know. Witches know everything."

"Nonsense," Jack said. "You have shown us already how good you are at keeping secrets. This will merely be another one. When anyone asks you what transpired here today, you must tell them that Aunt Emily's jewels were found in your bedchamber and that I have punished you for stealing them."

"But I didn't—"

"Protest your innocence as much as you like to the people you tell," he advised her. "Keep them thinking about the jewelry, and we will come off like winking. On Wednesday afternoon you will go the village just as you have been doing, but this time I shall be lying in wait in the woods. When your witch trots along to get her money, I will capture her."

"No, oh, you mustn't, Cousin Jack! You don't know how powerful she is. She can do anything. She told me so!"

"She will have to show me her power before I will believe in it," he declared grimly.

When Melanie looked as though she might become hysterical out of her fear for Jack, Emily said practically, "Cousin Jack will not be alone, you know, darling. I will be with him."

"No, you will not," Jack retorted.

"Well, perhaps not," she agreed, noting that her words had agitated Melanie more than ever, "but you ought to have someone along, and not those ridiculous Runners, either. Once they knew what was planned, neither Tickhill nor Earswick could be trusted to keep a still tongue in his head." She paused briefly, thinking. Then a look of mischief lit her face. "I know," she said. "I know precisely who will help. Melanie, do you think your witch would dare try to cast a spell over Mr. Scopwick?"

Melanie looked at her in awe this time. There was a long silence before she said thoughtfully, "He is not my family."

"No," Emily agreed, "but even if he were, I believe he would be more than a match for any witch, don't you?"

The little girl nodded, appearing for the first time to believe that something could actually be done.

Jack reminded her again that she was to speak only of the jewelry found in her bedchamber and of nothing else.

"Giles will demand to know everything," Emily told

her. "He was most concerned about you. Do you think you can manage to tell him only that much and no more?"

Melanie nodded. "Giles believe what I tell him, and he will not expect long explanations from me."

When she had gone, Emily turned to Jack and said cheerfully, "I am so pleased to see her behaving more like a normal child. Do you really believe we can capture her witch?"

He was regarding her with a quizzical look in his eyes, but he replied evenly enough, "Certainly. The woman is no doubt only some goody from the village who has known her for years."

"But if Melanie had recognized her, she would have told us."

"She may have disguised herself." He paused, then added abruptly, "Look here, Emily, I had to do that to you, you know. You were already relaxing, no longer afraid of what I mean to do, and we needed a tremendous shock to loosen Melanie's tongue. I thought at first that fear of her own punishment would turn the trick, but when it didn't, I was only too willing to follow your lead. Then you nearly ruined everything. If she had noted that you were no longer fighting me, she would never have spoken up."

Reminded, Emily rubbed her backside and shot him a straight look. "I will pay you back one day."

He chuckled. "Oh, I don't doubt that for a moment."

"You enjoyed it!"

He shook his head. "I was angry with you. Never doubt that. Indeed, you ought to be pleased, since your object was to make me as angry as you could. Even through my fury, though, I recognized your intent. I cannot say you have never ripped up at me in front of anyone else before, but your temper usually flashes and your words spill out, noun over verb, without thought or reflection. This time there was clear calculation in the things you said, and you were sarcastic, something you rarely are. But you almost went too far. You made me damned angry, almost too angry to realize in time what you were trying to do. You might just as easily have ended in the lake again, you know, and that would not have served our purpose nearly as well.''

"You did not have to strike me so hard," she said.

"I believe I did. If your shriek had not been entirely real, I doubt that Melanie would have been shocked out of that stupor she'd fallen into." He stood up and looked down at her with gentleness in his eyes. "I'll not deny that aggravation lent strength to my arm, lass, but you cannot blame me for having been angry with you. Though I did not then know the truth about your accident in the woods, you have done many other things of late to vex me, have you not?''

"Don't be foolish," she said, stepping back to put distance between them. When he caught her by one shoulder, she looked first at his hand and then up into his face. "Release me, Meriden."

In answer, his free hand moved to her other shoulder and he drew her close again. When she opened her mouth to protest, he silenced her with a kiss that instantly stilled her protests and inflamed her emotions. With a soft moan, she melted against him, and some moments later he set her back upon her heels and said quietly, "You cannot respond like that one moment, Emmy love, and the next expect me to believe either that you feel no tenderness toward me or that you think I feel none toward you.''

Breathless, wishing her passions would not betray her so, Emily tried to glare at him, but his smile informed her that the result was not a success.

"What exactly do you intend to do about Melanie's witch?" she asked, trying to put the conversation back on a course she could deal with.

His smile broadened to a grin. "I mean to do precisely what I said I would do. I will discuss the matter with Scopwick, of course, but I daresay he'll agree with me that the best course is to capture this witch. Whether we then deal with her ourselves or present her to a magistrate remains to be seen.''

"You are assuming, of course, that the vicar will listen to anything you wish to say to him," Emily said, noting as she spoke that her breathing was returning to normal. "Also, will you not need Melanie to draw the witch out of hiding?"

"Yes, but the child will be perfectly safe, I promise you. All she need do is to walk to the village and back again, just as she always does. I will see to it that she is watched every step of the way. When the old woman approaches her, we will catch her. There is nothing that can go wrong."

"I want to be with you or to be one of the watchers," Emily said firmly.

"No," he replied. When she bristled, he said, "I'll use lads of my own from the Park, men who know the moors and woods so well they can blend in with the deer and the chaffinches. You could not do that. And you cannot stay with Scopwick and me, because you would have to give reason for your absence from the house. Both Sabrina and Miss Lavinia would demand to know where you were going, and you are no great dissembler, lass."

"But I have left the house before without—"

"Perhaps," he said very gently, "now is as good a time as any for us to discuss what happened the last time you wandered off on your own. My sisters were never allowed to set foot beyond our gardens without protection, you know, and I would wager that your father never allowed you to do so either."

"I am a woman grown, Meriden, and—"

"Why is it," he asked plaintively, "that I sink to being 'Meriden' again whenever I dare to disagree with you?"

"You are not disagreeing," she retorted. "You are merely attempting, as usual, to exert your will over mine. Surely you do not believe I did anything foolish or dangerous merely by following a child to the village or an old woman into the woods!"

"Subsequent facts prove that to be one of your more fatuous declarations, my dear."

She flung out her hands in frustration. "You know what I mean. Of course events proved otherwise, but the simple fact of following Melanie's old woman was not an action anyone of sense would have conjectured beforehand to be dangerous."

"Life is dangerous," he said severely.

"Oh, for goodness' sake, Jack, you put me all out of patience with you when you talk like that."

"I am certain," he said in that same grim tone, "that you would as lief put an end to this conversation altogether, but I have several things I still wish to say to you, not the least of which is to express my displeasure over the fact that you knew what Melanie was doing and said nothing to me about it."

"I gave her my word," Emily said. "Surely you would not have had me betray her trust."

"No," he agreed, "where we differ in our opinions is with regard to your having given your word to Melanie at all in such an instance. By doing so, you were aiding and abetting her in an unquestionable wrongdoing. That was a betrayal of your duty as an adult toward the child."

"I . . ." Emily hesitated. His words put the incident in a different light, and she knew suddenly that he was right to be displeased with her. When the thought brought a lump to her throat, she told herself it was because she hated so to have to apologize to anyone. But she knew that that wasn't really the case. Apologies had been part and parcel of her life, for she had always been quick to see when she was wrong and to say so. With Jack, things were different, but she wasn't certain why that was so. She only knew she would rather have cut out her tongue just then than have to admit to him that she had been wrong.

"You were saying?" he prompted dulcetly.

Emily swallowed the lump. "I . . . I thought I was doing the right thing," she said. "Perhaps—"

"Perhaps?"

"Oh, very well, then," she snapped, "I wasn't thinking clearly at the time, if you will recall, but I see now that I ought to have brought her straight along to confess her sins to you. You would have punished her, and she would very likely never have told us the truth of the matter or ever have spoken to me again, let alone confided in me, but that would have been the right thing to have done, would it not?"

Jack grimaced ruefully. "I had forgotten that you were making decisions then with a muddled head. Perhaps we had better lay this discussion to rest before you remind me of anything else I had rather forget. Arguing with you, my lass, is, as always, a lesson in humility."

She shook her head, finding it easier now to say what had to be said. "No, you are right. I did tell her she ought to come to you and tell you everything. I even told her I was certain you would not be as harsh with her if she would but let you help with whatever was troubling her. But when she refused, it was easier to tell her I would keep her confidence than to insist in the face of her distress that she confess to you."

Jack put his arm around her. "Don't torment yourself, lass. It is always easier to know what one ought to have done than to know what one ought to do next. I have made mistakes myself."

"No, have you, sir?" Her eyes were twinkling when she looked at him, and she was astonished at how much better she felt. When he grinned at her, her breasts swelled with pleasure, and she waited, lips parted, for him to kiss her again.

Jack looked at her, bent a little toward her, and then, as Emily waited breathlessly, an enigmatic expression crossed his face and he drew back again. "You had better go now," he said quietly, "and you had better fix it in your mind what you will say to anyone who asks questions about your jewelry. It will be best, I think, to profess dismay and perhaps some disbelief in Melanie's guilt."

Those feelings, Emily thought, staring up at him, would not be difficult to project at all. She was feeling them sweep through her as she stood watching an expressionless mask descend upon Jack's countenance.

He had been about to kiss her again; she was certain of that. But then he had not. Instead, he had withdrawn from her altogether and without comment.

Slowly, hiding her disappointment, she turned away and moved toward the door. Reaching it, she turned back to see that he had seated himself in his chair behind the library table and was thumbing through the ever-present stack of papers.

He looked up. "Was there something else you wished to say?"

She shook her head; then, feeling that some sort of comment was called for, she said calmly, "I was going to ask if there was anything at all that I can do to help on Wednesday, but I suppose we can discuss all the details later, after you have spoken with Mr. Scopwick."

"We can, of course," he said, "but mind this well, Emily. You are not to attempt to do anything on your own on Wednesday. I know you believe yourself capable of anything, but I will be very angry with you if you try to take part in that business just to show me how useful you can be. Some unconsidered action on your part might well overset all our plans."

She sighed. "I will try not to interfere, sir."

He nodded and turned his attention to the papers in front of him, and she opened the door and went out.

13

EMILY TRIED TO FIND AN OPPORTUNITY TO DISCUSS THE situation with Jack before Wednesday, but he seemed to be avoiding her and always had something more important he had to attend to when she approached him. On Tuesday afternoon, having seen nothing of him all day and determined to discover what plan had been made for the following day, Emily went in search of him, only to be told by Edgar Harbottle that his master had business with some of his tenants at Meriden Park that day. Finally, in desperation, she turned to Melanie for information.

They had walked to the pond for the little girl's swimming lesson, so Emily, knowing they were quite alone, waited only until they were lying side by side on the flat rock, drying their chemises, before putting her first question.

"Are you frightened about tomorrow, darling?"

"Oh, no," Melanie replied. "Cousin Jack has promised that he will let no harm befall me."

"He has talked to you about what he wishes you to do, then?"

"Yes, we went for a ride yesterday, and he explained exactly what he wants me to do." She frowned slightly, remembering. "I am to wait until Miss Brittan leaves, just as I always do, and then I am to walk into the village. I must remember to walk very fast through the woods, even though I am not frightened of them anymore, and then I am to walk more slowly coming back. When she comes out to get the money, I am to give it to her and pretend to be frightened and hurry away. They will do nothing until I have moved away from her, he said. That way, she cannot grab me and will have no time to cast a spell before they catch her."

"I see. I didn't know you had ridden out with Cousin Jack."

"Oh, yes. In fact, we rode on Saturday afternoon too. He said it was time we came to know each other better."

"But you said nothing to anyone else about your rides."

Melanie chuckled. "I am still rather quiet at the house, Aunt Emily. Cousin Jack said it would be much better to continue to behave as I did before. Safer, he said, since word gets around so quickly about anything that happens at the Priory."

Emily nodded. It was odd, she thought, how a grown woman could suddenly feel such intense jealousy toward a small child. Jack had not so much as spoken to her yet about his plan, nor had he invited her to ride with him again. For that matter, she mused, she would have enjoyed riding with them both.

Such thoughts continued to bedevil her mind throughout dinner that evening. Meriden was not at the table, but he was present in her mind as she racked her brain to think what she could possibly have done to offend him. Since she could not ask him, she was left with only her reflections for company and found it difficult to attend to the conversation around her. Since Mr. Saint Just was planning to leave for York the following day, she did manage toward the end of the meal to pretend some small interest in the farewell festivities, but she was grateful when Sabrina gave the signal to leave the gentlemen to their port.

Dolly having airily announced that she meant to retire early, Emily was left with only her sister and Miss Lavinia for company. Sabrina chatted about the lesson for the next evening's church service, and Miss Lavinia made appropriate responses without looking up from her tatting while Emily flipped through the pages of a fashion magazine in silence. At last she set the magazine down and arose from her chair.

"I think, if you will excuse me, that I will not wait for tea, for I seem to have a headache starting. No doubt an early night will do me good."

Sabrina immediately expressed concern, echoed by Miss Lavinia's demand to know if she should order a tisane prepared.

"No, ma'am, I am in need of nothing but rest. Martha will look after me, and by morning I shall be as fit as a fiddle."

She walked up the stairs, her head still full of thoughts of Meriden. Really, she chided herself, she was behaving more like a lovesick schoolgirl than a woman grown. She ought to know better. If she had any sense at all, she would take herself firmly in hand.

Her meditation was interrupted as she passed the closed door of Dolly's bedchamber by the sound of angry voices from within. Curious, Emily pushed the door open to discover her elder niece and nephew in the throes of a violent quarrel. Neither noted her entrance for several moments.

"You ought to be thrashed!" Oliver stormed, shaking Dolly.

"And who would do such a thing?" she demanded, wrenching herself free of his clutches and turning, arms akimbo, to glare at him. "Papa is dead and you have no authority over me, Oliver. I shall do as I please. You cannot stop me."

"The devil I can't! I dashed well ought to slap some sense into you, Dolly, and by God—"

"You wouldn't dare. He would call you out if you did!"

"That's all you know. He can't call me out. He's in the wrong, and so you would know if you had a brain the size of a pea in that addled head of yours, but you don't know the first thing about anything, and so you have been but putty in the hands of the first loose screw who's ever whispered pretty things in your ear. You ought—"

Dolly's hand whipped up and smashed against his cheek, bringing flames of wrath leaping to his eyes.

"Dolly!" Emily cried, rushing to intervene before Oliver could retaliate in kind, as it certainly appeared to her that he meant to do. "Stop that at once! What is the meaning of this?"

Recognizing a probable ally, Oliver said bitterly, "She thinks she is going to York with that rattle Saint Just, that's what. All for that stupid assembly. Perhaps you can talk some sense into her, ma'am. I cannot. But I promise you," he added with a grim look at his sister, "she is going nowhere with him tonight. Not if I have to tie her to her bedpost."

Dolly snapped, "You cannot do that, Oliver. No one will allow you to tie me to my bed, will they, Aunt Emily? Tell him!"

"Not only will I not tell him any such thing," said Emily, holding on to her temper with great difficulty, "but I will hand him the bindings myself. No, do not say another word, Dolly," she commanded when the young lady drew a deep indignant breath. "I tell you, I cannot be held responsible for my actions if you speak. Where is Mr. Saint Just now, Oliver?"

"You needn't concern yourself with him," Oliver said. "I left him in his cups, which is how I came to learn of this mischief in the first place, and he can thank my upbringing for the fact that I didn't take further advantage of his condition to drown him in the lake. But I can handle Mr. Bloody Saint Just." He shoved a hand through his hair. "God, to think I brought him here. I promise you, he'll leave first thing in the morning."

"No!" Dolly cried. "You cannot, Oliver. He is the only person here who cares about me."

"If I didn't care about you—" her brother began.

But Emily interrupted brusquely, saying, "Never mind that now, Oliver. Just go make certain your erstwhile friend is not down at the stables attempting to make arrangements for a pair of fast horses. It would not do for him to prate of this disgraceful nonsense before the grooms or anyone else."

"Good Lord, I never thought about that. But what about Dolly? You ought not to have to deal with her alone, ma'am."

"Do you think I cannot do so?" Emily demanded.

"No, of course not! That is, perhaps I ought to fetch my—"

"Your mother? Don't be a nodcock, Oliver. Your mother would promptly succumb to a fit of the vapors, and I haven't got a supply of feathers by me to burn. Nor do I require the services of Miss Lavinia. Do you go now and attend to Mr. Saint Just and leave your idiotish sister to me."

He regarded her doubtfully, but only for a moment. Then, with a final glare at Dolly, he took himself off, prudently shutting the bedchamber door behind him.

Dolly sniffed. "Since I have no wish to hear what you have to say to me, I shall go to bed." Turning away with a flounce of her muslin skirt, she moved to ring the bell.

Emily said quietly, "If you so much as touch that rope, Dolly, you will awaken in the morning to the news that Meriden desires to speak with you in the library. And if you think that, having got yourself into this kind of scrape, you will escape with no more than a tongue-lashing, you would do well to think again. He has not been in the best of tempers of late."

Dolly stopped where she stood. For a long moment Emily was uncertain as to whether her words had really sunk in, for the girl's spine was stiff and her shoulders hunched forward. She seemed poised on her toes, uncertain of what to do. Tempted though Emily was to add to what she had already said, she remained silent, waiting.

Finally Dolly turned. "You will not tell him anything if I listen to what you have to say?"

The answer to that question was easy. "I will certainly tell him if you do not; however, I will make no other promise. You have done very wrong, Dolly, and you deserve to suffer the consequences of your actions."

"Well, I think you would be very mean to tell him when you must know that he will be furious with me," Dolly said, pushing out her lower lip.

Strongly suppressing the familiar urge to throttle her niece, Emily said patiently, "What occurs must be on your own head, Dolly, not mine. It is you, not I, who have done this foolish thing."

"I do not see what is foolish about wanting to have fun."

"That is not the point. What is unconscionable is your plan to travel with no other escort than Mr. Saint Just."

"But he is the only one who would take me to York!"

"Dolly, it is improper for an unmarried young lady—or a married one, for that matter—to travel with an unmarried gentleman who is not related to her. Surely you know that."

"Fustian, that's all such rules are. What could possibly happen when Mr. Saint Just is Oliver's friend?"

Balked for a moment by the simple fact that she felt strangely unequal to the task at hand, Emily tried a different tack. "Dolly, you were forbidden to go to York at all. That is the fact of the matter, plain and simple. To entice Mr. Saint Just into helping you defy not only your mama's orders but also your Cousin Jack's was very wrong. You know it was."

Dolly shrugged. "I do not know that I enticed him at all. He suggested attending the assembly when first he arrived, and I agreed that it would be the very thing to cheer everyone up. Then fusty Harry told Oliver it was not to be, and Cousin Jack flew up into the boughs—as though he has never bent the rules himself, which everyone knows he has—and everyone was cross with me, but Mr. Saint Just laughed at them and said he was mad about me and that we'd think of something else. We could have been in York before morning, and though Lettie has vexed her mama and is not to go, after all, Mr. Saint Just knows of an inn where I can rest and change to my ball gown—"

"Dolly, you cannot want to be ruined," Emily said desperately.

"I don't know that I would be. When Lettie went to stay with her Aunt Catherstoke in Bath, everyone said she would be ruined, but she had a wonderful time and set up any number of flirts, so that when she went to London for the Season this year, she already had lots of friends, and she said that that made everything much nicer than if she had known no one."

"Goodness, Dolly," Emily said testily, "I have met your friend Miss Bennett but once, and even I could see what a flighty little puss she is. I do not doubt that people hereabouts expected her to ruin herself. I daresay she may thank her Aunt Catherstoke that she did not.

But that has nothing to say to the purpose. Has no one ever explained to you what can happen to a young woman who has no one to protect her?''

"She will be ruined," replied Dolly complacently.

"Oh, we are talking in circles," Emily said, barely stopping herself from pushing a hand through her hair as Oliver had done. "Look here, have you any idea what that means? Have you any idea what men and women do? When they are married, I mean? No," she said, answering her own question when her imagination boggled at an attempt to envision Sabrina discussing such a subject. "Of course you do not. Well, you are about to find out."

"But how do you know? You have never been married."

"I have sisters other than your mother," Emily said, hoping her smile hid the fact that she, too, would prefer not to discuss such a subject. "Sisters who talk about everything. And I have friends too, for that matter, who clearly discuss more interesting matters than you discuss with your friends. Now, sit down in that chair and listen to me carefully."

Twenty minutes later, there fell a heavy silence in the room, and Emily found herself wondering if she had gone too far. Sabrina would certainly not thank her for putting Dolly in possession of the facts of married life. Indeed, at the moment it did not look as though Dolly, who was shocked to silence for once, would thank her either. Emily leaned forward in her chair. "Do you understand all that I have said to you? Do you realize now that by traveling alone, at night, with Mr. Saint Just, you would have been laying yourself open to just such treatment?"

"He wouldn't," Dolly said in a choked murmur, but for once doubt sounded in her voice.

"It wouldn't matter if he didn't," Emily said brutally, "because after you had spent so much time in his company, everyone in England who knew about it would assume that he had, and that, my dear, is the nut with no bark on it."

Dolly burst into tears, leaning over to hug her knees while she sobbed, "It isn't fair!"

"Life is often unfair," Emily told her, then grimaced and looked at the ceiling when she remembered her own reaction after Jack had made a similar, equally sanctimonious statement to her. Fortunately, from her point of view, Dolly neither looked up nor reacted as Emily had done. She sobbed louder instead, setting her aunt's teeth on edge. Emily bit her tongue and let the girl cry, but when Dolly straightened a few moments later in an attempt to catch her breath, Emily said bracingly, "That will do now. You will ruin your complexion if you keep on this way."

Dolly hiccuped but made an effort to regain control.

"That's better," Emily said. "Take a few deep breaths now, and you will be composed again in no time."

While she obeyed, Dolly watched her aunt with wide, disbelieving eyes, and when she could speak without stammering, she said, "Was that all true, Aunt Emily, or did you make it up to shock me?"

"It is true, darling, every word. I do not know from my own experience, of course, but I am told that with the right husband the whole business will be very pleasurable."

"Whoever told you that must have been lying," said Dolly flatly, making a moue of distaste.

Emily's eyes twinkled. "That is entirely possible, I suppose. One will simply have to wait and see. But I hope that now that you understand the matter better, there will be no more talk of forbidden assemblies or of dashing off into the night with only a single inebriated gentleman to bear you company."

Dolly made a face. "I shan't go as far as to the bottom of the garden alone with any man!"

Emily chuckled. After a brief silence she said, "Are you composed enough now to seek your bed, my dear?"

Dolly nodded, got to her feet, then looked at Emily searchingly. "Must you tell Cousin Jack about all this?"

Tempted to promise to keep Dolly's confidence as a reward for her change of attitude, Emily hesitated briefly, but she had learned her lesson. She reached out to touch her niece's shoulder as though to soften the blow that was to come.

"Never mind," Dolly said with less bitterness than might have been expected. "I daresay he will have to know what we were going to do. Mama, too. Oh, Aunt Emily, I would not have had her know! Not for anything."

"She would have known soon enough if you had done the thing," Emily pointed out. "Maybe after this you will think your actions through more carefully. In any case, I believe Oliver will tell your Cousin Jack all about this at the first opportunity, since he is blaming himself for having exposed you to the attentions of a man like Mr. Saint Just."

"But I liked his attentions," Dolly protested. "Oliver should not blame himself."

"Yes, he should," Emily countered. "He is your brother and is therefore responsible for your well-being. He ought to have known that your very innocence in such matters made you unable to deal with Mr. Saint Just on your own. Indeed, we all ought to have realized that and, accordingly, to have kept our eyes open. You were that much more vulnerable to his charms, my dear, because of what you did not know."

"He knows all those things you told me?" Dolly's eyes were wider than ever. "Does Harry Enderby know them, do you think? Does Oliver?"

Grinning now, Emily said, "Miss Lavinia would no doubt assure you that all men know such things from the cradle." Then, more soberly, she added, "I believe Saint Just knows what he's about, certainly. Jack didn't like him from the start, and I cannot say that I took to him much either, but neither of us suspected that he would dare attempt such a thing as this."

"Cousin Jack will be very angry," Dolly said unhappily.

"Yes, but if Oliver does tell him, it will be Oliver who

bears the brunt of it," Emily assured her. "By the time he speaks to you, he will have burned off the worst of his temper."

Dolly managed a watery smile, then leaned forward and put her arms around Emily. "I'm sorry I was such a beast," she said.

Emily returned her hug. "Ring for your maid now, my dear, and get to bed. Things will look more cheerful in the morning."

In her own bedchamber a few moments later, she wondered if she had spoken truly. Sabrina would be in a dither once she heard what had been planned, and no matter what he said to Oliver, Jack would not be as sanguine afterward as she had led Dolly to believe. Emily was certain he would be pleased by the change in the girl's attitude, but she knew he would not believe, any more than she did, that Dolly would be all roses and light to live with from now on, any more than she had been before. Dolly had been shocked, Emily knew, by what she had learned about men's ways with women, but that shock would dissipate rapidly and would do little to alter her fundamental selfishness. Indeed, knowing Dolly as she had come to know her, Emily was more than a little afraid that her niece might develop a desire to experiment with what she had learned. In the long run, she thought fretfully, she might well discover she had done Dolly a disservice.

Once her head hit her pillow, however, all thought ceased and she fell into a deep and dreamless sleep. Not until daylight filled the room did her reflections return to disturb her peace of mind. Knowing that only action would calm her, she hurried through her breakfast, grateful that Sabrina still slept and that Miss Lavinia appeared to be engrossed in some sketches she had made of her latest scheme for the garden.

"Nearly time to set bulbs for spring," she said cheerfully, looking up when Emily took her seat. Emily nodded, and silence fell, broken only by the sounds of silver against crockery and the whisper of Anna's footsteps when she brought Emily's tea.

As soon as she could decently leave, Emily hurried downstairs to the library. William, on duty in the hall, nodded when she asked if Meriden had arrived. "Is he free?" she demanded, not wishing to interrupt any more distressing scenes.

"Aye, miss, free as air." He moved quickly to open the double doors for her.

Jack stood up when she entered, and only when the smile of greeting on his face faded as rapidly as it had appeared did she remember that he was somehow out of charity with her. She had no time to consider that now, however.

"Has Oliver been to see you?" she asked abruptly.

He nodded.

"Then you know what took place here last evening?"

"I do. He said you dealt with Dolly. I hope you smacked the stupid chit."

Emily shook her head. "I was not so violent, but I did shock her, I fear, and I do not know that you will approve of what I have done, any more than Sabrina will."

He raised his eyebrows but said nothing, merely motioning her to a chair. When she had seated herself, he sat back down in his chair behind the table, moved to put his feet up, and then, appearing to think better of it, tilted back in his chair and folded his hands across his flat stomach. When she still had not spoken, he said, "Well?"

"I told her all about men and women," Emily blurted.

"All?" He grinned.

"All."

"You cannot possibly know very much yourself," he said flatly. "Tell me what you said to her."

Emily blushed fiery red. "I will not. It was difficult enough for me to discuss such a subject with Dolly, but I saw at once that she had absolutely no comprehension of the dangers involved in her relationship with Mr. Saint Just, so it was clearly my duty to explain them to her."

"I hope you frightened the little cat senseless."

"Well, she was shocked, of course, but that will pass. You do not think I did wrong?" Suddenly it was of prodigious importance to her that he should not think that.

He shook his head. "Best thing you could have done under the circumstances."

Emily sighed, surprised by her deep relief. "I thought, you know, that I might have put new ideas into her head, worse notions than were already there."

He chuckled. "I wouldn't be surprised if you had, but you needn't concern yourself if you did. Dolly's own selfishness will protect her. She means to make a good match, and she must know—if she doesn't, you must make sure to tell her—that no man of high estate will be interested in damaged goods."

"Well, I did tell her that," Emily said on a note of satisfaction, "and I told her also that I would not conceal from you what she had done."

"Very proper." He smiled at her. "I won't insult you by suggesting that you recalled that Oliver would tell me—"

"Of course not! I told you—"

"I stated that badly," he admitted. "You could not have known, after all, that Oliver would tell me anything. He might have decided to protect his friend instead."

"I could not have thought that after seeing him last night," Emily said honestly. "Has Mr. Saint Just departed?"

"It seems," Meriden replied carefully, "that he had passed out at the table before Oliver returned to him last night. Unable to wake him, Oliver caused him to be carried to his bed, and being a conscientious host, he has determined that he ought not to wake his guest before he's slept his fill."

Laughter gurgled in Emily's throat. "He didn't say that! That sounds much more like something Harry Enderby would say."

Jack nodded, his eyes twinkling. "Not at all the thing

to disturb a man when he'll wake to a raging head, not to mention an order to take himself off at once." He became more serious. "Don't mistake me, though. Young Oliver is very angry, with himself as well as with Saint Just. The lad seemed to expect me to tear a strip off him for what happened."

"Well, didn't you? I confess that I was persuaded you would. He brought that scoundrel here, after all."

"But he didn't make him into a scoundrel. I told Oliver that I was content to leave his friend to him, that I had other, more important things to do today and thought him thoroughly competent to attend to Saint Just."

"When do you meet Mr. Scopwick?" Emily asked bluntly.

"Shortly before noon. I have given it out that I have business at Enderby Hall today, so no one will think it odd when I leave the Priory at that time. Melanie knows what to do."

"Yes, I know, for she told me. Are you quite certain she will be safe, sir?"

"Yes, so don't you think for a moment about lending your protection to ours." When Emily flushed guiltily, he nodded. "I thought so. You hear me, my lass. I have already had all the uproar I can tolerate this week, so don't you provoke me again. I've done all I can think of to keep you out of this and I mean you to stay out. You stay right here at the Priory and keep your long nose out of those woods. Is that understood?"

Emily nodded.

"I'd like to have your word," he said with a level look.

Emily stiffened. "Haven't I said I will not leave the Priory grounds? You insult me, sir, demanding that I give my word like a half-baked schoolboy. Shall I cut my finger and mix my blood with yours? Would that satisfy you? Or must it be in writing and witnessed by a dozen men? Only say what you want, Meriden, and I will endeavor to provide it for you!"

"Lord, what a temper!" Jack stood up and moved toward her, causing Emily to jump to her feet and skitter away from him. But when he laughed, she stopped where she was and glared at him. He shook his head. "What did you think? That I would shake you, or worse?" When she did not answer, he chuckled again. "Very well, Emmy love, I won't insult you. I will merely state once more that if I find you anywhere near Melanie or that path through the woods, I will deal with you as you deserve."

Emily fled, glad only that he had not forced her to give him her solemn word. She had said she would not leave the Priory grounds, and she would not. But neither could she let Melanie go off alone. Jack had not considered what would become of the little girl after they caught her witch. He seemed to think Melanie would just run along home again. Emily knew the child would do nothing of the kind, for she was certain that curiosity would win out over good sense and that Melanie would stay right there. If an altercation ensued, she might be hurt. And, too, Jack seemed to have forgotten about the old woman's accomplice. No old woman had struck her down. Of that she was certain. Only a strong arm could have accomplished such a feat. Emily intended to be on the scene to see that such a thing did not happen again. And she could do that without leaving the Priory grounds. Indeed, she thought smugly, she could walk nearly all the way to the village without leaving Staithes property.

If there was a cloud over her satisfaction, it was the fact that Jack would not see the matter as she did. There would no doubt be a reckoning afterward, but she would deal with that when it came. In the meantime, there was no way she knew of by which she could sit quietly at home and let Melanie walk alone into danger. Thus it was that when, from the window of the drawing room, she saw the little girl setting forth, Emily waited only long enough to be certain Melanie was well on her way before she hurried downstairs, determined to follow her.

She had reached the front hall when she heard her name urgently called from the landing. Turning, she saw Dolly waving a single sheet of paper.

"Aunt Emily, where are you going? I must speak to

you at once. Oh, it is dreadful. You will never believe—"

Casting a glance at the interested William, Emily interrupted the flow of words, saying matter-of-factly, "I see that you are big with news, Dolly. Do you come with me into the library and tell me quickly, for I am just going out."

"Oh, but you cannot! Indeed, when I tell you—"

"Come down at once," Emily said more sharply. "Cheltenham drama has no place in your mama's front hall."

"Well, you would not have said so if you could have seen the plays Mama and Papa and their friends got up when they had a house party here several years ago," Dolly said, coming rapidly down the stairs as she spoke, "but only wait until I tell you—"

"Be good enough to keep silent until we may be private," Emily said, firmly telling herself that Melanie would be safe until she returned from the village, by which time Emily would be in her place in the home wood, a place from which she could see the path clearly and watch the area where Meriden and the vicar would be hidden. She had no doubt that the two men would conceal themselves in the shrubbery, but there was a tree . . .

"Aunt Emily, attend to me," Dolly said fiercely. "Oliver has challenged that dreadful Mr. Saint Just to fight a duel!"

14

"WHAT?" EMILY STARED AT HER NIECE IN DISBELIEF. "Nonsense, Dolly, you musn't let your imagination carry you beyond the line of being pleasing."

"But it is true. And Mr. Saint Just accepted his challenge. Only look at this." She handed the sheet of paper to Emily and watched her rapidly scan the words, adding helpfully, "As you see, Oliver writes that he is leaving his bay gelding to me and his school ring and his embossed saddle to Giles. To Melanie—"

"Hush, Dolly, I am trying to read," Emily said impatiently. "Mercy me, he truly means to do this terrible thing. Where is Bishop's Clearing?"

"Why, it's near the main road through the woods. There used to be some sort of little chapel there before they built Mr. Scopwick's church—only of course it wasn't Mr. Scopwick's church then, for that was centuries ago when the Priory really was a priory and the bishop was used to come occasionally to say the Mass or whatever in the little chapel."

"Enough! Do you mean to say the clearing is near the vicarage?"

"No, didn't I just tell you? It is near the top of the road a short distance before it emerges onto the moor."

"Merciful heavens, 'tis near where I was struck down, then. They will be dueling not a hundred yards from . . . from the road," Emily said, just stopping herself from revealing too much to Dolly. "But no doubt they mean to fight with swords."

"As if that would be better!" exclaimed Dolly. "But they won't, for Oliver don't know one end of a sword from another, and even Saint Just wouldn't be so unsportsmanlike as to take advantage of a man he calls his friend. They will fight with pistols. Oliver says as much, there, in his letter."

"So he does," muttered Emily, reading again. "Oh, what a pair of ninnies they are! Come along, Dolly, we must stop them, and I might not find the clearing quickly enough by myself."

"But they must be there by now," Dolly protested. "Oliver didn't expect that I would read this until much later in the day, for I hardly ever go to my bedchamber at this time, you know, only I wanted to fetch my shawl—"

"Well, you didn't fetch it," Emily said, looking her over, "but that cannot be helped. Don't argue with me, Dolly. Just come at once. You don't want Oliver to be killed."

Dolly agreed that such an outcome was unthinkable, and Emily waited not a moment longer. Her greatest fear was not for Oliver but for Jack, Melanie, and Mr. Scopwick. She had no confidence that either Oliver or Saint Just would shoot straight, and she had no knowledge of how many shots each would be allowed. The thought of stray bullets flying around the woods near the road terrified her. Taking Dolly by the arm, she dragged her along, hurrying through the hall and out to the drive.

Releasing her hold on Dolly, Emily hurried into the woods, but as she neared the point where the road forked, she realized that she would have to take care. Haste was important, but not so important that she wished to risk running full tilt into either Melanie's old woman or Jack.

Dolly caught up with her as she moved into the shrubbery. "It is much faster to stay on the road. Why do we go this way?"

"Look here," Emily said quickly, "I did not tell you the whole before, but Meriden and Mr. Scopwick are attempting to catch someone who has been—"

"Oh, the jewel thief!" exclaimed Dolly. "Do you know who it is, then? Oh, how exciting! Where are they?"

Deciding to accept Dolly's assumption rather than to attempt to explain what was really taking place, Emily gestured with a nod of her head. "Somewhere up yonder, lying in wait. That's why I was so shocked to hear of the duel being fought nearby. A stray bullet—"

"Oh, my goodness! We must hurry!"

But Emily caught her impetuous companion by the arm. "We must go carefully, Dolly. It will do no one any good if we run into the . . . the thief, or into the vicar or your cousin, for that matter. Explanations mean delay, no matter how quickly we make them, so it will be better to stay off the road."

"But I have never walked through the woods except on the paths or the road," Dolly protested. "If we go charging about, I shan't know precisely where Bishop's Clearing is. There is a narrow path from the road that leads directly there. And should we not warn Cousin Jack of the danger at once? They could shoot at each other before ever we get to the clearing."

Hesitating, Emily realized that Dolly was right, especially if the girl could not lead her quickly and quietly to the clearing. The thought that Jack might be injured, even killed while she dallied, lent wings to her feet, and she hurried back onto the road. To warn the men first was certainly a better notion. She had avoided doing so at once because she had known she would have to face Jack's anger with her before she could explain anything to him. As for running into Melanie or her witch, she had no idea now how much time had passed since Melanie had left the house. She could only hope the child had not yet had time to reach the village and walk back again.

Back on the road, they made good speed, though Emily warned Dolly to go as quietly as she could. "We do not want to startle the villain unless we must," she said.

As it happened, the two of them rounded a curve in the narrow road in time to see Melanie directly ahead of them, face-to-face with the same old woman Emily had seen before. Emily stopped dead and Dolly walked straight into her just as the woman turned, uttered a shriek of fury, and whirled toward the narrow path, only to run straight into the arms of Jack and Scopwick, who had been concealed in the shrubbery on either side of it.

Breathing a sigh of relief, Emily hurried forward to warn them about the duel. Before she could speak, however, and before Jack could give utterance to the words of fury she could see leaping to his tongue, Mr. Scopwick snatched the scruffy gray wig from their captive's head, revealing brown hair arranged in a tight bun at the nape of her neck.

Melanie, who had stood frozen in place, gave a gasp of dismay. "Miss Brittan!"

"Miss Brittan, indeed," bellowed the vicar with strong satisfaction. "Never did believe in any witch. Stands to reason I'd have heard by now if there were anyone about who could be described as such. What's your game, woman?" When she glared at him, he chuckled and gave her an admonitory shake. "No point in silence. You've stolen enough from this child to land you in a peck of trouble. Daresay we shall see you hanged."

Miss Brittan gasped, "Hanged? You cannot. You are a

man of God. Moreover, the child gave the money willingly."

Jack had been glaring at Emily, but at these words he turned his attention to the captive. "Not willingly, madam, as well you know. You have betrayed a solemn trust by what you have done, and you deserve to suffer the harshest punishment."

"I needed the money," the woman said pitifully.

"That is scarcely reason enough to terrorize the child entrusted to your care," he retorted.

"Not to a cold, unfeeling Englishman, perhaps," she said, recovering her spirit. "In my country, love is sufficient reason for any act."

"Your country?" Dolly said. "But you told Mama your home is in Kent."

Miss Brittan shrugged. "A trifling lie, that is all."

"You are French, are you not?" Jack said.

The woman nodded, and Emily, remembering that her own reason for being on the scene at all was an urgent one, turned to Jack. "Meriden, you must—"

"Hold your tongue!" he snapped. "You and I will talk at length later, I promise you, but for now, if you value your hide, you will keep silent."

"But—"

"Hands up! Nobody move!"

Startled, everyone turned toward the new voice to discover that a thin, wiry, dark-haired man had emerged from the shrubbery on the south side of the road, opposite to the place where Jack and the vicar had concealed themselves. In his right hand he held a wicked-looking pistol that he pointed first at Scopwick and then at Jack, but the anger flashing in his dark eyes was directed at Miss Brittan.

"Fool," he snarled, his accent even in the few words he had spoken proving him beyond anyone's doubt to be a Frenchman.

"Why do you show yourself, Antoine?" Miss Brittan asked fretfully. "Leave at once. Protect yourself!"

"Not without the money," the man said. "You told me you would bring it, that you would meet me after you had seen the girl today. I waited, only to hear you condemn us out of your own mouth. Where is the money and the jewels?"

"The jewels!" Jack exclaimed, staring at Miss Brittan. "You took the missing jewels?"

The Frenchman answered scornfully, "Of course she took them. We require money to pay the men in Scarborough who will give us passage back to our country. Once we knew there would be enough, for me to elude my foolish English guards was a simple matter, and Felice gave me excellent instructions about where to meet her. But she said," he added, glancing murderously at his accomplice, "that there will be no trouble, that we—but, no, Englishman, you must not!"

When the Frenchman had looked away from the others toward Miss Brittan, Jack had tensed himself to spring, but the villain sensed his movement and drew the pistol sharply back so that it was pointed directly at him.

Seeing the muscles in the man's hand begin to tighten, Emily hurled herself at him without the slightest thought for her own safety. As she struck him, she felt a sharp pain in her right arm and heard two shots ring out so quickly that the second was but an echo of the first. Reflecting vaguely that she hadn't realized his pistol could shoot more than one bullet, she clutched at him. Then, as they fell to the ground in a tangled heap, there was a third explosion, nearer at hand but more muffled than the others, and she felt the body beneath her jump and go limp. Dazed by shock and stunned by her fall, she made no effort at first to move. Then, so certain was she that Jack had been killed despite her efforts, she was afraid to look up.

His voice aroused her. "Emily! Good God, lass, you are bleeding! Did he shoot you? Whatever made you do such a damn-fool thing?"

"Pick her up, lad," Scopwick said from behind him. "Oughtn't to let her just lie on him like that, you know."

"What?" Jack looked back over his shoulder at the vicar and then down at the Frenchman. "Why isn't he moving?"

"Pick up Miss Wingrave and perhaps he will be able to do so," the vicar said practically.

"Antoine! Oh, Antoine!"

"Never you mind about him, woman," said the vicar, tightening his grip as Miss Brittan lunged toward her fallen compatriot. "Just stand still and behave yourself."

"Heard a lot of bangs," said Miss Lavinia, stepping from the shrubbery, dressed in her fishing attire.

Giles was at her heels. "We were looking for the vicar to go fishing," he said. "What's happened here?"

"Dammit, woman!" bellowed Scopwick, turning on Miss Lavinia angrily. "What are you thinking of, dashing about without so much as looking where you're going, and bringing the boy with you? Those bangs you heard were pistol shots that, come to think of it," he added in a distracted tone, "could not both have come from the Frenchman's pistol. Say, Meriden, is that fellow dead?"

"His pistol appears to have discharged when he fell," the earl said in a strange voice.

Dolly piped up excitedly, "Then you killed him, Aunt Emily, you killed him!"

Emily closed her eyes. Her arm ached abominably where Jack held it. She thought at first that he was holding her too tightly, but then she realized he was doing what he could to slow the bleeding. When she opened her eyes again, he was looking into her face as though he wished to ascertain whether she was conscious. She smiled hesitantly.

"I'm not dead yet, sir," she said. "Is he?"

He nodded. "As near as makes no difference, I think."

"He would have killed you," she murmured.

"Hush, we'll talk about that later."

"I was afraid of that."

"I said, hush. I'm going to hurt you a trifle."

That his notion of a trifle was not the same as hers became instantly clear. He squeezed and probed the wound, sending sharp, stabbing flashes of agony through her that made her gasp and fear that she would disgrace herself by being sick all over him. Then, wrapping the wound tightly with her handkerchief, he said, "That's all. Wanted to be certain no part of the bullet remained. Fortunately it appears only to have creased your arm and didn't penetrate the flesh by more than a half-inch at the worst. Best to make it bleed a bit, however. Daresay the village leech will wish to cup you otherwise."

"Not if I can stop him, he won't," she muttered.

"Coward. That will hold you, however, until we can dust it with basilicum powder and get it properly bandaged. Then, my lass, you and I are going to have a serious talk."

Dolly's demanding to know how the Frenchman had managed to shoot himself and Emily too, and with only one bullet, if he had been meaning to shoot Cousin Jack, drew Meriden's attention before Emily could protest the innocence of her actions.

"He didn't shoot your aunt," he said crisply. "Scopwick, where did that other shot come from?"

"The duel," Emily mutterd, trying to sit upright.

"The what?" Both men stared at her, but before she could elucidate, sounds of new arrivals were heard, and a moment later four young men appeared, strolling together along the narrow road. Emily, leaning her head against Jack's shoulder, recognized three of them.

"Goodness," said Dolly, "what is Lettie Bennett's brother doing with Harry and Oliver and Mr. Saint Just?"

The four young men, upon seeing the crowd in the road, had come to a halt. Then Oliver, noting that Emily was being supported by Jack, rushed forward, exclaiming, "Good God, what happened here? Aunt Emily, are you all right? Good God, there is blood all over your arm!"

"Harry," demanded Dolly, "what are you doing with that dreadful Mr. Saint Just?"

"Ain't with him," he said, regarding her with disapproval. "With Oliver. There was a bit of a dust-up, you see. Oughtn't to mention it, of course, but since they made a mull of it, there's no point keeping mum. His second, don't you know. But more to the point, my girl, what are you doing hovering about where, if I don't miss my guess, there's been mischief afoot?" He lifted his quizzing glass and surveyed the scene. "That fellow's dead," he pronounced in a thoughtful tone. "Look here, Meriden, you been shooting poachers? Oughtn't to do that sort of thing in the presence of ladies. Agitates 'em."

"Poachers," snorted Miss Lavinia. "What I want to know is what Miss Brittan is doing here and why Eustace Scopwick is hanging on to her as though he fears she'll fly away."

"Because she's like to do just that," snapped Scopwick, glaring at Miss Lavinia. "She's the cause of all the riot and rumpus that's been going on hereabouts. She took your blasted rubies, that's what. Oh, Lord, what now?" he demanded. He was looking back down the road toward the Priory, and everyone else turned to look. Sabrina was hurrying along the road, holding her skirts up at a scandalous height.

"I was walking to the vicarage when I heard the most awful row," she called out when she saw them looking at her. "First shots, then shouting. I recognized the vicar's voice, so I came to get his help. Jack, can that dreadful man who struck Emily down be back in our woods? You must find out who's been shooting. Merciful heavens!" She had seen Emily and the Frenchman. "What has happened here?"

Swiftly, letting Emily fend for herself for the moment, Jack stood, swept off his jacket, and dropped it over the Frenchman's head and torso. Mr. Scopwick had released his captive's arm and was striding angrily toward Sabrina. "Didn't I tell you not to set foot out-of-doors without a good strong footman beside you? What are you thinking about? You've got no better sense than Lavinia Arncliffe!"

Miss Lavinia said sharply, "Now, see here, Eustace Scopwick, you've no call to go saying such things. If a body's wanting to go fishing and is looking for the friend she usually fishes with and hears two pistol shots, it is only natural that she—"

"Oh, cease your piping, woman, and go fishing or wherever else you can think to go!" Scopwick shot over his shoulder as he rapidly approached Sabrina and grabbed both of her hands. "And take that boy with you! Do not go any nearer, my lady," he added quickly as Sabrina moved to pass him. "The sight is not a pleasant one."

"Shots?" said Harry. "Two shots? Guess Ollie and

Allie are to blame for those. A duel, don't you know?" he added when all eyes turned his way.

"Well, we know that," Dolly said, lifting her chin a little. "They were fighting over me, after all."

"If you are wise," said Mr. Enderby, favoring her with a chilly look, "you won't refine too much upon that, my girl, for there is nothing at all romantic in having two gents making cakes of themselves like they did. Bad *ton*, that's what it is, and that's what I told them both from the onset. Dashed bad *ton*."

"You're only saying that because you don't like it that Mr. Saint Just paid heed to me," snapped Dolly.

"Dashed loose screw," Harry retorted. "Said so all along. Man don't go about seducing his friends' sisters under their own roofs. And you, Saint Just, don't go thinking to call me out for saying as much, because you know it's true."

"I don't ever call anyone out," Saint Just said blandly. "Oliver did the calling. I've apologized to him, and I'll apologize to anyone else who will listen, before I take leave of you all."

"Oliver oughtn't to have called you out at all," Harry said, frowning. "Dashed awkward."

"What!" exclaimed Dolly. "You think Oliver did wrong to defend my honor? How can you say such a thing?"

"Didn't say it," Harry told her. "Said he was wrong to call Saint Just out. Guest under his roof, don't you know. Man don't threaten to shoot his guests. Only think what a precedent that would set. Told him so. Wouldn't listen."

"Well, of course he wouldn't listen," Dolly said angrily. "He was certainly not going to sit back and let that man do what he wanted to do to me, what I didn't even know he wanted to do until Aunt Emily explained the matter to me. Why, I think you're perfectly horrid, Harry."

"Should have thrashed him for his insolence," Harry said, still following his own train of thought. "Would have done it myself if anyone had told me what was going on."

"Like to see you try," murmured Saint Just dulcetly.

Oliver turned on him. "No, you wouldn't, because saving Cousin Jack, Harry's the best man with his fists in

Yorkshire. You'd have suffered a lot worse than you did from my pistol."

"Well, no one but the birds you frightened suffered from that," said Harry, adding for the others' benefit, "Both shot wide, which goes to show. Of course, Saint Just did it on purpose—deloped into the air. Oliver's just a naturally bad shot." His breath caught in his throat suddenly, and he looked the scene over again, lifting his quizzing glass to his right eye as his gaze came to rest upon Emily. "I say . . ."

"Which way were you facing, Oliver?" Jack demanded.

Oliver flushed to the roots of his hair as understanding swept over him. "I don't know precisely. We just faced each other, and—"

"South," said the helpful Mr. Enderby in a thoughtful tone. "Daresay he was pointed directly toward you lot." Looking back at his principal, he said, "Looks like you didn't fire so wide after all, Ollie, if your bullet touched Miss Wingrave and went on to put paid to that fellow there."

Wrathfully Jack turned toward the hapless Oliver, the look on his face causing that young man to take two hasty steps backward. Jack said, "The Frenchman fell on his own pistol, causing it to discharge. The only thing you hit, you young idiot, was your aunt. And when I finish with you, you'll be lucky if you can sight a pistol again, let alone fire one."

"Jack, no!" Emily cried, trying to get to her feet. "Oliver never meant to hurt me. That was an accident." Standing, she took a step toward him with the intention of stopping him physically, but the shock of the wound she had suffered made her dizzy and she stumbled.

Sabrina's cry of alarm stopped Jack. Seeing Emily swaying on her feet, he leapt to catch her before she fell, but his temper was more inflamed than ever. Catching at her arms without thought of the pain he was causing her, he shouted, "You are right to defend Oliver, for it was your own idiocy that nearly got you killed. What were you thinking of to leap in front of the damned Frenchman's pistol that way? In fact," he bellowed, "what were you doing in the road at all? You promised to remain at the Priory, to stay out of all this."

"I promised to stay on the Priory grounds," she said without thinking. "The woods are still—"

"Damn you, Emily," he snapped, giving her a rough shake, "I am going to teach you the folly of playing such tricks with me. Before this day is out, you'll get such a lesson that you'll never dare to do such a thing again."

"We came to warn you about the duel," Dolly said, "and I don't care what Harry says. I don't believe that Oliver did anything wrong. Though I do think," she added musingly, "that it is rather nice that Harry wants to thrash Mr. Saint Just."

"Just you come along with me, my girl," said the exasperated Mr. Enderby, "and I'll explain this business to you in a way that you will understand clearly. I never knew such a brainless wench in all my life, and that's a fact. You need a good strong-minded man to look after you, so you just come along with me right now. And mind, Dolly, I'll have no back-chat."

"Yes, Harry," Dolly said meekly. "Please don't be vexed with me. Perhaps I didn't properly understand, after all."

"Dashed right, you didn't," said Mr. Enderby.

Watching them go, Emily remembered Dolly's assurance that she wouldn't go to the bottom of the garden with any man. Harry, however, was not a man whose motives need trouble anyone, Emily decided, turning her attention back to the earl.

He was staring in stupefaction at Mr. Scopwick. "I should what?" he demanded, making it clear to Emily that another conversation had been going on besides Harry's with Dolly.

"Well, you cannot do the things you have been threatening to do to her if you *don't* marry her," the vicar said, chuckling and throwing a wicked glance at Emily. "It's not, as our Harry would say, at all the done thing. Certainly, as a man of God, I could not condone beating a woman who is not your wife. Moreover," he added, looking down at Sabrina and speaking gently, "you'll need someone besides young Oliver there to help you run the Priory. I mean to take his mama off your hands if she will have me."

Ignoring the bulk of the vicar's comment, Jack said flatly, "Oliver is going back to Cambridge. Whether he likes it or not, I mean for him to finish his education."

"I'll go," Oliver said quietly. "I've a deal to learn before I shall be fit to run Staithes properly or to look out for the children as I should."

"Mr. Scopwick," Sabrina said faintly, clutching tightly at his hands, "whatever did you mean by what you said?"

"Mean to marry you, that's what. Been thinking about it for a long time, but didn't think you liked me well enough or that I ought to speak before you were out of mourning. Can you stomach being Sabrina Scopwick after so many years as Lady Saithes?"

"Goodness," Emily said while her sister looked up at the vicar in speechless dismay, "I had my mind all made up to a match betwixt you and Miss Lavinia."

The vicar roared with laughter. "That heathen wench? I'd be ripe for murder within a week. No, ma'am, a peaceable man like me needs a peaceable wife."

"Peaceable," snorted Miss Lavinia. "That will be the day. Sabrina would need to sit on you in order to have peace if she were daft enough to marry you. Don't you do it, Sabrina. We go on comfortably enough without him."

Sabrina shook her head, still clearly unable to speak, and there were a number of chuckles from the others. Favoring them with an air of reproval, Miss Lavinia added primly, "Having known Eustace all my life, I can assure you all that I should certainly never be so lost to my senses as to marry him or any other man. Men are but foolish creatures at best, and a sensible woman steers clear of them. If dear Sabrina is so misguided as to agree to take on the burden of sharing life with you, Eustace, I shall fashion some thick earmuffs for her. At least, thus, the worst of your bellowing will be muted."

"And what of your megrims, you old bat?" demanded the vicar. "No doubt we shall be forced to take you in as well. 'Twould be a crime to force you on young Oliver, and that's a fact.''

Sabrina spoke at last, weakly. "I couldn't possibly," she said. "N-not possibly. Oh, dear.''

Scopwick smiled gently down at her. "You will change your mind, I think," he said. "Already you look to me for help when you need it, do you not?"

Again she was silent, looking up at him with eyes that were round with astonishment.

"If Sabrina ever does agree to marry you," Jack said quietly into the silence that followed, "Miss Lavinia can live with Emily and me, and welcome."

15

EMILY HAD BEEN WATCHING JACK FOR SOME TIME, trying to decide if he was still furious with her for nearly getting herself killed and, incidentally, for disobeying his orders. She realized now, without surprise, that although she had been almost as surprised as her sister to hear Mr. Scopwick's proposal, she had not been nearly as astonished by the vicar's suggestion that Jack marry her, and she had been even less astonished to hear Jack make the offer he had just made regarding Miss Lavinia. Before she could search her mind for logical reasons for this surprising turn of thought, Sabrina spoke up, diverting her instantly.

"Before anyone gets married," she said rather quickly, still looking up wide-eyed at Mr. Scopwick, "should we not remove that odious person from the roadway? I am sure Melanie and Giles, at least, ought not to be standing here talking about such things over the body of a dead man. It is not at all the thing, you know. And what are we going to do about Miss Brittan? She certainly cannot continue as Melanie's governess, although I am sure she has repented of all her dreadful deeds.''

Miss Lavinia sniffed. "No doubt it was the man's fault, anyway. Probably he's the one clouted Emily."

"Do not blame Antoine," said Miss Brittan stiffly. "He was still in the prisoner camp that day. When I knew that Miss Wingrave had been so foolish as to follow me, I merely stepped behind a tree, and when she passed me, I hit her with a rock. I do not apologize. It was necessary that I not be recognized. And please do not call me Miss Brittan anymore. I am Felice de Bretagne, and my family is an old and proud one.''

"But we were kind to you," Sabrina protested, looking away from Scopwick at last in her surprise.

"You provided me with a place to live near my beloved Antoine, that is all. Your country would not permit me to visit him when I asked to do so. Indeed, I was forced to pretend to be a citizen of Belgium to pass your stupid customs. I had an English governess when I was a girl, and I speak your language like my own, so once I was here there was no difficulty. Now that Antoine is dead, I shall die too.''

"You'll go to prison, more like," said Scopwick, "despite what I said before. Don't hold with hanging females, myself, so I'll speak for you, I expect. Daresay you won't like Bridewell, but there it is. Where are those cursed Runners of yours, Meriden? We could use them now.''

"At the tavern in the village," replied the earl, who was watching Emily closely. "I'll send someone to fetch them.''

"I'll go," Oliver volunteered.

Meriden glanced at him. "An excellent idea," he said curtly, "but don't think to play least in sight afterward, my lad. I've still a few things I want to say to you about your duel, you know.''

Oliver nodded, returning his look manfully. "I know, and I deserve to hear them. We never thought about how close to the road that clearing is. Even Harry didn't consider that, blast him." He glanced at Mr. Bennett, who had been watching and listening without making his presence felt. "Your nag's in my stable, Ted. Want to ride along with me?"

"What about him?" Bennett asked, gesturing toward the Frenchman's body.

"Lord, he ain't going anywhere," said Oliver.

"Nevertheless," said the much-tried earl, "someone must stay here until the Runners arrive to deal with the body and to take Miss Bri—that is, Mademoiselle de Bretagne in charge. There is no point that I can see in taking either one back to the Priory."

"I can stay," offered Scopwick, chuckling again.

"No, I want you to look after Sabrina," Jack said, ignoring that lady's small gasp as he turned his gaze upon Emily again. "Miss Lavinia and Giles can take Melanie fishing with them, if she wants to go, but Sabrina will no doubt wish to continue with her visit to the vicarage, and I want a few words alone with Miss Wingrave."

His tone of voice made Emily look at him sharply. He was looking grim again, and she was by no means certain whether he meant to propose marriage in style or to throttle her.

Mr. Bennett expressing his willingness to remain with Miss Brittan while Oliver fetched their horses, as well as a pair of stout grooms to take Bennett's place while the two young men went in search of the Runners, the others were easily persuaded to leave the scene.

Sabrina said nothing about the decision made with regard to where she would go, but expressed concern lest some unsuspecting wanderer come upon the Frenchman's body.

Scopwick assured her that there was no cause for worry. "Man'll have to be carried somewhere, I expect, so it'll be best if the lads bring a hurdle or some such to carry him on. Runners'll take Miss Whatever-she-chooses-to-call-herself in charge, but they ain't going to want to be burdened with a dead body any more than anyone else would." He looked at Meriden. "Daresay the churchyard's the place for him. I'll see to it if you like. Just have the lads take him along there once the Runners have had a look at him. Ought to notify the folks at Stilington Camp that their wanderer's been found, too."

"If they've even noted his disappearance," Jack said. "What are you waiting for, Oliver? You have your orders."

Nodding, Oliver took himself off at a lope. Miss Lavinia, casting a glance at the earl, quickly gathered up Giles and Melanie and disappeared with them back into the shrubbery.

Sabrina was earnestly explaining to Mr. Scopwick just then that since she had no intention of marrying him, he ought not to take her to task for her actions, and that, contrary to what he believed, she had indeed brought a footman with her when she ventured out-of-doors. The man had been carrying her poor-box offerings for her and she had sent him on ahead to the vicarage when she had turned off the path in search of the vicar.

Emily, noting that her sister no longer seemed as frightened of the big man, found herself wondering how her parents would react if Sabrina should even hint that she might accept his proposal. *Sabrina Scopwick*! The name certainly had an odd ring to it, to be sure.

She snapped out of her reverie when one strong arm embraced her shoulders and another moved to the back of her knees. "What are you doing?" she demanded of the earl.

"Taking you back to the Priory, where you ought to have stayed in the first place," he said, scooping her up into his arms. "And if you know what's good for you, my lass, you won't keep bleating at me along the way."

Since her mouth was already open to voice her protest at being manhandled, Emily stuck her tongue out at him. To her relief, he grinned at her.

"Very pretty behavior, Miss Wingrave. You have surely made your reputation with young Bennett there."

Having forgotten Mr. Bennett's presence, she started and looked back over her shoulder, only to relax again when she saw that the young man had perched himself upon a fallen log near Miss Brittan and was engaging her in conversation.

"He is too busy to notice what I do," she said.

"Learning to speak French, perhaps," the earl replied dryly.

"I would never have taken her for a Frenchwoman," Emily said with a sigh, leaning her head against his shoulder and thinking how very comfortable that position was. Her arm scarcely ached at all now.

"She fooled us all." His tone was grim, and she knew he did not like the thought that he had been taken in by the governess as easily as everyone else had been.

Not wanting him to think badly of himself, she offered a distraction. "I could just as easily walk, you know."

"No."

She looked up at him from beneath her lashes. "Do you mean *no* in the sense that I cannot walk or *no* in the sense that you do not mean to allow me to do so?"

He stopped and looked directly down into her face, his eyes narrowed. "Miss Wingrave, do you ever do as you are bid?"

She blinked. "Often. What particular error have I committed this time? To make you demand such a thing, I mean," she added hastily, not wishing to hear a list of her misdemeanors and perfectly certain that at the least encouragement he would provide one. The fact that his eyes gleamed told her she had been right to qualify her question.

He said gently, "I told you not to bleat at me all the way back to the Priory."

"You make it sound as though we're miles away. Am I too heavy for you, sir?"

He chuckled and began to move rapidly forward again. "You are a featherweight, as you know perfectly well. Look here, Emily, do you really want me to put you down?"

"No." She felt warmth surging to her cheeks and looked quickly away. His arms tightened, and the warmth in her cheeks spread immediately to the rest of her body. Looking up at him again, she saw that a tiny smile was playing on his lips, but he continued to look straight ahead. No doubt, she told herself, he did not wish to embarrass himself by tripping over something in the road. He made no attempt to engage her in conversation, and she decided to show him that she could keep her mouth shut if she wished to do so. Bleating, he had called it, as though she were a chatty ewe.

Relaxing, she closed her eyes, the better to enjoy the sensation of being carried in a pair of strong arms while resting her head against a solid, well-muscled shoulder. What, she wondered, would it be like to be married to Jack, to owe him her duty and obedience, to feel his hands upon her body whenever he wished to touch her? The last thought brought a rush of unfamiliar sensations washing over her, and her eyes flew open.

She had been dimly aware of the crunch of pebbles beneath his feet, so she was not surprised to see that they had reached the drive. Jack was still gazing straight ahead, and she took the opportunity to look more closely at his face. He was truly a handsome man, she thought, although from her present angle his eyes looked more deeply set than ever. Indeed, she told herself fancifully, his heavy brows overhung them like ocean cliffs over the shingle, shadowing the dark, mysterious recesses beneath.

He looked down at her suddenly, and so focused was her attention upon his countenance that he startled her. Jack grinned, his white teeth flashing in the sunlight, his eyes twinkling at her confusion, but still he said nothing. When she opened her mouth, wishing only to break the odd silence that had fallen between them, he grinned wider and murmured, "Bleat, bleat," and she shut it with a snap and closed her eyes again determined not to give him the satisfaction of making her speak or look at him.

The rhythm of his stride changed as he hurried up the stairs, and once inside the house, he gave rapid-fire orders to Merritt and to William as he carried her into the library and laid her down upon the sofa.

"Sit up," he said to her then. "I want to see if you are still dizzy."

"You might have learned that much by allowing me to stand before now," she said.

"I might have. Now, do as I bid you."

She swung her feet to the floor and sat upright, surprised to discover that she did indeed still feel dizzy. "Surely I did not lose so much blood as that," she said, looking up at him in bewilderment.

"You suffered a shock," he said. "The dizziness ought to pass quickly now, but don't attempt to stand up just yet. I want to get that wound cleaned up and get a proper bandage on it."

"You're a doctor now?"

He gave her a direct look. "I will certainly send for Dr. Prescott and hope he treats you as you deserve, but for now I am perfectly capable of doing what must be done. The bullet passed through the wound cleanly, but there is always risk of infection. You will need to take care for a few days until we may be certain there is none."

Sobered by the thought that infection could mean her death, she made no reply. To her infinite gratitude, once William and the butler had brought him the items he required, Jack rejected their offers of assistance and sent them out of the room again, but it took more effort than she would have thought possible to withstand his attentions when they had gone.

"Scream if you like," he said grimly as he poured over her arm a liquid substance that stung like the fires of hell.

"I will not scream," she said through gritted teeth, "and damn you, Jack, that stuff's whiskey. I shall smell like a gentlemen's club."

"I know what it is. Brandy was more readily available to Merritt than vinegar or turpentine, either of which would have done the job as well and both of which, in my opinion, would have reeked even worse. How do you know what a gentlemen's club smells like?"

She grimaced at another sharp slice of pain. "Must you be so brutal? I only imagine what it must be like, of course. Why must you soak me in that stuff?"

"I am not soaking you. I am only doing what I may to prevent infection." As he dusted the wound with basilicum powder, wrapped a clean bandage around it, and fastened the bandage securely, he added, "Instead of complaining, you may be grateful that you are not a soldier in battle, for

I can assure you that you would find having hot tar or pitch poured over your wound a good deal less enjoyable than this.''

"I think, considering the state of your temper a short time ago, I ought to thank the Fates instead that there is no tar or pitch at hand," she said tartly.

He did not smile this time but said, "I realized from what Dolly said that you meant to warn us about the duel and did not purposely break your faith with me, but your behavior, for all that, was nonetheless foolish."

Remembering that her first intent had not been innocent at all, Emily had the grace to blush, but Jack took little note of the fact, and if he thought it unusual of her not to respond immediately, he did not say so. Instead, he said quietly, "What devil possessed you to leap at that villain as you did? Good God, Emily, you might well have been killed! Indeed, for one awful moment I thought—"

He was still kneeling in front of her, and when he broke off, his jaw working strangely, she reached her hand out to touch his face, noting the roughness of his cheek but thinking more about the gentleness of which this volatile man was capable.

"You have been vexed with me many times," she said in a low voice, "for failing to think before I act. I fear this was but one more such time. Are you still vexed, sir?"

"Was that the only reason you acted as you did?" He was looking directly at her again, his gaze oddly intense.

She swallowed carefully, wondering if she was about to commit a fateful error. "No, Jack, that was not all."

He sighed with relief. "Well then, my love, will you?"

"Will I what?" she demanded, stubborn to the end.

"Will you marry me, of course?"

A silence fell.

Finally Jack said, "Well, love?"

Emily looked at him, feeling suddenly rather shy. "I thought you were angry with me even before this business today. You have scarcely spoken to me, after all."

He touched her hand. "I have known for some time that I had fallen in love with you, but when I let my feelings show the first time, you froze up like a winter lake."

"I thought you were playing games again," she said, "like last Christmas. I couldn't believe you really loved me. I suppose I feared being hurt again, and then you said such cutting thing about Stephen Campion. True things," she added, looking away, "but painful nonetheless."

"I know." He grimaced. "I was a brute, but when you accused me of playing a game with you, I took it hard. At first I was angry, but then I began wondering if I really was in love after all these years, and wondering, too, if you could ever love me. It occurred to me that I might just be believing what I wanted to believe. I wasn't certain that you knew your feelings either, despite your response to me when I kissed you, so I decided to give you time to be sure of them without overbearing influence from me." He smiled at her. "I knew the answers to all my questions when I saw you leap at the Frenchman and feared for my own sanity when I thought he might have killed you."

"You were so angry," she murmured, her hand gentle against his chest. "I was afraid too, Jack, for you."

His eyes narrowed again and he covered her hand with his, squeezing tight. "I understand why you did it, Emily, but I hope you will understand me, too, when I say that if you ever frighten me like that after we are wed, I will make you wish you had never been born."

Emily lifted her chin and gave him a challenging look. "We will fight all the time," she said, thrilling within to the thought of many years spent pitting her mettle against his.

"No doubt we will," he agreed, smiling again. "You learn slowly."

"As do you, sir, though I am not nearly so brutal as you are. You will beat me."

"Certainly," he said, grinning broadly now. "At least once in every fortnight if I've got any sense at all." Then, more seriously, he said, "Will you risk such a fate, lass?"

"Well . . ." She paused, watching him, satisfied when he began to look a little anxious. "Very well, I'll risk the consequences if you will, but hear this, Meriden. You are not the only one who can make good his threats, you know. I promise you by all you hold holy that I will make you very sorry if you ever so much as lay a hand on me."

"I intend to lay hands upon you often," he said huskily, pulling her to her feet and suiting action to words.

As he caressed her, Emily's senses stirred to respond to the fire his hands lit in their wake. She raised her arms and put them around his neck, lifting her face to his, aroused to a passion she had never experienced before by the increasing heat of her own body. As he bent his head to kiss her, Jack's right hand cupped her left breast, igniting new, more fervent sensations. Emily pressed her body against his, trembling one moment, delighting in the hardness of his muscles beneath her moving fingertips the next. The pain in her arm forgotten for a time, she kissed him harder, opening her lips in invitation to his exploring tongue. Moments later, when he lifted his head to look at her, she was breathing hard, as though she had been running, and her eyes were shining.

He said softly, "I'll never be sorry, Emmy love, never."